His
Kidnapper's
Shoes

ALSO BY MAGGIE JAMES

Fiction

Blackwater Lake
The Second Captive
Guilty Innocence
Sister, Psychopath

Non-Fiction

*Write Your Novel! From Getting
Started to First Draft*

His Kidnapper's Shoes

MAGGIE JAMES

LAKE UNION
PUBLISHING

Text copyright © 2016 Maggie James
All rights reserved.

Published by Lake Union Publishing, Seattle

www.apub.com

Amazon, the Amazon logo, and Lake Union Publishing are trademarks of Amazon.com, Inc., or its affiliates.

ISBN-13: 9781503941120
ISBN-10: 1503941124

Cover design by @Blacksheep

Printed in the United States of America

1

JUDGEMENT DAY

My body aches. The wall against my back grinds into my bones, as does the bench under my bottom; however much I fidget, I can't get comfortable. I guess they don't build police cells with such considerations in mind. There's no clock and I've lost track of how much time I've spent in this place. Two, maybe three hours? I wonder how long they'll keep me here. I remind myself it doesn't matter. I feel strangely disconnected from such things. All I can think about is my son.

The door swings open. I don't bother to look up, not at first. A pair of black shoes steps in front of me; slim legs encased in pale tights lead up from them. The police officer who arrested me; I register her voice telling me to stand. I glance up, observing the harsh judgement staring back from her eyes. She's young, probably mid-twenties. No ring on her left hand and I'd bet she doesn't have children. Her body doesn't look like it's ever split itself open forcing out a baby. This isn't a woman who spends her nights attempting to soothe a bawling child to sleep, while trying not to scream with frustration and sheer bloody exhaustion. She's not a mother. Had she found herself in my place, would she have done what I did? Perhaps not. However, she's not yet walked a mile in my shoes; if she's lucky she never will, so what gives her the right to judge me?

It seems she's taking me somewhere. They must be going to question me. Looks as if the doctor who examined me has decided I'm fit to be interviewed.

It's not going to do them any good. I won't be giving out any answers. Even if I talked for a week, a year, forever, I'd never make them understand. They're police officers; rules and their enforcement are everything to them, all black and white and rigid. According to them, I've committed a crime. I believe what I did was right and the only thing possible in the circumstances.

What's that saying, about the law being an ass? I reckon it's true. On the one hand, it states we're supposed to protect children from danger. Love them. Keep them safe. Punish those who hurt them. Yet I'm the one they'll put on trial. Even though I protected my son, took him away from harm. To my mind, it makes no sense for them to judge me with contempt. They're firing accusations at me that would only apply to somebody who doesn't love her son in the way I love Daniel. It's a crazy world we live in.

I hear your voice in my head, Gran, reassuring me, telling me not to worry.

The police officer orders me again to stand. This time her tone is sharper, and I get to my feet, thankful not to be sitting any longer on that unforgiving bench. It makes no difference where they take me anyway. Here or in a police interview room, I'll still need strong tea and time alone with my son. Doesn't seem like I'll be getting either one any time soon.

I follow the police officer along the passageway to another room. I take in my surroundings. This room's not built for comfort either. Magnolia walls, beige carpet. A table and chairs and some sort of recording device. Nothing else. A whiff of stale sweat hangs in the air.

The police officer yanks out a chair and orders me to sit. She thrusts a paper cup of water in front of me and I gulp it down, welcoming its icy coolness. My eyes focus on a chip in the wall. I let them wander over the blemish and idly wonder whether, if I stare at the mark long enough, it counts as meditation. Another part of my brain registers somebody pulling out the chair next to me and sitting down. From my peripheral vision, I see it's a man, suited in dark grey; I guess this must be some sort of legal representation provided for me. Somebody else is in the room too, a mental health social worker, I gather, from the words filtering into my brain, although I'm not paying much attention to what's being said. Two police officers pull out the chairs opposite me and sit down. One is the young woman. The other is male, considerably older. I continue to stare at the wall. I won't say anything. They can't make me.

My thoughts drift away. Your voice, gentle and soothing, is in my head again, Gran, telling me Daniel didn't mean to be so cruel. I draw comfort from your words. I was always able to talk to you, my beloved grandmother, something never possible with Mum, not with her being the way she was. You have to reassure me that everything will be all right with Daniel, Gran. He's the only one whose opinion I care about; I don't give a toss what anyone else thinks.

Ian is included in my indifference. My husband has never truly mattered to me. It sounds cruel to admit it, Gran, but I only married Ian for what he could do for Daniel. To provide my boy with the father figure he desperately needed. I wasn't interested in myself; finding a man to love was never on the agenda. I had my son for that, and he was all I had ever wanted or needed. Ian – I've grown fond of him, even if I can't love him, but it's always seemed to be enough. For me, anyway.

I think it's worked out well, despite my lack of feelings. Who says marriage has to be about love and living happily ever after? I've done my best to give Ian what he needs, even if I've always been out of reach for him emotionally. He's never been able to touch the true Laura, the essence within; I suspect it's been a disappointment to him. You see, Ian really does love me, and there's no denying he's been a good husband. He's given my son and me a home and security, as well as his name. He's provided me with the family life I craved, even though I never considered having a child with him. I'm not prepared to walk down that road again.

You and Ian would have hated each other if the two of you had ever met, Gran; chalk and cheese doesn't come close to describing it. He's Mr Conventional, with the career in financial planning and the golf club membership. The man who can't see any other way through life except doing what people expect of him. You know, Rotary Club dinners, drinks with business associates, that sort of stuff. All the things you, with your batik skirts from Bali and your silver earrings from India, would have scrambled to get away from as fast as possible.

Anyway, I know you understand. You always did. I'm certain you don't condemn me, not like the police officer who brought me here.

Not like Daniel either. Right now, he's judging me. I'll change that, though. I have to.

To lose my son for a second time would be unbearable. I won't lose him. I can't. I yearn to make things right between us. Since the day – when was it? Probably a few days ago, perhaps as long as a week, I'm not sure – when Daniel burst through the door, shouting, thrusting those papers in my face. The ones saying ugly things, making him turn against me. Ever since then, I've felt as if a fog has invaded my brain. I can't think straight and all I want is for Daniel to tell me it's all right. That he didn't mean those awful things he screamed at me.

It doesn't matter if they lock me away, if only Daniel will look at me and tell me he understands. Until he comes to me and says the words I crave to hear, I won't speak. I can't talk to him when he has such fury in his eyes; his forgiveness will be the trigger that releases my frozen tongue. Given the chance to be with him, instead of this place, I'd find the words to explain and everything would be all right. He wouldn't stare at me as if I'm something vile found stuck to the sole of his shoe. There'd be no more yelling or accusations, no tearing me apart with words loaded with blame and anger. He'd be my son again, my beautiful Daniel, and the world would be back to normal. I don't care if they lock me up in jail. That won't matter, so long as he doesn't hate me.

He's angry with me now, but I'll change that. He'll remember how I always loved him, even though, as a young child, he'd push me away when I tried to cuddle him. His rejections always pierced me, every time. I'd remind myself that being a mother is more than hugging your child. It's being there for them when they wake shouting and desperate from some night-time terror. It's nursing them when they're feverish, sponging them down when they're soaking the sheets with sweat. It's listening to stories of their day at school, plastering skinned knees, pinning their paintings of wobbly houses on the wall. I did all those things. I was always a mother to Daniel when it really counted. He'll realise that eventually.

He'll tell me he understands. Then everything in my world will be all right again.

I vaguely register words coming at me.

'. . . Laura Bateman, you knowingly and wilfully broke into the Cordwells' flat . . .'

'. . . quite deliberately . . . without thought for the distress and hurt you would cause . . .'

'. . . for reasons unknown at this stage . . .'

I don't deny the breaking and entering part. In that respect I admit I'm guilty. My mind spins back through the years and I remember my fear as I stood outside that flat, summoning up the courage to carry out what I'd decided to do.

I planned it very carefully. I'd thought of nothing else since I found they were going to take Daniel away from me. The only question was when to act, and sooner was better than later. My son's wellbeing was at stake.

More words filter through the fog in my brain.

'. . . psychiatric evaluation . . .'

'. . . best in his field . . . find out why she did it . . .'

They're so stupid. I did it to get my son back. What other reason could there be?

Except they say Daniel's not my son.

They say he has another mother.

There's that ugly word they keep throwing at me.

Kidnap.

They say I kidnapped Daniel.

2

TURNING THE CLOCK BACK

Daniel Bateman's hand strangled the neck of his half-drunk bottle of beer. Seconds later the bottle smashed against the wall, thrown with the full force of gym-bulked muscles. Long trails of beer dribbled darkly towards the floor; Tim would be pissed off but Daniel didn't care.

He'd lashed out verbally at his flatmate one night, frustration and rage fuelling his response at the suggestion that he might have drunk too much. Tim hadn't tried again and Daniel later regretted taking his fury out on him; the guy had only been trying to help. He realised his flatmate was concerned about him, but right now that was the least of his worries.

A few weeks ago, he'd been the closest to happiness he'd ever been in his life.

A lot had occurred since then; he had no idea how to cope with any of it.

Not surprising, really. Not many people would deal well with find-ing out their so-called mother had kidnapped them. Taken them when they were too young to remember. Stolen them from the parents who had given them their DNA and pretty-boy looks.

Small wonder he was a mess. Who wouldn't be? His name wasn't his name. He wasn't Daniel Bateman, but Daniel Cordwell, kidnapped twenty-two years ago by Laura Bateman, then Laura Covey, not long after his fourth birthday. Right now, he hadn't a single clue as to why. His mother – no, his kidnapper – wasn't talking. Not at all, not to anybody. God only knew whether she ever would. The police had told him she was undergoing psychiatric evaluations to establish how stable – or not – she was mentally.

Daniel snorted at the thought. She'd always been a bit flaky.

Ever since he'd found out the ugly truth about his life, he'd downed bottle after bottle of beer, trying to figure out what to do next. Much more alcohol, he thought, and he'd end up like his stepfather, with the paunch, spider veins and overall look of a man for whom self-care wasn't a priority. The thought, coupled with his fury, had been what made him hurl his beer at the wall.

Ian Bateman didn't merit a second thought. Unless it was to think of him dying a miserable death.

He'd started hitting the beer when the realisation struck him how different his sorry, messed-up life might have been if that bitch Laura Bateman hadn't kidnapped him. A knot of anger was swelling and twisting deep within him, and the booze was an attempt to drown it, submerge it in a flood of alcohol, in the hope it might start to unravel.

So far, it hadn't worked. He'd never been much of a drinker and before all this happened, he'd not seen much point in getting rat-arsed like some people did. He'd got pissed a few times when he first discovered booze, all mouth and bravado with his teenage mates, but since then, he'd kept his consumption low. Getting plastered didn't fit with going to the gym and keeping his face as pretty as most people found it. Dark hair, green eyes, the works. Not that his features were perfect; a tiny scar, the result of a sports injury, marred his left eyebrow. A purist might say his nose was a little sharp, but did women care? Not when the full lips below tempted them in for a kiss. 'A mouth I'd happily drown in,' Katie had told him.

Katie. As a result of the ugly truth that had blown his world apart, he'd lost the one person who really mattered in his life and with her the chance of something different. Something better.

Her loss was too raw, too painful. He couldn't think about her right now.

Anyway, his so-called mother occupied the epicentre of his thoughts. Laura Bateman. The woman who'd put his world through the liquidiser the day he'd confronted her, clutching the evidence of her deceit set out in cold typeface. Despite all his rage and accusations, she'd sat in front of him and denied everything. Hurt and betrayal seeped into him every time he relived the scene. She'd always told him how much she adored him, and he'd believed her. Seemed even that was a lie. Small wonder he'd reacted so strongly. He hadn't realised what a can of worms he was opening in doing the DNA test, and now he was powerless to reverse his error.

He could have ignored the test results; perhaps it would have been better if he had, walking away and never seeing Laura Bateman or his prick of a stepfather again. He could have moved to Australia with Katie, an opportunity now closed, and he'd never have uncovered his real identity. Far less painful all round.

He'd tried to punch the rage out of his system. He'd gone to the gym one evening, grabbed a punch bag and given the leather a pounding. He'd hammered away until he was barely capable of standing and his arms could hardly move. Sweat had blinded his eyes and drenched his T-shirt and he'd not stopped until Len, the trainer on duty, intervened.

'Enough, Dan.' Len topped six feet five, with a physique like a rhinoceros, but Daniel still tried to pull back to the punch bag. The other man wasn't having any of it.

'I said enough.' Len dragged him away, holding him by the arm. 'Look, mate, I don't know what's eating you or what's got you so pissed off. But you're not going to find the answers in that bag.'

Through the sweat blinding Daniel's eyes, he saw the concern on Len's face. 'Yeah, you could say I'm pissed off. I'm about as pissed off as I've ever been.' He swayed a little, exhaustion threatening to get the better of him.

'This have anything to do with that new girlfriend of yours? What's her name . . . Katie? Thought everything looked pretty peachy where she's concerned?'

He couldn't deal with this. Len was a decent guy but Daniel didn't do talking about messy emotional stuff with anyone and he wasn't about to start with Len. He'd begun to open up with Katie, especially in bed, but no way would they ever slide between the sheets again. Anyway, Katie hadn't been what drove him to the punch bag. She was collateral damage.

He realised Len was waiting for an answer. 'Look, I'm OK, mate. Really.' He pulled away, heading for the showers. Home was calling.

Now, on this drunken evening back at his flat a couple of days later, he decided Len was right. He wouldn't get the answers he wanted from a punch bag. Not from beer either. Maybe he'd go back to screwing things out of his system.

Sex had always been his drug of choice. With his looks, he rarely went home alone, always picking bed partners who just wanted a good time before saying goodbye. He never saw anyone more than three or four times, figuring after that he was in way too deep and he needed to get the hell out.

Because Daniel Bateman didn't do commitment. On the nights he felt good, he found a woman to screw. Any time things weren't so great – say, if he'd been brooding about his stepfather – he also went on the pull, but on those occasions he targeted a male partner. As to why, he didn't examine his motives too closely. Deep down he knew the truth;

such encounters served as an emotional Band-Aid. What other outlet did he have?

All that changed, though, when he met Katie Trebasco.

One thing was for sure: the punch bag and the booze hadn't provided answers; he doubted whether screwing around would either, but it was the only thing that had ever worked before. Not tonight, though. He felt too soused with the drink to do much in the sack and his current dark mood would hardly bag him a warm body for the night. It was too late to go out on the pull anyway.

He looked at the clock. Nearly midnight, with work in a few hours. He staggered to his feet, heading towards the bathroom. Best to be in bed before Tim got back. He couldn't face the meaningful looks and pointed clearing away of the empty beer bottles.

He needed his bed.

Along with turning the clock back a few weeks. Yeah. A miracle would solve everything.

3

ALCOHOL AND OPALS

I think I'm in some sort of psychiatric facility, although I'm not sure; I've not been taking note of what's going on around me. My confinement in this place must be because of my violence at the police station, when they forced me to provide a DNA sample. In contrast, the staff here must think I'm a model patient, always calm and compliant, although I never speak. I do what I'm told, when I'm told, to make life easier. I don't want to interact with these people; going along with whatever they decide is best for me is simpler. I have my own room and I can be quiet here.

In my mind, I'm back being questioned by the police, my lawyer sitting beside me, the mental health social worker off to my left. I still don't respond to anything that's said to me, or even show I understand what they want; my refusal is obvious, though, from my silence. No way will I allow them to take a blood sample or swab my mouth. I won't give them something they'll use against me, something to show there's no biological link between my son and me, even though I'm his mother in every way that matters.

They don't need blood or saliva, though; a hair sample will suffice, a fact already painfully familiar to me. What I don't realise is that they can employ force, if need be, to obtain it. I register this information and something inside, suppressed for a very long time, snaps. It's not going to happen. I won't let them. They decide to go ahead anyway; the rage erupts and I hit out at anyone I can before they restrain me, arms thrashing, screams of fury tearing from my throat, wild inarticulate sounds. The mental health social worker gets very involved and after that, everything's a bit of a blur.

None of that concerns me anyway. Daniel still occupies most of my thoughts. Anger like his can't last forever. He'll calm down, given time, and he'll visit me and I can explain. I won't speak if he's still full of rage, though. The only way I'll talk is if he's ready to listen to me.

I've plenty of time. Meanwhile, I lie on my bed and gaze at the ceiling, wishing you were here, Gran. I'd bury myself in your arms and you'd hug me tight like you always did and somehow the world would transform into a better place. You'd help me explain things to Daniel – the pair of you would get on so well, Gran – and I'd draw comfort in being with the two people I've loved the most.

I've not been granted a happy life, apart from having had you and Daniel in it. It's hard remembering some things, like when I lived with Mum. That small Hampshire town, home to three generations of Coveys, seems light years away now, after more than two decades of life in London. I never did tell you everything, Gran; I always tried to shield you from the worst of my troubles. You were so ill, and I didn't want to worry you. But such things shaped me, made me who I am, leading me to that flat in Bristol and to my son, my beloved Daniel.

It really did get bad for me at times. Take Mum's alcoholism, for starters. I think I'd turned eight when I realised not all mothers drank as she did. Up until then I thought it was normal to help my mother to bed every night after she'd drunk herself senseless. Apparently not, as I found out when I talked to the other girls at school. I learned not to say anything further, becoming vigilant about keeping up a façade of normality. Mum was a clever drunk, anyway. She'd get up in the morning as though she'd not touched a drop the night before, scrub all traces of the booze from her breath and go to work like everyone else. Wine was her favourite tipple although she wasn't fussy. She'd buy it by the box as well as the bottle and I'd watch her rip the bag from the packaging and squeeze out every drop.

You were always there for me when I needed you, though. I remember how I'd call you if she got bad and you'd come over. You'd help me undress her and get her into bed, your manner endlessly patient, your voice always so calm.

'Roll her onto her side, Laura, like this, in case she vomits in her sleep. She'll choke if she does, my love.'

I'd look at Mum's face on the pillow, her skin the colour of uncooked dough, snoring as she slept off the alcohol, her inability to be a mother a piercing regret to me.

Afterwards, you'd sit on my bed and brush my hair.

'Almost long enough to tickle your hips,' you once told me, the tug of the bristles against my scalp a panacea for my drunken mother snoring in the next room. 'Like soft golden caramel and every bit as thick.' You reached behind my ear and conjured up a sweet wrapped in shiny gilded paper, and I laughed, even though you'd pulled that trick so often before. You peeled off the wrapping and held the caramel up against my hair.

'See, Laura? Look how the colours match.' My hair was paler, I thought, but there wasn't much in it. You popped the sweet into my waiting mouth, and then patted my cheek, the oversized ring on your finger next to my eyes. 'Would you believe it? Another perfect match. Eyes of opal blue.' You stroked my caramel-coloured hair and for a while, I forgot I had a mother who was drunk and incapable of being a parent. You made it all go away, Gran, and that was the real magic you had for me, more powerful than any sweet.

'Why does she drink so much?' I remember asking you once, desperate to dig beneath the surface of the enigma that was my mother.

You sighed, at a loss to find the words to explain the truth to the unworldly eight-year-old whom you loved. You were right; I was too young to understand the ugly reality of what had happened nearly ten years ago. I needed to be older and a lot wiser before I truly grasped the reason Mum drank the way she did.

Sadness darkened your expression. You chose your words with care. 'Sometimes, Laura, men can appear nice on the surface, even when they're not. Especially when they want something from a pretty girl.'

'Like what?' I had no idea what you meant.

You didn't answer directly. 'Your mum was beautiful when she was younger. Too beautiful, Laura.' Anger seeped into your voice. 'She ended up attracting attention from a group of men, the type who aren't so nice on the inside. She didn't want to give them what they wanted, so they took it anyway.'

I had no concept of sex back then. I nodded, pretending I understood.

'They hurt her so badly.' Something in your expression told me you hadn't meant to say that in front of me. You said she'd needed to go to the hospital; she'd begun drinking heavily as soon as she got out.

'You see, Laura, my love, when your mum drinks, she's able to forget what those men did; for a short while, the world becomes a better place for her.'

I nodded again. That part wasn't difficult to understand.

'Your mother was never the same afterwards, sweetheart. Although she didn't want to let those men have what they were after, when she came home from the hospital she gave it to anybody who did. It can happen when women don't think much of themselves.'

You told me how you tried to talk with her, but you two were never close and she'd already built a wall, high and impenetrable, around herself. Then she got pregnant by one of several possible men and managed to quit drinking. Nine months later, I arrived; for a while, my mother continued to get better. She took care of me, didn't bother with the wine and you hoped, really hoped, she would be all right.

Slowly, though, she slipped back into that dark place where only a bottle of cheap red could make her forget and then you knew she'd never move past her pain.

By the time I turned twelve, I had you to be concerned about as well. I ignored the signs at first: how thin you'd become, how tired and frail. So long as I didn't ask you, I reasoned, I wouldn't hear the words I dreaded. You, being ever practical, didn't let me get away with the head-in-the-sand approach. You sat me down one day, doing your best to explain your illness so I wouldn't get too upset. I was a young twelve, after all, still unworldly.

'Laura, my darling.' Your voice, calm as ever, contrasted with the words to come. 'I know you've been fretting about me, my love, but there's no need. There's a lump growing inside me, something nasty that has no business being there. You mustn't worry, though. Those clever doctors at the hospital are going to operate to remove it and then everything will be fine.'

I didn't speak, too choked with terror. As ever, you were quick to reassure me.

'Don't get upset, my love. I'll need a course of treatment afterwards and then you'll have your old Gran back, good as new.'

My twelve-year-old self sensed your need to comfort me meant you were being sparing with the truth but I clung stubbornly to what you'd said, unwilling to believe you could be wrong. I convinced myself the doctors would make you better, just as you promised.

I'd visit you as often as possible, both when you were in hospital and when you came home; it was a long time before I believed you might get better. There were days when you hardly had the energy to talk, when your skin was as dry and dough-like as my mother's, and your trademark batik blouses hung on you like curtains. Some days I'd visit and not be able to return for a few days because I couldn't bear to see you so pale and exhausted.

You were ill for a long time, Gran. During that time, Mum got much worse. I think she relied on you being there to help and suddenly you weren't. You were too sick and you needed to put yourself first. Although the two of you had never been close – that skipped a genera-tion – I think she was terrified of losing you, her only living relative besides me. She drew comfort from the only source she knew – a wine bottle. Her drinking got even heavier and she started to pass out earlier and more frequently from the drink.

Soon it became harder for her to wake up in the mornings, or to wash and dress. Some days she didn't manage it at all and she'd lie there on the sofa, either sleeping or drinking more wine. Guilt stabbed me on those days that happened to be school days and I had to leave her, but the truth was, Gran, I needed to get out of the house. I had to distance myself from her wine-pickled breath and the empty bottles, from her open-mouthed snoring and the sight of her skirt riding up her mottled legs. I wanted to go to school, to be with normal people and forget for a few hours that I had a hopeless drunk for a mother.

Inevitably, she ended up being fired from her job and things got seriously bad, Gran. There was no food in the house and I remember rummaging through drawers trying to find money to buy groceries. I ate at your house as often as possible and I'm not ashamed to say I took money from Mum's purse as well. I did my best with the food, but the bills were another matter; soon angry letters started arriving, threaten-ing court action, and I grew scared, Gran. The phone had been cut off a long time ago but we still received letters demanding the arrears on the account. We had bills from the electricity and gas companies and Mum owed a couple of months' rent as well.

I thought about asking you for money but I couldn't, Gran. You needed to concentrate on getting well. Besides, I knew you were struggling financially. You had enough to cope with and I wanted to sort it myself, to make you proud of me.

In the end, I couldn't handle things any longer. I had no idea that day, seemingly the same as any other, would be the one where the pressure got too much. Mrs Davis, the maths teacher, asked me a question in class. I didn't know the answer because I hadn't been listening. I'd not eaten any breakfast and the urgent need to put food in my stomach, the growling pit at the centre of me, seemed a more desperate issue than solving algebraic equations. Tears pricked the backs of my eyes and suddenly I found myself crying. I didn't care about the entire class witnessing my meltdown, or the fact I had no tissue and used my sleeve to wipe away the snot. I didn't worry about the horrible sounds I was making. All I cared about was the hollow in my stomach and the overwhelming need to stop being strong all the time.

I cried for my mother, for the torment she so desperately wanted to blot out and which even my birth hadn't diminished. I cried for you, Gran, for your loss of zest for life, for your pale, unhealthy skin and dull eyes. But most of all I cried for myself, for the exhausted and hungry fourteen-year-old who didn't have a life like her classmates, for the girl who had to stop her mother vomiting in her sleep and who stole from her purse to buy food. I wanted, more than anything, to crawl into bed, sleep for a week and wake up to find food in the house and Mum sober. When I was younger, daylight chased away any childhood nightmares. This time I couldn't wake up.

I'm not sure what happened after that; it's all a bit of a blur. Social workers came to the house. They looked at Mum, lying soused on the sofa. They saw her red-veined eyes, the raddled face, the empty wine bottles. They asked to read the threatening letters and I showed them. They fired off searching questions about what we ate and I told them there was no money for food.

'Any other relatives?' one of them, all brisk efficiency, asked.

'Only my grandmother.' The need to protect you while you were so ill battled with my longing to run to you, to seek comfort. 'But she's sick. Really unwell.' I told them about your illness, how you were the best Gran in the world but you had to look after yourself and you couldn't cope with me as well as getting better. The two social workers exchanged glances.

'If she goes to live with her grandmother, she'll still be the carer. She'd merely be swapping a drunken woman for a sick one,' said Brisk Efficiency.

The earnest people from Social Services had to do something with me, the solution being foster care. I ended up in a family placement. My foster parents meant well but I couldn't connect with them in any way. I'd never known real family life; their house always seemed too noisy, too full of people, what with three children and relatives always visiting. I felt the weight of their kindness oppressing me; their apple-pie family only served to mock me, thrusting in my face what I'd never had.

I visited Mum as often as I could bear. I'd go after school and most of the time she didn't even realise I'd arrived, being too drunk to notice. The house, always a grimy mess, smelled foul and the bills were still piling up. It could only be a matter of time before the landlord evicted Mum. I thought about the homeless drunks, filthy and apathetic, who lived in tattered cardboard boxes under the flyover nearby. I was sure she'd end up like that if he threw her out and in a way, it didn't matter. It would be one step closer to the oblivion she craved.

It never came to that, Gran, as you know. At a time when you needed to concentrate on yourself, and when I should have been a carefree teenager, we lost the woman who had always been between us from a generational point of view. Now I didn't live with her, nobody was around to make sure she didn't vomit the alcohol back up and one night she did, and choked on it. She lay there for a couple of days until the landlord forced the lock. He'd hoped to collect the rent but instead found Mum's dead body, dried vomit pooled on the carpet and in her lungs. She was thirty-four years old and when I last saw her alive, she looked fifty.

'She finally has the peace she yearned for, Laura.' Your comment echoed my thoughts, relief that her suffering had ended soothing my grief.

By then, I'd accepted I'd have to make the best of foster care. I tried to integrate more with my foster family, choosing to stay with them once I turned sixteen rather than try a supported living scheme. I saw you whenever I could, Gran. You were getting stronger and more like your old self, but, oh, so slowly. And when I saw you smile, when you told me how glad you were I'd found a good family, life got easier. I'd have done anything not to worry you.

Then I turned seventeen and met Matthew Hancock.

4

TIME WE GOT HORIZONTAL

Maybe, thought Daniel, he'd have done things differently, given the gift of hindsight and the ability to wind back the clock. Three weeks ago, he'd started to believe things could turn out good at last, that he could forge a new life for himself, outrun his demons. Back then, the envelope confirming his lack of shared DNA with the woman who called herself his mother hadn't arrived. Three weeks ago his life, and his bed, had Katie Trebasco in it. On the evening that set him on his current path, he'd been getting ready for a date with her, the hotter-than-hot woman who had every fibre of his being wound so tight he couldn't think of much else. Tim had been talking to him from the doorway of his bedroom.

'You going out with your new woman tonight, Dan?'

'Yep. Checking out a new Thai restaurant that comes highly recommended. Katie wants to try gai pad prik. Normally, with her, she'd be talking about the Thai equivalent of the *Kama Sutra*, but this time it's food she's after.'

'Jeez, mate. You've got me worried here. Who are you and what did you do with the real Dan? What's been your limit before this – three dates, then you bail out?'

'Sounds about right. What's more, I'm not even considering bailing out. I can tell you're impressed.'

'Gobsmacked, more like. You've been with this Katie longer than anyone else and you've not mentioned other women since you started dating her. What's so special about this one?'

'Can't put my finger on it. She's not my usual type at all.'

'You have a type? I thought you'd go for anything female and breathing.'

'Ha, ha, you're such a comedian.' Daniel grinned. 'I'm not sure what it is about her. It's not just that she has a brain, unlike the gorgeous but not quite Mensa material I usually date. It's more than the fact she's pretty damn good in the sack . . .'

'Whoa! Spare me the details.'

'Sorry. I forgot how prudish you are about sex. The thing is – I simply don't want to get laid anymore with some woman who may be hot but whose name I can't remember in the morning.'

'Sheesh. You've got it bad for this Katie.'

Talk about an understatement. He'd started to think he was falling in love with her. They'd met when she came into the shop-cum-art gallery he managed and started browsing through the Balinese sculptures. He'd given her the once-over, as he did with any decent-looking woman under forty. She definitely passed muster. It was more than simple sexual attraction, though. Something about her seemed familiar, and yet if they'd ever met before he knew he'd have remembered her.

His first thought had been that she was one classy piece of skirt. She was unusually tall, a shade under six feet, and sported glossy brunette hair reaching just below her shoulders, clipped to one side with a silver barrette. She teamed it with a mouth too wide for conventional beauty but which sat exactly right with her melted-chocolate eyes and longish nose. She was dressed in skin-tight jeans and a man's plain white shirt, pulled into a knot above the waistband, simple but stylish at the same time. Her accessories were what gave her look an unusual twist. Large hoop earrings strung with blue and black beads; thick silver and turquoise bangles around both wrists; a chunky buckle on her belt. She'd taken the cowgirl-next-door look, added a touch of Eastern spice, thrown in a dollop of pure Katie, and created a wet dream on legs. They'd gone out that night, ended up in bed, and Daniel had been hooked ever since.

'Yeah. Got it really bad for her. Scary stuff, I tell you. What's happening to me, Tim?'

'You're growing up, Dan. Happens to us all. Next thing, you'll be looking in jewellery shop windows, choosing an engagement ring for her. Then it'll be all dress suit and buttonhole for you in front of the altar. A year later, you'll be signing the forms for a Mothercare store card.' He laughed and dodged Daniel's punch. 'Hey, you can't deny I'm right. It's only a matter of time before I need to advertise for a new flatmate.'

'You're way ahead of me there. All I know is, I don't want anyone else. What's more, I'd be jealous as hell if she hooked up with another guy. Listen, I'm going to be late if I don't get my arse in gear. Catch you tomorrow, mate. I won't be back tonight.'

He grabbed his jacket and grinned as he thought of what he had coming to him. They'd eat some great food, chat and he could gaze into those melting eyes all evening. Then back to her place, sex their dessert. Except with Katie it felt more like making love. His need for casual fucks was morphing into something tenderer and more fulfilling, thanks to this woman. A realisation that scared him to the bone, and not just a little. How the hell had she managed such a transformation?

The whys and wherefores of it all buzzed in his head as he walked to her flat. Katie opened the door as soon as he rang the bell. 'Well, hey, lover boy.'

'Hey, yourself.' He took in the arousing combination of tight trousers and lacy top, which gave more than a hint of what was underneath, and pulled her in for a kiss. 'Mmm. You look good enough to eat. Perhaps we should skip the Thai food and I'll have you for dinner instead.' He nuzzled her neck, inhaling her musky perfume. 'Missed me?'

'Don't flatter yourself. I only saw you this morning. Come on. Much as I'd like to get those arse-hugging jeans off you and get you horizontal, it will have to wait. We're booked in for eight, and I'm one hungry woman.' She trailed a finger down his cheek, her touch cool, her smile a promise on a plate. 'I'll make the wait worth your while.'

Five minutes later, they were walking through the door of the Royal Thai restaurant, Daniel noticing the glances Katie got from the other diners, male and female. She commanded attention wherever she went and it wasn't simply because of her looks; her height ensured that she was usually the focus of interest. She didn't wear flat shoes like so many tall women. Instead she often wore heels of two or three inches, putting her on a level with Daniel and sometimes an inch over. Daniel liked it. It was a novel experience for him to touch toes and lock eyes at the same time with a woman during sex.

They ordered and Daniel reached across the table to grab her hand. 'So how was your day?'

'Hectic. No different to usual.' Katie sighed. 'There's more talk of cuts, we were short-staffed again due to one of the other doctors calling in sick – physician, heal thyself! – and to top it all we had a god-awful car crash to deal with. Shit, I hate working in a hospital sometimes.'

'No, you don't. You'd be looking for some other line of work if you did, instead of thinking of heading off to be the sexiest doctor in Australia.' The hulking great elephant in the room, as far as he was concerned. 'You thought any more about going?'

'All the time when work is like it was today.' Katie shook her head. 'I've got the visa, as I've already told you. Doctors – they don't have any trouble getting immigration visas to Oz.' She smiled. 'Ever since I went

24

there in my gap year, I've wanted to live Down Under. You'd love it, Dan. The weather, the beaches . . . life is good in Australia.'

'Any idea where you'd go in Oz?'

'Thought possibly Sydney or Melbourne, get some Aussie work experience under my belt and then . . . promise me you won't laugh?'

'As if I would.'

'I thought about applying for any vacancies they might have in the Flying Doctors. Not sure what it is about the place, but I really liked Alice Springs. I could imagine myself living and working in the Red Centre. It's beautiful, Dan. And it really is red. You're laughing, you pig.'

'Not laughing at you, Katie girl. Just can't believe I'm with the kind of woman who wants to be a Flying Doctor. Hell, the main ambition of most of my exes has been to have the latest pair of Jimmy Choos.'

'You've been dating the wrong type of woman.'

'Something I can't argue with. Come on, Katie; put me out of my misery. You going to Oz or not?'

'I'm not so sure anymore.' She squeezed Daniel's hand. 'A complication has come along.'

'A complication?'

'Yes. He's . . . let me think, he's six feet two, far too handsome for his own good and boy, does he know it . . .' Daniel laughed. '. . . and the type of man my mother warned me to steer clear of. I wonder if that's part of the attraction?'

'You really want the sort of guy your mother would pick for you? Some accountant with his head up his arse and clueless about what to do in bed? Speaking of which . . .' He lowered his voice and leaned across the table. 'This complication of yours . . . is he good between the sheets?'

Katie kissed him. 'Oh, yeah,' she whispered. 'He's really, really good. That's part of the problem.'

'Him being skilled in the sack is a problem?'

'Yes, stupid as it sounds. You only get the way he is in bed with plenty of practice. With lots of women. The thing is – I've not been with him very long. He's making all the right noises, sure. He's been a player, though, and I'm a one-man-only kind of woman. I need to be sure I can rely on him.' Her expression was serious. 'Can I trust you, Dan?'

He'd have run like crazy from a conversation like this before Katie came on the scene. With her, though, he didn't feel the slightest inclination to do so, a novel turn of events for him. Tim might have a point; perhaps he was growing up at last. 'You can trust me, Katie, I swear. There's been nobody else since I met you. I admit I've played the field, long and hard, in the past. I'm telling you, though – I don't want or need that anymore. Listen, about this Australia thing. Don't go.' He squeezed her hand. 'I want you here with me. Perhaps that's selfish, but it's true.'

Katie didn't answer for a while. Her gaze dropped to the table and Daniel wondered if she agreed he was being selfish, trying to stand in the way of her new life when she'd hardly had a chance to get to know him properly.

A sliver of fear pricked him. Had he scared her off, risked losing her, by admitting his feelings?

Eventually she looked up. She had an expression on her face he'd never seen before. It took a moment for him to recognise it as unease.

'Can I suggest an alternative, Dan?'

'Which is . . . ?'

'You could come to Australia with me. As my established partner. My de facto is what they call it.' She dropped her gaze, seemingly unable to look him in the eyes, focusing her attention on her plate instead. This new, hitherto undetected, vulnerable side of Katie amused Daniel. She was normally so self-assured, so confident. If she was worried she'd frightened him off, she needn't be. No way. The old Daniel, playboy Daniel, was definitely in retreat.

The noise from the other diners faded away as he considered her suggestion. He'd not seen this one coming. Not at all, but he liked the idea. A lot. Not just the thought of a fresh start in Australia, although that held a strong appeal. What caused hope to swell within Daniel was the fact he'd be going with her.

'You'd want me there with you? Really?'

'If you fancy giving it a go. You'd love Australia, Dan. I can't think who wouldn't. We can always try a holiday first, find out if you like it. We could make a great life for ourselves in Oz.' She paused. 'I know we've not been together long, but would you at least consider the idea?'

'Yeah, I'll think about it.' The suggestion of a new life Down Under definitely had its merits. Not just being with Katie, and the sun, sea and lifestyle. At the back of Daniel's mind a welcome thought emerged. He might never have to see his stepfather again.

'I don't want to push you, Dan . . .'

'You're not, babe. I've told you already; the way I feel about you is different. I know it's early days with us, but what the hell. Let's keep Australia in mind and see how things go. I presume I'd have to get a visa on the strength of being your . . . what did you call it, your de facto partner?' He laughed, but without mirth. 'I can't see me getting one based on my job. The demand's probably not too strong Down Under for guys like me. Manager of a shop selling overpriced goods from the Far East to those who want to give their homes that authentic Oriental touch. Oh, and don't forget, as my stepfather would tell me if I ever spoke to him, pathetic wannabe artist.'

'No, no, mister.' Her gaze locked with his, her look a gentle rebuttal of his words. 'Don't put yourself down like that. This art thing of yours fascinates me. Are you ever going to let me see any of your paintings?'

'Might do. One day.'

'Hmm. Sore subject, obviously. OK, point taken.' Katie laughed. 'Time to shift the conversation to safer ground. Listen, if we do decide to live in Oz, we'll need to check out how it would work for you, regarding a visa. I think it's probably way too soon for them to accept us as a couple. I'm guessing here, but we'd most likely have to prove we'd been living together for a year, two years even.' Her expression turned serious again. 'I don't want to rush you. Or myself, for that matter. I reckon we're still some way off getting a place together, don't you?'

'Probably, although if things keep up this pace, I'll be moving my stuff in before you know it.' He couldn't believe it, but he felt good, even excited, about the prospect. 'Besides, Tim will be glad to get rid of me. Perhaps you ought to talk to him before you decide we should live together. He'll fill you in on all my revolting personal habits that as yet you're blissfully unaware of.'

'What, you, Mr Perfect? I am going to meet Tim sometime, right? Although I think you said your flat has paper-thin walls.'

'Too right. You can get loud in bed, remember, sweet pea. Might be too much for someone of Tim's sensitive nature.'

He grinned when he saw the look on her face. He knew what it signalled, but pretended not to. 'What're you thinking, Katie girl?'

'All this talk of getting loud . . .' She flashed her come-to-bed smile and Daniel's jeans grew tight around his prick. 'I think it's time we got horizontal, don't you, lover boy?'

5

CHERRIES AND WHIPPED CREAM

Matthew Hancock. Oh, how I remember when I first met him. I don't think I ever told you about that, Gran. When we did talk about him, it was because you were getting me through the mess he dragged into my life. The romantic part came before the crap, though; I was young and foolish then. The naïveté of being seventeen, although I'm not sure I'm a whole lot wiser these days. It seems obvious now what would happen. There was never a chance things would go any other way.

I met him at the local Sainsbury's where he had a Saturday job; he had dark hair and puppy-dog eyes and looked like all the pop stars rolled into one. He spotted me when I walked in and to my surprise started chatting me up. I was mesmerised by his dark charm, stunned that he would want to talk to me, mousy little Laura Covey. Matthew Hancock, all swagger and endless self-confidence, was temptation on a plate to my inexperienced self, and he came with cherries and whipped cream on top. My teenage hormones stirred into life for the first time and shot into overdrive; I couldn't resist and didn't even try.

I walked out of Sainsbury's with the thrill of knowing he went to Fairfield High, he was three months older than I was, and we'd be meeting later at Burger King. I did the proverbial walking on air in my head, Gran. It all seemed so romantic. Well, not the Burger King bit, but I was too smitten to say anything. The hours couldn't pass quickly enough until we met again, even if it would be over greasy burgers and chips.

He was late and terror shot through me. What if he didn't turn up? He was so gorgeous and I had no idea why he'd want to spend time with me. Eventually he walked through the door, all strut and charm, and I babbled something inane in relief. We ordered cheeseburgers and thick milkshakes but I don't recall eating much. I remember looking into his eyes, so dark and melting, picturing us walking hand in hand down country lanes on hot summer days. We'd drink wine at a candlelit table at Bella Pasta and order something wildly sophisticated like spaghetti with clams and we'd be oblivious to everything else because we were so much in love.

For now, though, cheeseburgers would have to do and if Matt – everyone called him Matt – wanted to be with me, nothing else mattered.

He didn't ask any questions about me, thank goodness; after all, my life didn't hold much of interest. Instead, I gazed into those deep brown eyes as he talked about how he and his mates had formed a band and once they'd finished school, they'd be the next big thing for sure. I pictured myself as the adoring girlfriend – no, fiancée – waiting for him after concerts and kissing him on hearing the news that the band's latest album had stormed up the charts.

He held my hand as we walked home and I couldn't believe my luck when he said he wanted to meet up again. We decided on chips in the local park in a couple of evenings' time.

He turned up late again but I told myself I couldn't expect a creative type like him to worry about being punctual. We bought bags of thick greasy chips, poured salt and vinegar on them, and splashed out on bottles of Fanta. We sat by the lake in the park and ate our chips and afterwards I felt a bit queasy but oh so happy to be with Matt, him of the dark eyes and hair.

He told me more about himself; I learned he'd picked science subjects at school with a view to studying mechanical engineering at one of the London universities.

'Gonna go, keep my dad quiet, like you have to, but I reckon I won't need to bother much with the course. I'll be discovered by some hotshot music producer, with or without the band, before long.'

I said nothing, in awe of his self-confidence.

'Can't wait to leave. This place is a dead-end dump.'

Hurt cut through me at hearing him say that, but I realised someone with Matt's abilities couldn't stay in a small town like this. He was right; he needed to be in London, ready for his talent to be discovered. I wasn't going to be selfish and if Matt had to move away, I'd go as well. I'd get a job, any job, and we'd be together.

We finished the chips and Fanta and he squeezed his arm around my shoulders. He pulled me towards him and on that old bench spattered with pigeon shit I had my first kiss, our mouths greasy from the chips and tasting of vinegar and Fanta. I had no idea what to do, unlike him – after all, a boy as good-looking as Matt must have had any number of girlfriends – and he didn't seem to think I did too badly. He kissed me again, his hand sliding under my T-shirt towards my breasts.

I was almost relieved when the first few drops of rain fell on us.

'Better be getting home,' I mumbled.

He took his hand off my breast. 'My parents are going out Sunday afternoon. You can come over.'

Sunday came, and I went to his house, my stomach twisting into knots at the thought of what he'd expect. I'd never had any experience with boys, Gran, apart from the kiss on the park bench. Remember what you said about my mother? How she gave her body to anyone who wanted her, and why? Well, I could have given her some stiff competition back then – now as well – in the low self-esteem stakes. I was the teenage daughter of a deceased alcoholic, after all, and fatherless to boot. Losing my virginity to Matt that afternoon was as inevitable as my mother choking on her own vomit. He wanted me, and I didn't even think of saying no.

We started kissing, and I found myself sprawled on the bed, with Matt on top of me, his hand snaking under my T-shirt again. His touch caused me to shiver, whether from nerves or excitement I couldn't tell. I knew I was going to go through with this, but a prickle of fear stabbed me. Would I measure up to the girls he'd had before? Would he still want me afterwards?

He had a condom ready, so we did it, all uncomfortable and awkward, and I didn't get anywhere near coming, and then he finished, to my relief. Not just because the discomfort had ended, but also because I'd finally had sex. I was no longer a virgin. Matt had plucked my cherry well and truly and if I hadn't enjoyed the experience, well, plenty of girls probably didn't the first time. I know you won't mind me telling you this, Gran. You always were a woman of the world, and totally unfazed by sex.

We started dating regularly, usually a couple of times a week, sometimes less.

'Got band practice most nights,' he told me. 'Have to put the music first.' I understood, even if I didn't like it. He was going to make the big time, after all, and I wouldn't do anything to get in his way.

Next time the sex wasn't so uncomfortable, and I felt more confident. So what if I didn't get much pleasure? I knew I was in love and if he'd not yet told me he felt the same, well, I could wait. We were seeing each other regularly, making love, as I liked to call it, every time, and I couldn't have been happier.

Then everything changed. A motorist who believed he could drive with more beer than blood in his veins cut short my foster father's life one night. His wife went into emotional meltdown after his death and, unable to cope, asked for a new placement for me. Too old at seventeen for another foster home, I ended up in supported lodgings with a family.

I didn't like the change at all. The man made me squirm with revulsion and I did my best to avoid him. I'd catch him staring at my bottom if I wore tight jeans and he always talked to my breasts rather than to my face. The woman was pleasant and did her best to make me welcome, so I tried to stay close to her and she'd chat away, being one of those people who liked to talk and didn't expect a great deal of response. They had one child, an eight-year-old boy, who spent his spare time out playing with his friends. I spent most of mine in my room, when not in school.

It was a time of upheaval, what with the funeral and the change of living arrangements and I didn't get to see Matt for a few weeks. I phoned him as often as possible, though.

'I miss you,' I'd say every time we spoke. I never did find the courage to ask if he missed me. Instead, I'd listen to the smooth velvet voice that would take him to stardom and impatience to see his soft brown eyes again would shoot through me. Once things became more settled, we arranged to meet at his house the coming weekend.

His dark good looks overwhelmed me once more and we had sex straight away; only later did I realise we'd forgotten to use a condom. I convinced myself it would be OK; we were normally so careful and it wouldn't be fair if I got pregnant after one little lapse. I carried on meeting Matt whenever he could spare the time and didn't think too much about the fact I'd had bare flesh instead of latex thrusting inside me that day.

Then I realised I'd not had my period for a few weeks and I got scared. I waited a bit longer; still nothing happened. By now, I was seriously frightened. I went to the chemist and bought a testing kit, unable to look the cashier in the eye as I handed the money over. I took it home, read the instructions and prayed things would be all right, hoping I'd wake up tomorrow to find menstrual cramps replacing the knot of tension twisting in my stomach.

It didn't happen, of course. I woke up the next day and my period still hadn't come, so I went into the bathroom and peed on a plastic stick, and I chewed my nails and thought of what Matt would say. He had London and his career ahead of him or at the very least his engineering course, and then I thought about me. I was too young to have a baby; I was looking forward to London even if Matt hadn't mentioned me going as well, and I had the whole world before me. Or so I thought.

Things didn't work out like that, as you know, Gran. I stared at the plastic stick and the realisation punched me in the gut that I'd managed to get pregnant, however unfair it might seem after one moment of carelessness among all the condoms we'd used. I had to tell Matt, but hey, maybe that would be when he told me he loved me.

I called him and we arranged to meet the next evening in the park. The wind was cold, a hint of rain in the air. We'd only just sat down on our usual bench when I blurted it out.

'I'm pregnant.' I couldn't look at him as I spoke so I never did see his initial reaction.

'Are you sure?' His voice sounded tight, as if caught in his throat. I'd taken him by surprise but he'd be all right eventually, or so I hoped. He had a lot to take in.

'Yes. I'm way late. I've done a test too. Remember the time we got carried away and didn't use anything?'

'Yeah, but . . .' He didn't seem able to look at me, his fingers fidgeting with the zip on his jacket. It must be the shock, I decided. He'd be fine once he got used to the idea.

The silence tightened between us. I craved to hear him say it would be all right, for him to give me the reassurance I desperately needed. To pull me close, tell me he loved me. When he did speak, his words dropped like acid on my teenage hopes.

'Is it mine? How can you be sure I'm the father?'

I couldn't reply for a while. Eventually I managed to force some choked-up words past my dry throat. 'There's been no one else. It's yours.'

Silence again. Then:

'Can't you . . . you know . . . get rid of it?'

With those words, Gran, my dreams of London and the perfect boyfriend shattered. A chasm as wide as the world stretched between us, a gulf I realised had always existed. Only my naïveté and lack of self-love had made me believe otherwise. I saw myself for the gullible fool I was, a girl now left to carry the baby, and alone as well. Matthew Hancock was worthless, immature and completely undeserving of the love I'd thought I felt for him. No love existed in my heart then, not when he made it clear I should take myself off and get our baby pulled out of me and washed down the drain. However sick I'd been at the thought of being pregnant, I'd never once thought of abortion. Never. I stood up and walked away from him, leaving him where he belonged, on that old bench covered with pigeon shit. I didn't look back.

6

FAMILY TALK

Daniel glanced at the alarm clock on the bedside table. One in the morning. Beside the clock stood a stone statue of Shiva, bought by Katie when she first came into his shop, one of several Oriental carvings around her flat. He picked up the statue, running his fingers over the cool stone.

Katie was lying next to him, wearing what he liked to think of as her thoroughly fucked look. She glanced at him, smiling at the slow slide of his hands over the marble. 'A souvenir of that fateful day we met. You'll have noticed I'm partial to sculpture, especially anything from the Far East. Never thought it would lead me to Fulham's hottest male.'

Daniel laughed, putting the statue back. There was silence for a while, before he trailed his finger down her cheek.

'Penny for them, beautiful.'

'A penny's all they're worth?' Katie settled herself among the pillows. 'Maybe I was wondering how I got so lucky, finding a hot slice of man like you. But if that were the case . . .' She grinned at Daniel, her expression feral. 'I wouldn't tell you anyway. I reckon your ego is big enough without me swelling it even further.' They kissed lazily for a few minutes; sated, relaxed kisses now they'd taken the edge off their mutual lust.

'Hmm. Not just your ego swelling around here.' Katie reached down a hand to grasp Daniel's cock. 'You have no recovery time?'

'Not when I'm in bed with Putney's hottest female.' He put one finger under her chin and upped it. 'Think a lot of you, Katie girl.'

Katie pulled back to look at him. 'Me too, Dan.' They'd not mentioned the word love yet, but every time they'd seen each other recently it seemed to be there. Hanging in the air between them, teasing them, baiting them with the idea that now might be the right time to say it. This was new territory for Daniel; he was undecided as to whether he was sinking or swimming in the uncharted waters of Katie Trebasco. Australia, moving in together, being – what had she called it – de facto partners? Sheesh. Fast going for someone who'd not got beyond three dates with any woman – or man – before. At this rate, he'd soon be tossing shrimps on the barbie somewhere hot and dusty on the other side of the world.

And it wasn't so terrible a thought. He laughed.

'Share the joke, why don't you?'

'Just picturing me Down Under, doing the stereotypical Aussie male barbecue thing. Tongs in one hand, beer can in the other. You at my side, smoking hot in a bikini. Hey!' he said, as she punched his arm. 'Seriously, Katie. It's got to beat English rain and fog.'

'You'd better come up with a more compelling reason to go than the British climate. Sounds like you're thinking about it, though.' Was that hope he detected in her voice?

'Said I would, didn't I?' Hurt crossed her expression, sparking the realisation he'd played it too casual. 'To be honest, I've not thought of much else.'

She smiled. 'I appreciate it's a big decision. What would your mother and stepfather think, Daniel? You don't talk about them much.'

'Not much to say. Don't see a great deal of them.' Katie talked about her parents a lot, obviously close to them, the adored youngest child of a seemingly perfect family; it made his chest grow tight with jealousy when he thought of it.

'Any particular reason?'

'Yeah. Doesn't sound like my family's much like yours.' He opted for his standard tactic, deflection. 'Tell me about them. Names, ages, all that sort of stuff.'

'All right. I'll start with Mum and Dad. My father's called Richard and Mum's name is – wait for it – India.'

'That's a bit offbeat.' Daniel pulled a face. 'I thought Trebasco was a strange enough name. But India?'

'My grandfather travelled a lot in Asia, hence Mum's name. I think they wanted something unusual to call her.'

'You're close to your parents, right? You talk to your mum every day?'

'Every day. We're like best mates. She had me when she was forty. My sister Sarah was born straight after they got married, when Mum was twenty. They never meant for her to be an only child, but for some reason Mum didn't conceive again. They did all the tests; the doctors never found anything to explain why Mum couldn't get pregnant for a second time. They told her to keep trying, but in the end, I think they accepted it wasn't going to happen. Perhaps that's what did it. Often happens with women. The pressure to conceive goes away, and boom! Nine months later, I came along.' She laughed. 'A surprise baby for them in their forties. They spoiled me rotten. So did Sarah.'

'Was it difficult for your sister? Her being so much older than you?'

'No. We get on fantastically well, always have done. She was amazed, but delighted, when she found out she was going to have a brother or sister and, as I said, she spoiled me. She's been like a second mother. She was married by the time I came along, what with there being so much of an age gap. And then . . .' Katie's voice trailed off. He couldn't fathom the expression on her face.

He hugged her. 'Hey, what's up? You look kind of . . . sad.'

'Nothing. Think I'll keep that one for another time. You've got this impression of us being the stereotypical happy family – well, we were. We are. Apart from the skeleton rattling around in the closet. Dan, do you mind if we don't go there? It's not something I want to talk about right now.'

Reluctance to discuss family matters was something Daniel understood only too well. Unsure how to respond, however, he resorted to flippancy. 'Aw, you've got me all intrigued. You will tell me, right? One day? Going to open the closet door and let the skeleton out?'

'Yes, I'll tell you. Just not now.' She looked away. He'd never seen her like this – withdrawn, reflective – and it upset him. He realised he didn't like seeing her unhappy.

Ah, well. He'd prise it out of her eventually.

He needed a little deflection again. Australia would do nicely.

'Are your family going to be OK with their precious baby girl living on the other side of the world? Anyway, what about you? You're not going to miss them?'

'Of course. I'll miss them like crazy, but they love me to bits; Mum and Dad would never want me to hold back on anything because of them.'

'Do I get to meet them sometime?'

'Yes. You do. Don't look so worried. They'll like you.'

'Katie, you're a doctor. You've been to medical school. You save lives for a living. What was your dad before he retired – some sort of high roller in the financial world? I manage a small shop-cum-art gallery and it's not even mine. I just run it for someone else. Am I going to be what they want for you?'

'Dan, this isn't the nineteen-fifties. You don't need permission from my dad to date me. They won't care what you do work-wise.'

'Are you sure?' He appreciated her attempt to reassure him, yet a nugget of doubt persisted. Would a shop worker be good enough for Katie's parents?

'Yes. Dad may have done well in his stockbroking career but he's not a snob. Neither is Mum, or anyone else in my family. They're all pretty down-to-earth people.'

'But you've not told them much about me, have you?'

Katie sighed. 'Not a lot, no, but not because I'm ashamed of you, or whatever you might be imagining. Oh, don't pull that face. I've not known you long, but I can guess what you're thinking a lot of the time.'

'Scary. Now even my thoughts aren't private anymore.' He kissed her. 'So what's with the secrecy, if you're so close to them? How come you've not told them about the handsome sex god you're dating?' He belied his flippancy with a smile.

She responded by pressing close, her skin soft against his. 'It's partly because you're becoming, shall we say, pretty important to me, that I've not said anything. You're right. Mum and I are really tight, and usually I tell her every last detail about who I'm seeing, straight off.'

'Yeah. That makes perfect sense. You meet Mr Wonderful – that would be me, in case you're in any doubt – and you don't tell your mum. Whereas every Mr Wrong who's passed through your life gets a mention?'

'Hey, it's not like I haven't talked about you. Mum knows I've been seeing someone. That's another thing. Every time we speak on the phone, she asks me a hundred questions about you. I'm a wicked daughter, Dan.' She laughed, a relief to him after her earlier withdrawal. 'I love keeping Mum in suspense, teasing her. I've not even told her your name yet. She knows you're my toy boy and yes, being two years younger than me does qualify you as a toy boy. I've let slip you're tall and look like you've stepped off a Hollywood movie set and that's about all. She's threatening to camp out here in my flat until she meets you.'

'OK. I get the bit about liking to wind your mum up. That all there is to it?'

'No.'

'You going to let me in on the rest this side of Christmas?'

'It's hard to explain.' Katie sighed. 'This may sound crazy but the reason I've not told them much about you yet is because of the way I'm starting to feel about you. It's like when you're a kid, you know? Talk about something and you jinx it. I'm eight years old again in my head and you're a wonderful secret I'm carrying around with me. I want to keep you all to myself for a while longer. Make any sense?'

Daniel laughed. 'Strangely enough, yes.'

'Sounds mad, I know. Listen, I will tell them about you, and soon. Anyway, Mr Hypocrite, I bet you've not mentioned me to your mum and stepdad yet.'

'I did say I've been dating someone. The thing is – I've only seen Mum a couple of times since we started going out and it was the usual with her, you know? She treats me as if I'm a kid – "Are you eating properly?" "Are you wearing enough warm clothes?" It never stops.'

'You're going to have to tell me about them, Dan. I'll be meeting them someday, if this goes anywhere between us.'

'I know. It's just . . . well, from what you say you had a happy childhood. You're close to your parents. Some of us don't come from that sort of background.'

'You're right. I guess I'm one of the lucky ones. You really can't tell me about them?'

He couldn't go on avoiding the subject. No, he'd tell her the bare bones, and with any luck that would be enough. For now, anyway.

'OK. Mum had me when she was young, at eighteen. Her mother had died a few years before. Her only other living relative was her grandmother, on her mother's side.'

'Was she a single mum? What about your father?'

'An engineering student. Aspiring musician too, from what she's said. They'd been saving up, planning to get married once he'd finished university in London. Then do the living happily ever after bit. Except things didn't work out like that.'

'What happened?'

'He died in a car crash. Huge pile-up on the M4. She was seven months pregnant at the time.'

Katie expelled a breath. 'Christ, Dan! She must have gone through hell.'

'You're right. Must have been incredibly rough. I can't imagine how Mum coped, to be honest. Might explain why sometimes . . . she suffers on and off with some sort of depression, Katie. Withdraws, barely speaks, needs medication.'

'What was your father like? You a chip off the old block?'

'I've never seen any pictures of him. She never talked about him when my stepfather was around. Chip off the old block? Yeah. Mostly, from what I've been told. Apparently, he was tall, with dark hair, like me. Brown eyes. Not like me. Good-looking, she always said. Definitely like me.'

Katie laughed, before her expression sobered. 'Sounds like your mum had life tough at a young age. No father, no mother . . . she had a grandmother, you said?'

'Yeah. I'm not sure when she died; I get the impression Mum finds it hard to talk about her. They were really close, you see, in a way she doesn't seem to have been with her own mother. At least, that's what comes across from what she says. Which isn't much. Must run in the family, the not being close to your mother bit.'

'How old were you when she got hitched to your stepfather?'

'She met him when I was nearly five. Married the bastard a year later.'

'Hmm. I'm getting the impression, loud and clear, you two don't get on.'

'Yeah. You could say that.'

'Is he that bad? Why don't you like the guy?'

'You mean apart from him being a total arsehole?'

'Yeah, but what makes him an arsehole? Look at me, Dan. Please.'

Daniel's emotions squeezed tighter than a clamshell. He'd tell her enough to keep her from asking too many questions, but nothing else. Ian Bateman was a sore spot he had no intention of probing.

'He's one of life's stereotypes, Katie. One of those who never have an opinion against the norm. Supports Fulham because he's a guy and hey, guys from round our way all support Fulham, so he does too. Same reason he plays golf on Sunday. Oh, and of course . . .' Sarcasm curled Daniel's mouth. 'He's a complete philistine, despises anything to do with books, music or art. All art, but especially mine. "Artists are hippies and fools and should get a proper job." A common refrain with him.'

'Is he the reason you've never pursued your art as a career? When I've noticed every time you talk about it, your eyes light up like crazy? And there's this animation in your voice you don't get any other time. Is that why you think he's an arsehole?'

'You got it. When I first mentioned doing a degree in art, he didn't stop banging on about it for days. You'd have thought I wanted to study paper folding, for God's sake.' He tensed, hearing his stepfather's searing contempt in his head. 'He said I was a waste of space, a dreamer, and if I believed I'd ever make a living out of slapping paint on canvas I was even stupider than he'd thought. Told me no way would he ever pay one penny towards me doing an art course.'

'Didn't your mother stick up for you? What did she say when he spoke to you like that?' He heard raw anger in Katie's voice, her vehemence temporarily drowning out his stepfather's contempt. Not that it ever left him for long.

'He never behaved that way when she was around. He saved it for when she went out. Not that he was exactly warm towards me when she was there, but he never did or said anything out of line. She was surprised I never studied art at college, but she had no idea he was the reason. She doesn't have any money of her own, or I presume she doesn't, given the fact she gave up work when she married him. I wouldn't have asked her anyway. I think she always expected my stepfather would provide the funds if I wanted to go to college, so when I didn't, she thought I didn't want to.' He laughed bitterly. 'Not the case. I'd have given my right arm to study art.'

'Except then you wouldn't be able to paint. Yep. Your stepfather sounds like a complete arsehole.' The anger in Katie's voice cheered Daniel. This woman understood, making her a keeper if ever there was one.

'See, apart from art, there was nothing else I wanted to do. So I left home as soon as possible, did delivery work, bar work . . . ended up managing the shop where we met. I do art classes as and when I can.' He fought, without success, to prevent resentment seeping into his tone.

'You've not seen much of them since?'

'Not really. He plays golf on Sunday. I go round then to see Mum. She cooks a traditional Sunday roast because she's not convinced I eat properly now I don't live with her. I leave as soon as I can and always before he gets home.'

'So what about your mother? How come you don't get on with her?'

44

'She's what I call a smother mother. Always has been. Promise me you'll never fuss over whether my socks are warm enough.' Daniel realised his words sounded brusque. 'I don't mean to sound uncaring. She's just a bit much at times.'

'Perhaps you're being too hard on her. Isn't that what mums do? Mine still worries about me. I know my gap year was tough on her.'

'Yeah, I know, Katie. She doesn't have a great deal in her life, I suppose, and she's always made me the focus of it. It's a bit difficult to deal with, although I try not to get annoyed with her.'

'She get on OK with your stepfather?'

'Yeah. In her way. She's always been a traditional wife. Shirts ironed, washing done, his meals cooked.'

Katie laughed. 'All the things I will never be doing for you.'

'The funny thing is – I may think he's a prick, but she doesn't. She really does seem to feel affection for him, hard as that is for me to understand. I always thought he cared more for her than the other way round, though.'

'Do you think he does care about her? Or is it the fact he has an on-tap maid service?'

'That's the weird part. When I lived with them, he genuinely seemed to love her. Showed it in little ways . . . I don't know, like the way he looked at her, his tone of voice, although he could be pretty controlling towards her.'

'What's your mum like?'

'She's nothing like me. Petite, comes up to just under my shoulders. Not bad for her age . . . she was really pretty when younger. She has a picture of herself, when she was eighteen, holding me not long after I was born. Dark blonde hair and big blue eyes. Heard my stepfather tell her enough times her eyes were what drew him to her when they first met. He actually sounds romantic – except that's not a concept you'd associate with him – when he says it.' He yawned. 'You finished interrogating me about my family? Can we get some sleep now?'

'Yep. Don't think you're completely off the hook, though.' She grinned, before her expression sobered. 'I'm aware you're reluctant to talk about your family. I'm here for you, though, Dan.' She stroked a finger down his cheek. 'Remember that.'

He did, as he fell asleep, her body spooned against his. Tonight marked a turning point, he decided. A while back, talk of Ian Bateman would have triggered a desperate hunt for sex. Not anymore. Somehow Katie made all the angst melt away.

7

HIS WORD AGAINST MINE

My already fractured world was about to split apart even further, and the hopelessly naïve girl I was back then had no idea.

The woman from the house where I was lodging had gone out for the evening and the eight-year-old boy was at a sleepover. The man sat downstairs drinking beer, as usual; he didn't figure in my thoughts for even a second. I lay on my bed, Gran, planning how to tell you about my pregnancy, hoping you would understand and not be too disappointed in me. I thought I could come and live with you; I'd be the best mother ever and give my child the love and stability I'd never had. Maybe I'd take some courses at the local college, get some qualifications after my baby's birth. It'll turn out all right, I promised myself.

I was jolted out of my daydreams by the door banging open. The man walked in.

He'd never come into my room before. Every part of me instinctively backed away from him, wanting him gone.

He sat on the bed, amid a cloud of boozy breath, belching beer fumes my way. I inched away from him, drawing my legs up beside me.

'So,' he said. 'You still seeing that boyfriend of yours?'

His words startled me. I didn't think anyone knew about Matt. I'd never actually lied about him, but every time we'd met, I'd given the impression I was going to see a female friend from school. I thought I'd face fewer questions that way.

'I saw the two of you.' He edged closer. 'One evening. Going into Burger King. Holding hands. I thought to myself: Laura, she's bagged herself a boyfriend. Not surprising. Pretty girl like you.'

'He's not my boyfriend.' I had no idea why I told him that. 'We broke up.'

'You don't say.' He wetted his lips, his eyes nailing themselves to my breasts. 'You shouldn't be too upset. Like I said, a pretty girl like you . . . you could have your pick.'

Oh, God. I swear my flesh tried to crawl off my bones. I couldn't bear him being in my room, with both of us on my bed.

I twisted my legs onto the floor and made as if to stand up. His hand clamped around my arm, his grip crushing.

'Oh no, you don't. You're not running out on me. I want some of what you've been giving that boyfriend of yours.' He brought his face closer to mine and revulsion hit me as I saw the open pores on his nose, the veins in the whites of his eyes. His breath, reeking of beer and bad hygiene, hit me sourly in the face. I struggled to wrench my arm free from his grasp, but he tightened it even further.

I tried to fight back, Gran, but I couldn't. He had me cornered and there was no escape. I barely topped five feet two and weighed seven and a half stone. He measured six feet and weighed sixteen stone at least. I never stood a chance.

So I lay there, and the thing I thought couldn't be happening was, and I turned my head away and tried to pretend it wasn't. I was sobbing and thinking, no, he can't be doing this, he can't. There's a baby inside me and I have to take care of it and not let this happen. All the while, the man charged with giving me a safe and secure home lay on top of me, pinning me down with his weight while he rolled on a condom. The thought registered in my brain that he'd planned this; he'd come into my room prepared. Then he thrust into me, sudden and rough, and it hurt. He was heavy and slick with sweat, his flabby belly pressing tight against me, musty breath hot against my ear. I was bone-dry and getting sore and it seemed to go on forever.

Eventually he rolled off.

'It'll be your word against mine,' he said.

When I didn't respond, he stood up and left.

I lay there and I felt soiled, Gran, as if something vile and slimy had smeared itself all over me and I'd never be clean again. I wanted to turn up the shower as hot as it would go and scrub away the filth he'd put on me and not come out until I'd scoured every trace of him off my body. I didn't, because part of me was able to think clearly, you see, Gran, even if another part was screaming and wanting to pound my fists into the bed. I thought there might be some evidence to take to the police, like one of his pubic hairs or something.

His parting words came back to me, though. It would be his word against mine. I didn't have any fight left, Gran. Years of looking after Mum, finding out about my pregnancy, the betrayal by Matthew Hancock – and now this. I imagined stern police officers, looking at me, judging me, asking me if I was making it all up, had I consented to sex, after all I wasn't a virgin, was I? I thought of him telling a male officer how he'd tried to do his best for me, provided me with a home when I needed one, and the two of them nodding, agreeing that girls made things up, didn't they, to get attention. I pictured opening my legs as some hard-faced female doctor swabbed me for evidence. I thought of standing up in court while some stone-hearted lawyer tore me to shreds.

No. I couldn't do it. Far better to be a coward and run away.

I listened. I knew he was downstairs; I thought perhaps if I stayed very quiet, I'd be all right. He'd had what he wanted, so I reckoned I was safe for now.

A while later I heard the woman arrive back and the sounds of voices came from below, although I couldn't distinguish the words. Eventually both of them came up the stairs and went into their bedroom, down the hall from mine, and then into the bathroom. Someone flushed the toilet. The bedroom door clicked shut.

At last, there was silence.

I waited for at least an hour. Then I got off the bed, wincing at the soreness between my legs but moving as quietly as possible. I took the largest bag I owned and filled it with what few possessions I had. Once done, I grabbed my coat and hoisted the bag over my shoulder. I came out of my room, walked down the stairs and carefully unlatched the front door. Then I stepped outside into the frigid night air, the door shut behind me, my rapist sleeping, unaware of my flight. I would never set foot in that house again and my only thought was to get to you, Gran.

My bag weighed too much and the walk seemed to take forever, the cold slicing through me with every step, but eventually I arrived at your house. I took the key from its hiding place under the stone in the front garden, and I let myself in, desperately calling out for you.

You came down the stairs and I ran to you, dropping the bag, needing you to take away the pain and misery soaked through me. You asked me repeatedly what had happened, but I couldn't find the words to tell you. I felt guilty for putting you through this but I had no choice. You were my only refuge – where else would I go?

Eventually I broke away and rushed up the stairs into the bathroom, where I took the longest, hottest shower of my life. I grabbed a sponge and the soap and I washed myself all over, rubbing fiercely between my legs, scrubbing away the vestiges of the repulsive, flabby man with the musty breath and sweaty body, making myself even sorer but I didn't care. I could hear you outside, Gran, pounding on the door.

At last, I turned off the shower and opened the door and stood in front of you, still dripping, a towel wrapped around my body. You looked into my face and you understood what had happened. You pulled me to you and walked me into your bedroom, sitting me on the bed.

It all came pouring out then, Gran, and I told you about him, about the vile man who had seized his chance with a vulnerable girl half his size. I told you how disgusting he had been, how he'd hurt me. How I thought you'd make me go to the police and that was why I'd taken the shower, to wash away any evidence, because no matter how hard you tried to persuade me, I would never report my rapist. He'd go unpunished because however cowardly it might be, I didn't have the strength to go to the police, even with you at my side.

I've never been sure you really understood how I felt about that. You were reliving the horror you had gone through when my mother came to you bruised, bloody and battered after the gang rape. You were furious, mad at the man who had taken your precious granddaughter and treated her like shit stuck to his shoe. You stroked your fingers over my bruised wrists, swearing under your breath, something you never did normally. You told me he shouldn't get away with it but I think you knew you were fighting a losing battle. The shower had swilled down the plughole any pubic hairs or anything else that could place my rapist, panting and sweating like the vile pig he was, on top of me. Without evidence, it really did come down to his word against mine.

I woke up the next morning and knew I'd have to tell you about my pregnancy.

We sat in the window seat after breakfast, clutching steaming mugs of coffee, and I talked about Matt, how I'd thought I'd loved him. Unable to look you in the eyes, I told you about the baby. How Matt had wanted me to get rid of it, but how I couldn't contemplate abortion as an option. Not for a second. You didn't let me down. No judgement, no lecture about how I should have been more careful. You put down your coffee mug, pulling me to you, whispering into my hair how everything would be all right. You said I could come and live with you and you'd help me with the baby. Then you didn't say anything for a long while, just held me tight and I knew I'd found what I'd come for.

8

FIRST MEMORIES

The sex next morning proved a perfect counterpoint to the emotion of the previous night. It was ten o'clock before Daniel and Katie emerged from her bedroom, hair messed up and bodies sweaty, but too hungry to head for the shower.

Katie got going on breakfast. He watched her as she moved around the kitchen. So much for saying she'd never do that sort of thing.

Sometimes he thought she had the power to read his mind. She glanced at him over her shoulder, a smile on her lips. 'Look what you've done to me, Dan. I've turned into your mother already. Not sure how or when that happened.'

Daniel snorted. 'Trust me, Katie, you are nothing like her.'

She handed him his breakfast. Small talk prevailed as Daniel wolfed down bacon and eggs, the chitchat a welcome distraction. After they'd eaten, though, his girlfriend's expression turned serious. Dread pooled in his gut; he guessed what was coming, and he needed to forestall her, and quickly.

She spoke too soon, however. 'About your mother . . .'

He sighed. He should have realised she'd never let this go.

'You said she was a smother mother. OK, I can see why that would irritate you. But . . .' Daniel heard puzzlement in her voice. 'Plenty of mothers are a bit protective. Yes, it must be annoying for their kids, but they still want to spend time with their mums.'

'I visit her out of duty more than anything. Her fussing gets hard to bear at times.'

'What about her mental health issues? Are they a problem for you?'

'No. Not at all.' Daniel meant that. Over the years, he'd become accustomed to his mother's odd spells, as he called them. He hadn't been the only one at school with a parent who needed pills from time to time. He'd learned to ride things through until she emerged from whatever dark world she'd retreated into.

'Plenty of people don't deal well with mental health problems in others, Dan. Especially when a family member's involved.'

'It's not that.' Christ, he didn't like the way this was going. Anyone other than Katie, and he'd be deflecting the conversation. Fat chance of that with her, though.

'What, then? Dan, if we're going to make a go of this, you and me, I want to discover every dark secret you're hiding. Besides, I can't help it. I'm nosy.' She flashed him a smile potent enough to reduce any straight man to his knees. 'Come on. Tell Katie everything.'

Daniel looked at her, this classy, sassy woman who seemed to accept him despite his issues. He wondered how she'd react if he talked more openly about his relationship with his mother. His guilt at not loving her the way a son should. Would he be able to convey to Katie the beyond-weird thoughts he'd had in his head? Since . . . well, like forever. Right now, he had no idea how to tell her without sounding completely screwed up.

He'd never spoken of his childhood memories before, except with his mother, a long time ago, and every time he did, she'd brushed his questions aside with a laugh. Told him he was imagining the whole thing, although he'd never believed her. He wasn't a small boy anymore, though; time to step up and be a man. Katie wanted to know why he'd never warmed to his mother, why his emotions about her were so conflicted. Fine, he'd do his best to explain, as weird as the whole thing might sound. He knew – however much he might want to deny it – that he shouldn't shut Katie out on this. After all, he'd already revealed more to her about his family life than he'd ever done with anyone else. Time to trust her with this too.

He wouldn't tell her everything, though. Some things he couldn't put a voice to.

'Talk to me, Daniel.'

'It's complicated. It'll sound weird too.'

'So? Tell me anyway.'

'OK.' He sucked air deep into his lungs. 'Did you ever feel . . . like you didn't belong in your family? Like . . . you'd been adopted, or there was a mix-up at the hospital and they gave you to the wrong parents or something?' He grimaced. It all sounded so paranoid when voiced out loud.

She shook her head. 'No, not really, Dan. I've told you how much it meant to Mum and Dad when I came along, how I've always been close to them. So, no, I've never felt I didn't belong with them.'

Yeah. That figured. Sour jealousy squeezed his chest.

'But I remember other kids at school . . . they sometimes talked about believing they'd been adopted because they didn't think they fitted in with their family. Isn't that quite common, though, Dan? You do something out of line, your parents clamp down on you, and suddenly you're misunderstood and hard done by and life's terribly unfair. So you try to make sense of things by thinking you must have been adopted.'

'Perhaps. But that's not it.'

'What, then?'

'What are your earliest memories, Katie?'

She paused. 'I remember . . . let me think . . . the rag doll I had as a young child. The pink flowered wallpaper in my bedroom. Being told bedtime stories by my dad.'

'How old were you?'

'I'm not sure. I guess I can remember back as far as . . . three? Four? Hard to say.'

'You want me to tell you what my first memories are?'

'Well, yes, if this is all part of telling me what the issue is between you and your mother.'

'I remember being somewhere else.'

'What do you mean?'

'It's all quite vague, Katie. These are my earliest memories, as I told you. They're real, though. They might be indistinct, but they're genuine all right. I remember . . .' He shut his eyes, willing his mind back through the years. 'Someone else, other than my mum, taking care of me. A teenager, I think. She used to toss me a ball to catch. She had dark hair. Definitely not Mum. She's blonde, as I told you. There was another woman too. Older. I don't remember much about her. I can picture her, beside my bed at night. She'd sit there after tucking me in. Maybe she was telling me bedtime stories. I don't recall.'

Katie's expression was unfathomable. 'Dan . . . these memories . . . they might not be what you think. Perhaps the young girl was a baby-sitter who helped your mum out. The other woman could be the same thing. Some friend or relative doing your mum a favour. You said she was close to her grandmother. It might be her you remember sitting by your bed.'

'No.' He was sure of that. 'She wasn't anywhere near as old as Mum's grandmother would have been. There was no one else to help her, as I told you. She was an only child and she's never talked about any aunts, cousins, any other female relatives. The older woman . . . she was there more than the occasional night, Katie. It happened more frequently than a friend doing Mum a favour once in a while.'

'Did you ask your mother about all this?'

'Yes. Several times, when I was still very young, until I realised she wasn't going to tell me anything different. Up until the age of about seven, I suppose. I remember she'd already married my stepfather the last time I asked.'

'What did she say?'

'The same thing every time. She always said I was imagining things and laughed it off. She'd tell me I was her beautiful boy, how precious I was, how much she loved me. I always felt guilty for asking.'

'Guilt. Every mother's favourite trick.' Katie laughed.

'Thing is, I don't remember who these women are, but I'm not imagining them, Katie. They're real, although the details are foggy. They played some role in my life before Mum came along. See, that's the other thing. Every time I remember the girl with dark hair . . . the woman beside my bed . . . Mum doesn't figure in those memories. She comes along later. I know I was only a tiny kid at the time. However, I'm sure, as certain as I've ever been of anything. Mum wasn't around then. That's what I've never been able to understand.'

'Dan . . . I'm not denying what you say. Human memory can be weird and not always reliable, though. Especially when you think how young you were. Children don't usually remember anything before the ages of three or four, and boys recall less than girls do. Perhaps your mum told you some story which somehow got translated in your mind . . .'

'No.' He realised he'd spoken too sharply. 'That's not how it was.'

'Hey.' She reached across the table and squeezed his hand. 'I'm sorry, Dan. I'm not pooh-poohing what you're telling me. I'm simply saying our memories can be flaky things. You've probably heard about false memory syndrome, where people recall all sorts of stuff that never actually happened.'

'I'm certain of what I remember, Katie. Those women are real. I just don't have any idea who they are.'

'You thought about asking your mother again? Now you're an adult?'

'No. I don't think she'd tell me anything different. I guess both my stepfather and I, we've always steered clear of anything that might upset her. She's always been, well, fragile. The depression thing. About the only time my stepfather ever shows a shred of sensitivity is where Mum's concerned. But there's more. You ever get gut feelings, Katie? Those times when you're certain of something, even if it goes against all logic?'

'Yes. Doesn't everyone? Can't explain how it works, but yeah, my intuition's pretty spot on.'

'Then you'll get what I'm going to say. I'm sure, Katie, and I always have been, deep inside. Every time I think of the girl with the dark hair, tossing me the ball, and the woman beside my bed, I've always thought I belong with them. I have no idea who they are, but they're more real, more my family, than Mum. That's why I can't feel what I should for her.' He sighed. 'It's all pretty weird, right?'

Katie pulled a face. 'A bit different, I guess. You ever thought what might be behind this? Tried to find out who these women are and why your mother hasn't been straight with you?'

'Yeah, I've thought about it.' Over and over. 'Never known what to do. Talking to Mum, as I told you, is a dead end. She has no relatives I can ask. Sounds awful, but I've thought about going through her stuff, seeing if she has anything that might tell me what I need to know.'

'Could you have been adopted?'

'I don't think so. Mum was only eighteen, remember; there's no chance she'd have been able to adopt legally at such a young age, especially as a single woman. The only way it could have happened would be if it had been done in secret. Perhaps she had a younger sister who got pregnant but died, so Mum took me on. The thing is – that doesn't make any sense either. Why pretend she's my mother, if she's not? Why tell me she was an only child? Told you it was all a bit weird.'

'Dan, I don't want to throw a spanner in the works, but something else is a bit strange here.'

'God. As if this weren't messed up enough already. Go on.'

'One of the first things I noticed about you was your gorgeous green eyes. Green eyes and dark hair have always had quite an effect on me.' She laughed. 'You said your mum has blue eyes?'

'Yes. What attracted my stepfather to her, according to him. They're probably her best feature, big and an unusually deep blue. I didn't inherit them, as you've pointed out.'

'But you also said she told you your father had brown eyes?'

'Yes, that's right. Why? What does his eye colour matter?'

'I don't know if you ever did much in the way of genetics at school. Thing is, the odds of a mother with blue eyes and a father with brown eyes having a child with green eyes – well, they're quite low. It happens, but it's unusual.'

'So . . .' Daniel paused, trying to comprehend what Katie had said. 'You're saying the man who my mother says was my father . . . there's a good chance he may not have been? That might be untrue as well?'

'Yes. It's not impossible, as I said. We still don't understand a lot about how children inherit some characteristics. The whole thing's way complicated, Dan. But along with what you've already said, about thinking your mum isn't your mum . . . well, there does seem to be something not stacking up here.'

'Shit.' He'd thought this couldn't get any weirder. 'Shit, Katie. I had a mother who might not be my mother when we started this conversation. Now my father, this engineering student who she said died before I was even born, may not be real either.' He tried to joke it away. 'I'm having one hell of an identity crisis here.'

'Dan. Listen to me.' The firmness in her voice forced him to meet her eyes. When he did, her expression was warm and sympathetic. 'You either figure out how to deal with this, or else you put it behind you. Forget these doubts, the memories, and accept your life the way it is. If you can't – and I can understand if not – then you need to find a way to get to the bottom of what it all means.'

'Yeah. You're right. People say stuff about needing to find their roots, where they came from. Tim's a good example. Spends ages on those family tree websites, looking up birth and death certificates. No wonder he never gets laid.' He laughed shakily. 'Well, it's not bullshit. I honestly haven't a clue who I am. I have a mother who has never felt like a mother. Now even my father may not be who I've always been told he was. Who exactly are you dating, Katie?' He shook his head. 'Christ. Everything is so completely screwed up. You're right; I need to sort out which way to jump with all this.'

He stood up. 'I'm going back to the flat to think. I'll call you tonight.'

9

GOD'S LAUGHTER

I'm desperate to explain things to you, Daniel. I didn't find things easy, you see. I was only seventeen when I got pregnant, eighteen when I gave birth, and to begin with I was terrified of what lay ahead. I tried not to think about having a tiny baby dependent on me for everything. I was determined to be the best mum I could. My child wouldn't have a drunk for a mother who only cared about her next wine fix. I might not be able to give my baby a father but I'd give it everything else.

Gran was always a practical woman. She made phone calls to Social Services in which she made it clear I'd be staying with her, pointing out I'd turn eighteen in two weeks' time and be able to make my own decisions. We had a visit from my social worker; I refused to answer her questions about why I'd run away and Gran, thank goodness, said nothing. In the end, everyone agreed the best solution would be for me to stay with her.

I remember glancing at Gran after the social worker left, thinking she now looked her age. She'd always seemed much younger, what with her patterned skirts, exotic jewellery and endless love of life. Her illness had stolen all her zest, though, and she looked every one of her seventy-three years, and more. She had never regained her pre-cancer weight, being bony thin, her cheekbones prominent, her posture hunched. Her movements appeared slower, her thought processes not as sharp. The time had come for me to take care of her, this woman who had always looked after me when I needed her. I thought we'd help each other, play with the baby together and perhaps she'd regain a little of her sparkle. I saw us in the garden, dangling toys over the pram of a smiling baby and I saw some hope for the future. Right then I didn't dare to ask for more.

Besides, I had other things to think about. I'd struggled through the morning sickness and was feeling human again. My appetite had returned and I'd started to fill out. It was weird watching how my breasts and stomach swelled, blue veins appearing and thick red stretch marks joining them. I felt fertile, blooming, luxuriant, my burgeoning belly proof of the life kicking inside me. To my relief, my increasing desire to be a mother replaced my initial fears and I slowly grew more confident about the future.

One night I lay trying to sleep, unable to get comfortable because of my huge, at least that's how it seemed to me, pregnancy belly and then the pains started. Gran got me into a taxi, we went to the hospital and then I found out what pain really was. I'll end up splitting in two, I thought; I simply can't manage this. They tried to give me an epidural but the damn thing didn't work and the agony tore away at me, worse and worse. I struggled, sweated, cursed and prayed it would soon end, but it didn't. The birth took over twenty-four hours and right at the point where I thought I couldn't go on and I'd have to either push this baby out somehow or die, that's when it happened. I made one final effort and suddenly everything was over. I was a mother.

And when I cradled my baby close, this red, screaming scrap, all the pain melted away and a rush of incredible love surged over me. I knew nobody and nothing would ever matter as much to me as this perfect creature I held in my arms.

'What will you call him?' Gran asked.

I had no idea. I'd flicked through baby books at the library during my pregnancy, but had never come to any conclusions. I wouldn't be naming my child after Matthew Hancock; that was for sure. Eventually I settled on Daniel. It was an old name, still popular, and went well with the surname Covey. Second name – well, that didn't seem so important. I chose Mark. Daniel Mark Covey. It sounded good, distinguished even, and Gran approved. We went to register the birth after I left hospital, and then I took my son home.

Daniel, you have no idea how demanding babies are. Perhaps one day you'll be a father, although with all those girlfriends you have, that change every week, it doesn't seem likely any time soon. You're young, though, still sowing your wild oats, and in a few years you'll be ready to settle down and make me a grandmother. Then you'll find out what hard work babies are.

The first few weeks passed in a blur. I changed nappies, heated bottles and rocked my son when he cried. I snatched scraps of sleep as and when I could; I was permanently exhausted. It was all I could do to struggle through every day.

Gran was wonderful and I would never have managed without her. I fretted, though, worried that looking after Daniel and me was taking a toll on her when she'd never recovered her pre-cancer health. She got woken up at night when Daniel screamed with rage, frustrated with a dirty nappy or an empty belly, and often looked worn out.

I tell you, Daniel, I was desperate with worry when I found her sitting in the chair one day, her face ashen, fear and bewilderment evident in her expression. My frantic questions, fired at her out of terror, confused her even more; she had trouble getting her words out. When I eventually got her to talk, she told me she'd been heating some milk when she suddenly found herself on the floor, but with no memory of falling. I bullied her until she agreed to go to the doctor and I think she probably felt too tired to argue.

Her doctor told me Gran had suffered a mini-stroke, and once she'd had one, she'd be more prone to another. He prescribed medication, telling Gran she had to take life more easily. I realised that however exhausted I might get looking after my baby, I needed to take better care of my grandmother.

I started to fuss more over her, reminding her to take her pills, which she didn't always do, and making sure she got disturbed as little as possible at night. She still looked tired a lot of the time, though. I knew she was worried about finances and the state of the house. She'd bought the place after my grandfather died, being unable to endure staying any longer in the home they'd created together. She'd not had much money and all she'd been able to afford was a small, isolated and run-down place a little way out of town, which needed more cash to set it right than she possessed.

Anyway, I was telling you about how hard it was for me, how exhausted I got. The house added an extra strain on my depleted energy. I spent my days with primer and paint, trying to brighten up our tired home, checking the roof for leaks and replacing the old gaffer tape on the pipes under the kitchen sink. Gran smiled wearily at me, and I knew she appreciated my efforts. I made big pots of soup and pans of thick stew and coaxed her to eat as much as possible. I became even more exhausted but realised I'd have to manage somehow. I was eighteen, after all, and I needed to be strong, both for my baby and for my beloved grandmother.

In between decorating and looking after Gran, I stroked my fingers over my son's fat cheeks and felt his chunky limbs flail around as I held him. I thought about going to college and getting some sort of qualification, maybe in a couple of years' time; meanwhile, I'd look after my baby and Gran and life would be good.

Ah, Daniel, my beloved son. As the saying goes, people make plans, and God laughs.

Will you visit me soon, my love? I miss you. You're my son, the finest part of my life. I adore you; I've always taken care of you and tried my best to do the right thing, no matter what you think of me now. If I could see you and explain things, then you'd understand. You'd realise how it was for me, you'd stop judging me and your anger would melt away. We could rebuild some sort of relationship and the knot of pain in my gut would begin to unravel.

In the meantime, I get daily visits from an eager young man, presumably some sort of psychiatrist, who leaves my room every day looking less and less hopeful that he'll be able to persuade me to speak. Ian has visited me most days as well. I think he believes he'll be the one to get me to talk. He takes my hand and looks at me and I find it impossible to look back at him. I stare at the floor instead and every time he leaves he seems a little more defeated.

It's not his fault, Daniel. He loves me and he's always tried to be a good husband. All this must be hard for him. Ian has never been a man to like change. Suddenly he finds his wife accused of stealing the child who bears his surname, whom he brought up as his stepson. I know you and he never had the sort of relationship I would have liked but he still provided a father figure for you, gave you a male role model. I don't understand why you and he don't have any contact; it upsets me. I want to ask him to call you and tell you to visit me, but I don't. I need you to come without being asked. I won't speak anyway, not until you come. You'll be here soon; I'm sure of it. I hold on to that thought as I go through the motions of living and wait for you, my beloved son, to walk through the door.

Sometimes, though, as I wait, I think I can hear God laughing at me.

10

DIGGING DEEPER

Back at the flat, Daniel's emotions were veering all over the place.

He tried to marshal his thoughts into some sort of order. Take his mother and stepfather. Wasn't his dysfunctional family the core issue here, the real reason for his doubts? He'd always considered himself a bit screwed up by not coming from an apple-pie happy family like Katie's. He'd been saddled with a father he'd never known and a mother he couldn't relate to, hardly an unusual scenario. Did happy families exist anyway? Even Katie's seemingly perfect set-up contained its skeleton in the closet.

Be rational about this, he thought. His girlfriend was probably right about the memory playing weird tricks on people, twisting their thought processes so something false appeared real. Perhaps all this amounted to was some bizarre quirk in his brain cells breathing life into two women who had never existed.

There was the weird eye colour thing, though. Genetics had added a new dimension to this whole mess, although he didn't pretend to understand it. Science hadn't been his thing at school; he'd never paid much attention to anything other than painting, sport and girls. He hadn't a clue whether it made any difference; as Katie had said, it wasn't impossible for him to have green eyes with a blue-eyed mother and a brown-eyed father.

His father. Had he really been the music-loving undergraduate who had died in a tangle of twisted metal and broken bodies on the M4? Or had his mother invented the engineering student and his tragic death? If so, it added weight to the idea of him being adopted and his mother not being able to admit what had happened, for whatever reason. The problem being, as he'd pointed out to Katie, if he'd been adopted, it wouldn't have been official. There would be no records for him to check.

Wait a minute, though. Perhaps he'd been right in thinking the woman who called herself his mother was really his aunt. Laura Bateman might have had a sister who'd given birth and then died, and she took the child as her own. Maybe the death of this sister had traumatised her with grief, and so she never spoke about her. It would explain why Daniel had never completely bonded with her, if he wasn't her son. Might be the reason for the eye colour thing as well.

Both birth and death certificates would be on record if there had been a sister. Easily traceable, if he chose to do so. He could put Tim's fascination with genealogy to use, feigning a new-found interest in his family history to satisfy any curiosity from his flatmate.

It didn't explain, though, who the girl and the woman in his memories were, unless perhaps the woman was his maternal grandmother and the girl his birth mother. That didn't feel right, though. He couldn't shake the strong sense of connection with the woman beside his bed, as if she were his mother, not the girl with the dark hair. Something still didn't stack up here.

The same old story, he thought, as he paced his bedroom. Frustration clawed at him. He didn't have a clue what to do about the mess in his head. Should he even do anything at all? After all, he could always decide to live with the uncertainty and get on with his life. There was a lot to say for choosing the path of least resistance.

Shouldn't he resign himself to the fact he'd been dealt a less than wonderful family hand and move on? Perhaps not the ideal solution, but with Katie at his side, he'd get by.

Yeah, the easy option sure seemed preferable.

What had he once heard, though? How the hard way always got easier and the easy way always got harder.

He'd be taking the hard way, then, because he couldn't lie to himself. The old familiar feeling stirred in his gut. He'd never convince himself the memories weren't genuine. That Laura Bateman really had given birth to him. Especially now Katie had told him about genetics and eye colour. The doubts had doubled, tripled, multiplied out of control.

He dug into his memories, searching for the girl with the dark hair and the woman beside his bed. He saw the girl, her hair about shoulder length. The memory blurred in his head and he needed to concentrate to hold onto it. They were outdoors; he remembered the green of the grass, but he didn't recall any other details. All he could remember was the ball being tossed to him and the way the girl's hair swung as she moved. In his mind, she laughed at his infant self; in return he giggled with delight, a moment of bliss in an otherwise unhappy childhood. The same conviction he always experienced stirred again. The girl was real, and she had been important in his early life.

He dug down again, and brought up the unknown woman. This time, he was warm and comfortable in bed. This memory was even more indistinct, the room being in darkness. The woman sat on the edge of the bed as if she belonged there. He didn't remember her speaking or doing anything other than tucking him in. He didn't recall what she looked like. Whenever he thought of her, though, a sense of calm, of peace, came to him. This woman represented safety, warmth, security. No monsters lurked in the dark in that child's bedroom.

What struck him was the contrast between his feelings about his mother compared to when he remembered the woman beside his bed. Often a certain detachment prevailed when Daniel brought his mother to mind. Coupled with guilt at being a bad son. Yet when he thought of the woman sitting at his bedside, he always felt loved. Warm, safe and secure. He knew that was why, deep down, he believed this woman to be his mother rather than Laura Bateman.

The girl and the woman. Surely to God they must think about him, where he lived, what he might be doing? He wondered where they were, how he'd react if he ever met them again, which, God knows, didn't seem remotely possible. He didn't have a single clue to go on about their identities or where they might be, assuming they were both still alive. He had no reason to think they weren't; after all, the girl had been young, and the woman, well, she'd probably be in her forties or fifties now.

There remained the idea of searching through his mother's things to find answers, something like photos, letters or a diary. He dismissed the thought, as he'd always done before. No way would he sink so low as to pry through her possessions. He wasn't about to invade his mother's privacy without a very real expectation he'd find something, and he didn't have that. Besides, if he did find anything, he wouldn't be able to tackle her about whatever he came across. She'd never provided answers in the past and he didn't have any reason to think she'd start now.

His thoughts were turning in circles, ever-widening ones, without giving him any relief. Still, he now possessed something to go on, even if just a supposition. He'd talk to Tim as soon as his flatmate got home. Then, if he found Laura Bateman had once had a sister, he'd have something more solid with which to confront her.

Time to put the brakes on all this navel gazing, though. He was exhausted, strangely emotional too. He needed to talk to Katie. He pulled out his mobile.

'Hey, sweet pea. Missing me?'

'Don't flatter yourself.' He pictured the eye roll she'd be doing as she spoke. 'What've you been up to?'

'Thinking. I'm surprised you didn't hear the wheels turning.'

'Thought any more about what we talked about?'

'Yeah.' He briefly outlined what he planned to do.

'Makes sense. As you say, Tim can help you. I've never done anything along those lines, but these things are a matter of public record, aren't they? This idea of yours about her having a sister who may be your real mother: well, you're right. There'll be both birth and death certificates if she did exist and your mother, or aunt, covered it all up for some reason. But Dan . . . ?' Her voice held a warning.

'What?'

'You need to think about how to tackle this, if you do find your mother is really your aunt. You can't march in and confront her, if she's suppressed the memory of her sister's death, and if she's always suffered mental health issues. That would be cruel, not to say dangerous.'

'Yeah. You're right. One bridge at a time, though, OK? I'll talk to Tim tonight. Let's see if this hypothetical sister really did exist first. We might come up with nothing, after all. Perhaps Mum always has been an only child.'

'Have you considered what you'll do if that turns out to be the case? If you don't come up with a sister?'

'I'll be back where I started. Feet firmly planted on square one. Don't have a clue what I'll do then.'

'Not a problem. I have the answer. A pretty simple one too.'

'You what?'

'This conviction you have that she's not your real mother – well, I've thought of an easy way to prove that, one way or another. A private DNA test.'

This woman never ceased to amaze him. 'How do those work? Don't you need a blood sample?'

'Blood works best, sure, but plenty of other ways exist to get DNA. Hair, for example. You should be able to obtain some of her hair from her brush. With the roots attached. Take some of yours, send both sets to the lab, and they'll run the DNA. They'll be able to tell you for sure if she's your mother.'

He'd never considered such an idea but Katie was right. It would be easy enough to get a hair sample from his mother's brush. All he had to do was to go into the bedroom she shared with his stepfather the next time he visited her. She'd never know he'd taken the hair and if it did turn out she was his mother, well, he'd keep quiet and she'd never find out what he'd done.

'Dan? You still with me?'

'Still here, Katie girl. So tell me about these tests. How do I find somebody who'll do them?'

'Have a look online, Dan. You should be able to find plenty of companies offering DNA testing. You can do it through the post. It's usually used for proving paternity or otherwise, but DNA works for maternity testing as well.'

'I'll look into it. Do a Google search; see what I can come up with.' This woman was one to hang on to, if he possessed any sense in his messed-up brain. He'd thought he had no options available to him; he'd been convinced he had no choice but to live with the hazy memories plaguing him. Then she'd dragged forth his innermost thoughts and hadn't pegged him as weird but had been Katie, ever practical, coming up with answers when he'd thought none existed.

Realisation hit him. He loved this woman. Every cell of her, right to her core, although he had no idea how to tell her.

'Gonna go now, Katie girl. I'll call you later. Hey, Katie?'

'Yes, Dan?'

'You're one hell of a woman.'

11

SILENCE AND SCREAMS

Life seemed comparatively good back then, Daniel. I didn't mind the constant exhaustion; I went through my days happy and fulfilled, in a way I'd never been before. I'm the nurturing type, you see; all I wanted, all I've ever wanted, was to be a homemaker in a stable family set-up. Taking care of Gran and my baby, looking after our home – these simple things satisfied the nesting instinct in me, and I revelled in them. For the short time God allowed me to enjoy them, I mean. Because He was indeed laughing at me as I cooked, scrubbed and cleaned. He had His hands firmly on the rug of domestic bliss I was standing on, and I'd soon find Him wrenching it from under my feet.

One morning I woke up late, having slept well. I went over to check my sleeping baby, grateful for the unusual peace. Gran wasn't one of life's morning people; she wouldn't be surfacing much before ten o'clock. I scuttled back into the warmth of my bed, thinking about the chicken I'd roast later, followed by a trip to the park if Gran felt well enough. There was a new detective thriller on television that night we'd decided to watch. A perfect day stretched before me. I dozed off once more.

The unfamiliar silence was still there when I woke up again. The lack of sounds got me worried, you see, Daniel. The house seemed too still, too quiet, apart from the snuffling sounds from Daniel's cot; something jarred in my mind as being off-kilter. OK, so Gran wasn't at her best in the morning, but normally the noises from her bedroom as she moved around told me when she'd got out of bed. I'd not heard a thing.

I pulled on my dressing gown, shoved my feet into my slippers, and went to check on Daniel. Then I walked down the landing, hesitating before knocking on Gran's door. She might still be asleep; she'd been unusually busy yesterday, and hadn't gone to bed until late.

'Gran?' Silence came back at me. 'Gran, are you awake?'

Perhaps I should leave her be. Instinct, though, told me something wasn't right.

I tried again. 'Gran? Do you want some breakfast?'

She didn't reply. I shoved open the door and walked in.

I realised she'd died as soon as I looked at her. Her face was a terrible colour, the sort of shade no living human ever is, and her mouth hung open. Her head had lolled to one side and I saw where her spittle had stained the pillow. The left side of her face appeared distorted, as if some invisible hand had dragged her cheek towards her shoulder.

I remember the words no, no no, spinning round in my brain and I shook her, although I had no idea what good that would do, but I clung desperately to the chance she might be alive. A false hope, of course. She was cold beneath my hands; she must have died hours before. My wonderful grandmother, who had been the backbone of my life, had gone from me, and oh, Daniel, I had no idea how to bear her loss.

I was only eighteen and petrified. I was all alone now, except for a small, demanding baby who depended on me for everything. So I looked at my dead grandmother, lying grey and flaccid against her spittle-stained pillow, and I felt more scared than I'd ever been, even worse than when I'd been hungry and had no idea when I'd next eat. Being alone terrified me because everything was down to me now and I didn't know if I could cope.

I called an ambulance and the paramedics were so kind, as they're trained to be. A doctor came as well, telling me my grandmother had suffered a massive stroke, and calling an undertaker to transport her body to the mortuary. I finally broke down after everyone had gone. I was devastated, Daniel. Perhaps if you ever lose someone whom you love, although I hope to God you never do, you'll know what it's like. I wouldn't wish on anybody the agony I went through, slumped on the living room floor of the damp house I called home. I cried and I cried, both for my dead grandmother who had been torn away from me while still only in her seventies, and for myself.

I sobbed for the chicken dinner we wouldn't eat together, for the park we wouldn't visit, for the thriller that would go unwatched. I wept for her batik skirts and tie-dye blouses, the flash of her opal ring and the jangle of her silver bracelets. Most of all I cried for the loss of the only warmth and love I'd ever known. My beloved Gran was gone and somehow I had to carry on without her.

Eventually screams came from above, though, and I dragged myself up, and went to tend to my hungry and wet baby, mechanically changing his nappy, bringing him downstairs while I heated his milk and did my best to soothe his furious howls, tears running down my cheeks all the while. He must have picked up on my anguish because I couldn't settle him, but I didn't mind the loud wails, his flailing legs, because they told me he was alive, wonderfully and gloriously alive.

I went back upstairs and put warm clothes on my baby before settling him in his pram and walking into town. I found a funeral parlour and wheeled the pram in.

'My grandmother's died,' I said. Then I flopped into a chair, sobbing.

The next day, I looked through Gran's things. I found what I was searching for in her chest of drawers: a brown envelope, containing her will. She'd left everything to me, including the house.

I realised I couldn't stay there. Too many memories of Gran filled the place; besides, it needed too many repairs. I made up my mind. I'd go into town tomorrow and find a solicitor; when everything went through with the will, I'd sell the house.

Afterwards, I wanted a fresh start. Apart from the birth of my baby, I'd only known unhappiness in this small Hampshire town. Mum's drinking, Gran's illness and death, Matthew Hancock and the still vivid horror of my rape. I needed to get away. I'd rent a little flat for my baby and me somewhere else, perhaps in Bristol. Gran had once lived there, and she'd shown me pictures: the Avon Gorge, the Clifton Suspension Bridge, the Floating Harbour. It looked a beautiful city. What's more, it offered better opportunities for jobs and training. The more I mulled things over, the more a fresh start in Bristol seemed the right thing to do.

All actions have consequences, they say. I guess that must hold true for decisions as well. Would I have acted any differently, if I could have foreseen what would happen through moving to Bristol? My heart, gut and soul scream no, loud and proud, to me, Daniel. That choice led me to you, my dearest son. Your presence in my life is the consequence of that decision, made so long ago by a frightened and grieving eighteen-year-old, and you've always brought me such joy, no matter what you think of me now.

I'm painfully aware you believe you hate me. Perhaps you do right now, but what I'm going to tell you will make you understand why I acted the way I did. You already know why I decided to move to Bristol. Now I'll tell you the rest.

A few weeks after Gran's death, my solicitor had dealt with most of the legal stuff and things were moving along nicely, or so I thought. In my naïveté, I was making plans again, and I should have realised God would be in the background, laughing.

Anyway, life seemed good the day my solicitor told me I'd be able to put the house on the market in the near future. I'd soon be moving to Bristol, I thought; my new life beckoned. Gran's death still clawed at me, raw and painful, hitting me hard every single day. I knew she'd be happy I was moving on, though. I went to bed early, my head full of plans, checking a sleeping Daniel in his cot at the foot of my bed, transfixed by his tiny fingers sucked between his lips. He smelled of baby shampoo and contentment, his essence warm, delicious and utterly mine, and he enchanted every part of me.

I slept more deeply than usual. It was after eight when I woke up.

My intuition immediately kicked in, warning me something was wrong.

The most awful sensation, one I couldn't ignore, crept over me. Every instinct, every nerve in my body, screamed at me to get out of bed, right away. You see, normally there would be some sort of noise from Daniel, even when he was sleeping; my mother's ears were attuned to the sound of his breathing, however faint it might be. It was something I had come to take for granted; the faint snuffles he made when asleep, or the way his limbs bumped against the sides of the cot as he wriggled around.

No sounds came from my baby that morning.

Only a terrifying silence occupied the house. A silence so thick it sent shards of dread shivering through me.

I threw back the duvet, rushing to the cot. I grabbed the inert body lying face down under the quilt.

Daniel was cold. So cold.

No breath came from his tiny body.

And his skin; no baby should be such a pallid, unhealthy shade.

Cot death. I had heard of it, but such things happened to other people. I had never thought about it in connection with Daniel, my baby who had always been healthy and full of life.

Now he lay unresponsive in my arms and my voice rose high into the room, pleading, saying, 'God, no, no, no, no, no, please, God . . .'

I opened his mouth, and put my lips around the tiny ones I'd marvelled at the night before, trying to force life back into lungs I later realised had ceased working hours before. I pressed down on his chest, willing the heart underneath my fingers to start beating again, pushing reviving blood around his limp, pale body.

I don't know for how long I did all that. Time stopped when I grabbed my baby from his cot.

I blew into his mouth, and I pushed down on his chest, and all the while hot tears ran down my face and those shards of dread in my gut twisted, cutting my soul with denial that this had happened to my beautiful Daniel, to the baby who occupied the whole of my very existence. Impossible that life could be so cruel. It had already handed me my drunken mother, a brutal rape, and then taken my beloved grandmother. It shouldn't snatch Daniel from me as well.

It already had, though. My fervent pleas to some unknown God whom I didn't believe in went unheard.

I slumped back on my heels, my eyes unseeing through the tears, the dead body of my adored Daniel in my arms, and I screamed. Huge furious shrieks tore from my throat, filling the empty house with my rage and denial and utter devastation. There was nobody to hear them, in that house so far from town, and I screamed until I couldn't scream anymore, my throat raw. I held Daniel with one arm while I pounded the floor with the other until the hurt in my bruised and battered fist stopped me.

I lay on the floor, curled around the body of my baby, for the rest of the day. The room grew dark as night came and still I lay motionless on the cold carpet.

I'd stopped crying. Tears seemed pointless. No way could they ever express even a tiny part of the raw emotions within me. I had died inside, along with my baby.

I woke up on the floor the day after, cold and stiff, with my son even colder in my arms.

I knew I should tell someone he'd died.

But I didn't.

I don't know if you can understand all this, Daniel. Grief had probably obscured my judgement. I don't think I thought very clearly back then. Perhaps I believed if I didn't tell anyone, if I didn't register the death, then the unthinkable hadn't happened. My baby would still be alive.

Telling somebody would have made it all real, you see, Daniel. I'd have ended up with a death certificate in my possession, as I had with Gran, a stark piece of paper making it official, turning the nightmare into harsh reality. I'd have had to choose a coffin. At the thought of my baby's body in a tiny wooden box, I broke down all over again. Misery of such savagery and depth swamped me, the likes of which I hope to God you never have to deal with, Daniel.

On the evening of the second day, I knew I had to let go of my baby.

I washed and dried him and dressed him in his best clothes. Next I wrapped him up against the night air and placed him gently in his baby sling. Then I went to the shed at the bottom of the garden and took out a shovel.

I put on my coat, and left the house with my baby and the shovel, walking away from town, down the little track leading to the nearby woods, where I'd often walked with Gran. I was familiar with those oak-covered hills from my time living with her. Dog walkers came to let their dogs off the leash in parts of them. I didn't go near those areas. My baby had to be somewhere safe, out of the way, far from keen noses and digging paws, away from the sacrilege that would be to his beloved body.

So I carried him, held tight against me in his sling, along with the shovel, ever higher, away from where the dog walkers frequented. I panted up the hill until I stood, hot and sweating, deep among the trees. I found one that was still young, a sapling really, and it seemed the perfect tree under which to lay my baby. The sapling would rise and thicken with age, its roots would wind around his body and that way he would never truly die. This beautiful tree would hold him secure within its embrace and the life cycle in the trunk, the branches, the thrusting roots, would give some sort of existence back to him. I'd found the tree of life.

I started to dig. When my arms ached and my back hurt, and the hole was as deep as I could make it, I squeezed my baby tight. I kissed him for the very last time. Then I lowered him into his grave, so tenderly, along with the little teddy bear I'd bought for him after his birth. I covered him with the damp earth, sobs choking my throat all the time, patting the soil down and finally heaving some heavy stones on top. He was at rest now, and he'd sleep beneath those tree roots forever.

Darkness had fallen by the time I finished. Exhaustion, both physical and mental, overwhelmed me; I stumbled down the hill, back towards the house.

People talk about closure, but I don't think my grief would have been less had I registered the death and given Daniel a proper burial. How would a funeral have changed the awfulness of it all? Besides, I could never have had my baby cremated as I did with Gran; I found the thought of flames burning his delicate flesh utterly abhorrent. And

I didn't like the idea of burying him in some anonymous cemetery, flanked by the corpses of strangers. I realised what I had done was wrong in the eyes of the law but I didn't regret it. No, his grave was somewhere wild, beautiful and peaceful and the oak tree would take care of my baby forever.

Has your anger towards me lessened at all, Daniel?

12

CAN OF WORMS

Daniel stared at the monitor on his computer, willing his fingers to take the first steps on the family history website Tim had showed him.

His mother was forty-four, or so he believed. Any sister of hers who might have given birth to him would have been younger, he suspected, but he didn't think he should take anything for granted. Perhaps she had been older. Best to keep his search parameters reasonably wide. He'd research the online register ten years before and five years after her date of birth, for the town where his mother grew up. Covey wasn't the most unusual of names, but it wasn't exactly common either. With such a large timespan to look through, it took longer than he thought. His shoulders ached and his eyes hurt by the time he'd finished.

The only registered birth attributed to his grandmother, Madeleine Jean Covey, in that area of Hampshire during the time in question was that of his mother, Laura Susan Covey.

He tried again, this time not including Hampshire. He'd assumed there'd been no change of home for the Covey family, but checking was essential in case what his mother had said hadn't been accurate, or was an outright lie. This took even longer, but the result ended up the same. He found no trace of Madeleine Covey having given birth to any children other than Laura.

Time to try another angle; he'd search through the death register. If this hypothetical sister had died, it had probably happened around the time Laura turned eighteen. He had to hope she had never married and taken another name, otherwise he was screwed.

He scanned through for the death certificates of anyone named Covey during the timespan in which he thought the sister had probably died. None fitted his criteria. Nobody of the right age to be his mother, with the name of Covey, had died in the area of Hampshire where Laura Bateman had grown up.

From what he could see, there had been no sister. His mother wasn't his aunt. He rubbed his hand over his jaw, sighing. This looked like a dead end.

The phone rang. Shit. He'd been so wrapped up in what he'd been doing he'd forgotten to call Katie.

'You're neglecting me already.' He heard the laugh in her voice.

'I'm sorry, Katie. I got pretty tied up with this online family history thing.'

'You find anything?'

'Nope. Mum was indeed an only child as far as I can tell. No trace of any sister, in either the birth or death records.'

'Well, that's one avenue of enquiry knocked on the head. Don't forget you still have the DNA option to follow. You looked into that any further?'

'No. This has taken up most of my time. But I'll definitely check it out. Especially now the family history thing has proved a blind alley. I'm going to Mum's tomorrow. I'll get some of her hairs from her brush while I'm there.'

'Remember to find some with the root still on.'

'Will do. Anyway, enough of me and my weird family issues.' He lowered his voice, injecting a lorry-load of molten sex into it. 'You wearing that black silk thong I like so much?'

The phone call didn't end for another hour. Sated and grinning, afterwards he sat at his computer, typing 'private DNA tests UK' into Google. He browsed through a few sites, bookmarking one that, thank God, explained the science bits in plain language. The test could be done with hair samples and through the post, as Katie had told him.

He read further into the website he'd bookmarked. Apparently consent forms came with the kit they sent out; the testing company required his mother's agreement. Not that he'd be asking for her permission any time this century.

Daniel considered his options. All two of them.

First one. He could stop this, right now, and put the whole thing behind him.

Not going to happen.

Second one. He could falsify her consent.

By the time he clicked off the website, he'd ordered the test kit. No going back now.

The next day was Sunday, and he'd promised his mother he'd go over as usual for lunch. Guilt nagged at him about what he was intending to do. He'd promised himself he wouldn't invade her privacy, so what was sneaking into her bedroom to steal a hair sample, if not exactly that? He meant the world to her; betraying her trust was wrong, plain wrong. She'd be devastated if she realised he held more warmth in his heart towards the unknown woman from his memories than he did towards her.

I'm an arsehole, he thought, but I'm going to do this anyway. I have to.

It didn't prove hard to get what he'd gone for. He'd brought with him an envelope for the purpose. He excused himself shortly before the time came to go, saying he needed to use the toilet. Once upstairs, he went into her bedroom. No sign of a hairbrush on the dressing table. Then he spotted a handbag on the floor by the wardrobe. He pulled it open and reached in a hand.

Bingo. A large wooden hairbrush, complete with tangles of hair clogged in the bristles. There was plenty, surely enough for the test. Looking closer, he saw tiny pale bulbs attached to some of the ends. He started pulling hair from the brush, stuffing the soft wisps in the envelope, careful not to arouse suspicion by taking too much.

The test kit arrived two days later. He picked up the envelope of hair and sorted through the blonde strands. By the time he finished, he'd found six hairs complete with their roots. The bare minimum required, but it would have to do. He took another envelope and pulled hairs from his head, one by one, until he ended up with six with the roots attached.

He'd seen his mother's signature often enough to do a reasonable copy. Besides, the testing company would never know otherwise. The kit would go in tomorrow's post. They'd get it Thursday, postal service allowing. He reckoned he'd get the results by Friday of the following week, maybe earlier. He refused to think about what he'd do if the test showed she wasn't his mother. One step at a time.

After he sent the test kit off, he did his best to put the whole thing out of his mind. Katie played the same game. She merely nodded when he told her he'd posted it, asked him to call her as soon as he got the results, and changed the subject.

To pass the time, he turned back to his art, which he'd neglected since meeting Katie. Paint, brushes and canvas helped keep his demons at bay. He'd dabbled in all forms of painting since he was a child, finally settling on acrylics as his chosen medium, revelling in the thick, sensuous quality of the paints. His latest creation was the most deeply personal thing he'd ever attempted. The outlines were deliberately blurred and the colours muted, the shapes of the woman, girl and child fluid, as if they were melting. The whole mood of the painting was surreal, dream-like, in an attempt to portray the hazy quality of his distant memories. He found a soothing catharsis in purging the figures from his mind and transferring them onto the canvas; art helped him forget, at least for a while, his anxiety about the DNA analysis.

The waiting game ended Thursday of the following week. The test results were on the hall floor when he got home from work.

He ripped open the envelope at once. He held the test results in his hand, a couple of sheets of A4, along with a covering letter. Words jumped out at him. Genetic loci. DNA amplification. Testing process. They signified zilch to him.

Then words that did make sense floated in front of his eyes.

But in another way, they meant nothing whatsoever.

'Alleged mother . . . can be excluded . . . biological mother . . . no shared genetic markers . . .'

He read the words again. And again. A fourth time and they started to sink in at last.

Shit. Shit, shit, shit. His memories weren't false.

Neither were his gut feelings.

Laura Bateman was not his mother.

So who the fuck was she?

He'd done his best to convince himself the results would confirm her as his mother. It was the easy option. The one that meant nothing in his life would have to change. He'd have got closure on the doubts that had plagued him for so long.

Now, with the test results in his hand, he wished he'd never ordered them. Better to live in ignorance than face such betrayal. He slammed his fist repeatedly into his left palm, a vain attempt at releasing his fury. Impossible to vent the shock coursing through him.

Or his sense of loss. A few stark words had flayed his emotions, stripped him of the familiar, the comfortable. Laura Bateman represented safety, security, even if he struggled to return her love. Without her, life made no sense.

His hand was growing sore. When he raised it to his face, he discovered he'd been crying.

Eventually he reached into his pocket and pulled out his mobile. Katie answered on the first ring.

'Hey, lover boy.' She sounded upbeat. 'How are things?'

'I got the DNA results.' The catch in his voice betrayed him.

'Dan?' He heard her draw in a breath. 'Dan . . . are you all right? What did the test company say?'

'She's not my mother, Katie.' The words tumbled out in a rush. 'Got the results right here in black and white. We have no genes in common, none at all. Laura Bateman isn't related to me in any way. I have no idea who she is or whether any of what she's ever told me is true. My life is a big can of worms all right.'

'I'll be there in five, Dan. Let me grab a few things and I'll come straight over.'

'No.' He sighed, unsure how best to say this. 'I need some time, Katie. I can't deal with this right now. I'm finding it all too weird.'

'Don't shut me out, Dan.' Hurt in Katie's voice.

'I'm not, honest. Just got things to sort through in my head, that's all. You're not working tomorrow, right? Come over in the evening. I'll be fine by then, I promise.'

'Can't do tomorrow.' He heard her sigh. 'Or Saturday. My shifts got changed and I got dumped with a load of double ones. Sunday is the earliest I can manage. This is weird, really weird. But we'll sort it, don't worry.'

He didn't trust himself to reply.

'Dan? I'll see you Sunday. You take care until then, right?'

'Yeah, I will. Katie . . .'

'Yes, sweetie?'

'Thanks. For everything.' He almost told her he'd fallen in love with her. The words hovered on his tongue, teasing him, before he reined them in. Now wasn't the right time. He'd tell her once all this crap was over.

Daniel didn't move for a long while after the phone call. Such deception on Laura Bateman's part. Throughout his childhood, she'd plastered skinned knees, read bedtime stories, rocked him to sleep. A candidate for mother of the year, he thought bitterly. Oh, wait. Except for the fact she'd not given birth to him.

Small wonder her betrayal pained so much. Anger, hurt, loss all battled for dominance in his head. Right now, he hadn't a clue which was winning. The questions remained. Who was she? Why had this woman posed as his mother?

He knew he'd have to demand answers from her. Tonight wasn't the night, though. It was getting late, nearly ten o'clock. His emotions were bruised and bloody from being put through the wringer; he was too wound up, too out of control right now.

It would have to be tomorrow. He knew Ian Bateman always went drinking with his business associates on Friday evenings. He reckoned his best bet would be to go over to the house about seven thirty. He'd wait until his stepfather had left, if his car was still in the drive. Then he'd confront the woman who'd passed herself off as his mother and he'd make damn sure he got the answers he deserved.

13

ALL A MIRAGE

I'm sprawled on my bed, staring at the ceiling. So far, the shrinks have left me alone today. No doctors trying to probe inside my head, thank God. My thoughts are dark this morning, as if my mind has turned into a bolthole for my worst fears and insecurities, long suppressed. I'm thinking about Daniel, how much I love him. What he'd say, if I forced him to give an honest answer, about whether he cares anything for me. I wonder what my boy feels where I'm concerned, but however much I yearn to believe otherwise, I don't think it's love.

The thought forces its way into my mind, and I thrust it away the second it does, that Daniel has never really accepted me as his mother. I think back to when he was a small boy, when I had to cajole him to call me Mummy. I persuaded myself all I needed was time. Well, it's been twenty-two years; long enough, you'd think, but apparently not.

I've never allowed myself to dwell on this before. It's too painful, too unbearable, for me. Now, though, with all this time on my hands, it's like a scab. An ugly weeping sore on my psyche I can't stop probing. Half of me is reluctant to expose the raw emotions lying underneath,

and the other half can't help scraping away at it. I keep asking myself –
do I mean anything at all to Daniel?

Under the scab lurks the cruel conviction that Daniel has never
loved me. He'd never have done the DNA test if he did. I think again
about the results, with those long scientific words alleging I'm not
Daniel's mother but which ignore the fact I've fulfilled that role in
every meaningful way.

I lie here and I scratch and pick at the scab, and I can't understand
how things have turned out this way. Why doesn't my son love me? I
did all the right things. My love for Daniel has always burned fiercely;
being his mother fulfils me in a way nothing else ever has. Nobody will
ever love him the way I do. He's never been affectionate towards me,
though. Despair hits me when I think of all the times he's pushed my
eager hugs away, his coldness wounding me all the way to the bone.

My self-torture gets crueller. In my mind, I'm no longer in this
soulless psychiatric facility, but back home. I play the scene in my head
repeatedly, whipping myself with his punishing accusations.

I'm watching television one evening when he arrives. The front
door bangs open. Seconds later Daniel crashes into the room, clutching
some papers. I'm staggered by his appearance; he's enraged, face red,
eyes bulging. I can't take in what he's saying.

'I always thought something was wrong,' he shouts. 'Always knew
you weren't my mother. This proves it. Read this, you goddamn bitch.
It says it plainly here, in black and white. You're not my mother.'

Bitch. He called me a bitch. Daniel never, ever, speaks to me like
that, however coldly he may act towards me. I'm too much in shock
to grasp what he's saying, or to respond. When I don't reply, he storms
over and thrusts the pages under my nose.

'I've had a test done. A DNA test.' I'm taken aback. How and why,
I wonder.

'They don't lie. Read it. There's the proof we're not related. You're
not my mother.'

The words I've always dreaded. He's right, if you take into account the biology of the matter and nothing else. Yet on so many other levels, he's completely wrong.

I stare at what he's showing me, flinching from his rage, his cruel accusations. Words and phrases leap out at me. Some of them I can't understand. A lot is science-speak, incomprehensible jargon. I skip past the bits I can't grasp to the stark paragraph at the end.

And that's written in language even I can understand.

My life is a henhouse and the chickens are well and truly coming home to roost. I'm catapulted like a slingshot back into the past, not a place I want to revisit. Daniel has been a part of me for twenty-two years. For me, he's my son in every way. I hardly ever think about my desperate flight from Bristol so long ago. Now, though, the reality of what I did that night rises up before me, captured in the cold, heartless words I'm reading. Words that deny the truth of what it is to be a mother.

I think quickly. I'm caught in a trap; I can't admit what I did, or my reasons. Only one option remains: repeat the story I told Daniel all those years ago, keep telling him I am his mother. You see, I'm hoping if I carry on the same old lie, it will make it true. Ridiculous, of course, but I need Daniel to believe me so desperately. I'm clinging frantically to the perfect world of motherhood I've created, and I can't bring myself to let go. What else do I have in my life that means anything, besides him?

I realise as I speak I'm on a losing wicket.

'Daniel.' I look up into his face, so enraged yet so beloved. 'I don't get what you mean, my love. I'm your mother; of course I am. This test . . . I don't understand . . . how did you do it? Don't you need a blood sample?'

'I took hair from your brush. Did the test with that.' He pushes the papers towards me again. 'Read the last lines of the report. Plain enough, I'd say. We don't share any genes. So, tell me, for God's sake, who are you? How did I come to grow up as your child?'

Fury dominates his voice, but underneath I detect anguish. From his heart to mine, it seems. I feel his pain as my own; misery pierces me, almost driving me to my knees.

Hair stolen from my brush has unmasked me. I wonder exactly when my son's treachery took place. He must have eaten roast beef with me one Sunday, making casual conversation but hiding duplicity in his heart. All the while aware of what he intended to do. His betrayal cuts me to the quick, a pain almost as sharp as my misery. I don't have time to think, though; the need to carry on the lie is imperative.

'I'm your mother, my love. You grew up with me because you're my son, Daniel. How could you think otherwise, darling?'

He snorts with contempt. 'I've always known you weren't my mother. I remember asking you when I was still a small child. I asked you several times.'

I wind back through the years to those questions, to the terror they always produced in me.

'I remember another woman; she'd sit by my bed at night. The girl too. The one with the shiny, swinging hair. She used to play ball with me. I asked you over and over who they were.'

'You're mistaken, my love.' I'm desperate to convince him. 'I can only repeat what I told you before; those people are a figment of your imagination. They were never real. I can't tell you who they are, because they don't exist. I'm your mother, Daniel, in every way. I always will be. No one else could ever love you as I do. I cared for you when you were ill, when you had nightmares, when you fell off your bike. That's what real mothers do, Daniel.'

His rage seems to be increasing. He thrusts the papers in my face again. The hand holding them is shaking with fury. For the first time ever, I'm afraid of my son.

'The proof is here in black and white.' He speaks very slowly and deliberately. 'You might as well stop telling me all these lies. They're not going to wash anymore. I want you to end the bullshit, right now, and tell me where my real family is and how I came to live with you.'

Panic fills my throat, rendering speech difficult.

'Daniel, mistakes are made all the time. Just because somebody is a scientist and wears a white coat and has a string of fancy letters after their name, it doesn't mean they're infallible. Perhaps someone mixed up the samples in the laboratory or the results were misinterpreted. This test proves nothing, my love.'

'How can you carry on lying to me?' His hand, the one clutching the papers, falls to his side, and the pain in his expression twists my heart. 'You've always told me I mean everything to you. But that's a lie; it has to be. If you loved me, you'd tell me the truth.'

'But Daniel . . .' Despair almost chokes me. 'Darling, I am.'

'What about my eye colour?' The rapid change in direction throws me off-base. I don't understand what he means.

'My eyes. They're green. Yours are blue, and though I can't believe anything you tell me anymore, you said my father had brown eyes. The chance of a green-eyed child from parents with brown and blue eyes is low. Improbable enough to back up the test results. You're not my mother.'

'I don't know anything about such things, Daniel.' All this science stuff bewilders me. 'But surely it can't be that simple. There could be any number of explanations for your eye colour. Perhaps one of your grandparents, the ones I never knew, had green eyes.'

'I can't believe anything you say.' Bitterness, along with despair, drips from his words. 'For God's sake, you owe me the truth. Who am I? Was I adopted?'

'No, my love.' At least I don't need to lie about that. 'It's as I told you. You must believe me, darling.'

'Why should I trust anything you say?' I wince at the biting contempt in his voice. I'm trapped with no way out. So I carry on the lie. Even though my intuition tells me it's completely useless.

'Because I'm your mother, Daniel. All I can do is to tell you how it was; the only relatives I ever had growing up were my mother and my grandmother. I loved your father very much. We were going to get married and then we conceived you, right before my eighteenth birthday. I can't tell you something different, because there simply isn't anything else to say.'

'Prove it.'

'How?' I'm helpless in the face of such an onslaught.

'Take another DNA test. Voluntarily this time. I had to falsify your signature on the last one. Two tests can't be wrong. Provide a blood or saliva sample and prove you're my mother.'

My world is shattering; huge pieces are falling away from me, faster and faster, and even if I could piece them back together, the cracks would be too big, too vast. The urge to try, though, overwhelms me.

'No.' I grip tightly onto the cushion beside me. 'Don't ask me to do that, Daniel. I'm your mother, no matter what you think, and I don't need to prove it. Please, my love. Think about everything I did for you when you were growing up. I've always adored you, and tried to do my best where you're concerned. Why are you doing this to me?'

He shakes his head, and doesn't say anything for a while. Then he looks at me again, and the disgust in his expression wrings my heart.

'You never were going to give me any answers, were you? Just the same old shit as before. I hate you. Do you understand? I bloody hate you.'

My eyes fill with tears. Daniel stares at me with contempt and I'd do anything, anything at all, to tear such a look from his face. Ice grips my stomach, stills the breath in my lungs. My world shrinks to here, now, this moment.

Then he delivers his final blow. Straight through the heart.

'I've never loved you. Never.'

He turns away, making for the door. I grasp his arm to stop him, but he shakes me off and I let him go.

Pain, almost as devastating as when my baby died, slams through me. The sort of agony that slices into your gut and coils around your body, squeezing the life from you, making you try to scream away what's happening. Scream until your throat is raw and all you can do is lie on the floor with the tears pouring down your face and the word NO hammering through your brain. This time, though, I don't yell or pound the carpet. Instead a numbing fog creeps into my brain. My mouth goes dry and that is the last time I say anything.

Ian comes home to a wife he's never encountered before. It's not so much that I don't speak; I can't. Speech seems an utter impossibility. Daniel is the only one I want to talk to, but he's not listening to me right now. Will he come back, or should I visit him at that poky flat of his? Have I lost him forever? Panic overwhelms me and I run upstairs to bed. I drag the duvet over my head and shut out the sounds of Ian's footsteps on the stairs.

My husband cancels his game of golf the next day. I can register, with the part of my brain that still seems to function, that the not speaking thing worries him. Each time I've had one of my turns, as he calls them, I've never stopped talking entirely. Now, it's as if I've lost the ability and I never want to speak again. Unless it's to Daniel. He told me he's never loved me but I can't, I won't, believe he meant to be so cruel.

Ian mentions seeing the doctor, pills, getting proper help, and I understand exactly what he means. Well, I won't do it. I'm not going to allow some fresh-faced graduate whose experience of life is all from a textbook to probe around in my thoughts. Someone older wouldn't be any better either. I doubt any of them would have dealt well with the crap I endured in my early life; what right would they have to throw clichés like 'broken childhood home' and 'unresolved issues' at me?

I picture again the rage on Daniel's face, and right now, I can't fathom how to replace it with the understanding I crave. I tried my best, I really did. It's all been a mirage, though. I thought everything was perfect; I had the husband, the home, and what I wanted above everything else, my son. Now I realise the foundations of my so-called happy life were nothing but sand. I've been refusing to see the obvious; despite all my efforts, Daniel has never loved me, or regarded me as a mother.

I can't believe it has happened again. I'm not sure I can bear the agony of losing my son for a second time.

14

THE TRUTH WILL OUT

Daniel lay in bed, forcing down the fury still burning from the night before, evidenced by his clenched fists, the tightness in his jaw. One thing was obvious; he wouldn't get answers from Laura Bateman any time soon. If anything, his visit to her had heightened his confusion. Right now, his emotions were whiplashing between betrayal, hurt, rage and shock.

He was obsessing, but he couldn't help himself; his head was full of DNA results, genetic markers, blue and brown eyes. All swirling around and mixing themselves up with his hazy memories, resulting in total chaos. Understandable, though. Wouldn't anyone obsess, if they found themselves in a situation as weird as this? Right now he needed Katie; damn her double shifts at the hospital. He'd already texted her to tell her he planned to confront Laura Bateman, but hadn't updated her about the abortive result.

Amid all the confusion, though, a thought had surfaced, an impossible and yet compelling one, one that gripped him and wouldn't let go.

An unknown number of years ago, Laura Bateman had stepped into the role of his mother, for reasons still unexplained. The why might become apparent later. The how struck him as more important right now. Perhaps she'd kidnapped him from his real parents.

He pulled a face. The idea seemed so far-fetched, so bizarre. Things like that rarely happened and when they did, they happened to other people. Not to him, not to Daniel Bateman, an average guy from west London.

Abduction. Impossible. Ridiculous, even. So why couldn't he get the idea out of his head?

Because it seemed to fit the facts and he could think of nothing else that even came close. It would partly explain the two women of his memories. He didn't have a clue who the girl might be, but the woman by his bed, the one he'd always felt safe with – she had to be his birth mother, as he'd always thought.

Kidnap. It still seemed a crazy idea. It wouldn't do any harm to do some digging, though. Might turn out a waste of time. If so, he'd laugh about it with Katie; he'd let her common sense wash over him and together they'd figure out what came next.

He hesitated. It had been a rollercoaster couple of days so far and mentally he felt more than a little wrung out and washed up. Perhaps it would be better to run this by Katie first, see what she thought.

He'd need to wait, though, due to her shifts, and the notion of delaying action any longer was intolerable. Maybe he was obsessed, but the idea had taken root. He had plenty of time to spare anyway. The kidnap would have been big news in the national newspapers if his idea was right; they would probably be the best source of information. He'd start looking there.

He got up and switched on his laptop, opening up Google to type in 'UK newspapers archive'.

The British Library featured top of the results. He clicked on their website. They had an online search facility, but the link was broken.

He groaned with frustration. Shit. He needed to do this now, today. An online search wasn't possible, but what about the newspapers themselves? Anyway, where the hell was the British Library?

He found the answer: St Pancras, and they kept all UK newspapers from the seventeenth century to the present day, via microfilms. He'd need a pass card, which he'd get straight away if he provided two forms of identification. What's more, they stayed open until five. He didn't hesitate; he located his bank card and driving licence to serve as I.D., grabbed his jacket and keys, and set off.

Formalities completed, a couple of hours later Daniel was sitting in front of a reading machine in the British Library, a packet of microfilms in his hand. From what Katie had told him, his memories probably went back to when he was about four, so he'd start searching twenty-two years ago. If he found nothing, he'd widen his parameters. He slid the first microfilm into the reader, scanning through day after day, the first three pages only. A child kidnap would surely be front-page news, but just in case – he didn't want to miss anything.

His shoulders and neck started aching after an hour, and he'd only got up to March. Nothing in April. Nothing in May. He slid the next microfilm, starting in June, into the reader.

And there it was. The child kidnap that dominated the front page and most of the next two. The case that had shocked Britain at the time and sparked a huge nationwide hunt for the missing youngster.

Daniel dragged his chair closer, pulling a breath into lungs that suddenly seemed too small. He started to read.

On June 2nd twenty-two years ago, Daniel James Cordwell had been reported missing from his home in Bristol. The Cordwells had gone out for the evening, returning shortly before midnight. They arrived to find the police at the flat, their four-year-old son gone, and the fresh out of college eighteen-year-old nanny whom they employed hysterical.

It seemed the nanny, Alison Souter, hadn't had time to eat that evening. She'd grown hungry, fancied fish and chips, and figured the nearest fish shop was only a two-minute walk away. She'd checked on the sleeping Daniel, thought she'd be back in five minutes, no harm done.

She arrived back to an open front door and immediately dashed to Daniel's room. She found his bed and the rest of the flat empty.

There were no signs of forced entry or disturbance, simply the unoccupied bed. Alison Souter's screams had ricocheted around the flat, alerting the neighbours.

Daniel's chest tightened again. He looked, really looked, at the grainy black-and-white pictures accompanying the words. He scrutinised the snapshot of the four-year-old Daniel James Cordwell, at the dark hair, at the eyes giving no hint in the photograph as to whether they were green. This child was laughing, had longish hair, whereas Laura Bateman's photos of him as a young boy showed him unsmiling, his hair cropped. Was it him? Impossible to tell, especially given the blurry quality of the image.

He moved to the next photo. Alison Souter's face looked out at him and he took in her shoulder-length dark hair, hair he knew shone in the sunlight as she moved. Recognition stirred within him.

Howard Cordwell's picture: merely a photograph of a man, nothing more. Daniel felt no connection with him in any way. Dark hair, sombre expression, arm around his wife. Daniel's chest tightened further as he switched his gaze to her face.

He stared at her, at the woman who had suffered the theft of her only child, at her stricken expression, captured in the photograph of so long ago. The memory of the shadowy figure beside his bed, of the safety and warmth he'd experienced, crashed over him, bringing recognition. Certainty engulfed him; she was his mother. For some unknown reason Laura Bateman, then Covey, had found a way to break into the flat after the nanny had left. She'd snatched the sleeping Daniel and disappeared with him, leaving only an empty bed.

He'd found what he'd been looking for. He'd uncovered his roots, where he came from. He was Daniel James Cordwell, kidnap victim. The two women of his memories now possessed names and identities. He'd found a father as well, although he retained no memory of him. Not the handsome student Laura Bateman had described, killed in a car crash, but an ordinary-looking man, still very much alive; at least he was back then.

He carried on reading. The newspaper carried his mother's pleas for anyone who had seen or heard anything to come forward. He read her appeal to whoever had taken her son to bring him back, saying he was a tiny child who needed his mother. She spoke of her devastation, how much she loved Daniel, of her guilt at having left him. She said her life was on hold until she held her son, her precious Daniel, in her arms again. The article went on to state she had been too distraught to say any more and her husband had led her away.

Daniel leaned back in his chair, shock and confusion flooding his brain in equal measure. Weird didn't begin to describe the emotions in his head.

Impossible; there's no way you're a kidnap victim, logic said.

Wrong, retorted his intuition. You're Daniel James Cordwell.

He read the newspaper article repeatedly, sensing every time the same recognition of his mother, eventually convincing himself his instincts had it right.

A part of him clamoured for the safety of his comfort zone. Hindsight, such a wonderful thing. None of this weirdness would have happened if he'd taken the easy way instead of the hard one, concentrating on a future with Katie in Australia. A different reality would have stretched before him, his identity as a kidnap victim forever hidden.

He'd chosen the hard way instead, though, and another part of him savoured the triumph of sticking two fingers up to logic.

A warning bell of 'what the hell will happen next' sounded in his head. A crime had been committed, meaning he'd need to get the law involved. Telling the police seemed unavoidable, although he'd need more than memories, his gut feelings and a DNA test obtained by deception before he talked to them. He did have more, though. What with focusing on his parents and his nanny, he'd neglected something else mentioned in the newspaper article. A distinguishing mark, a mole, by which the missing child could be recognised if found. Daniel sported on his right hip that same mole, the pea-sized blemish proof of his identity.

A visit to the police seemed inevitable. Not yet, though. First, he'd tell Katie. He'd go to her flat tomorrow, once she got free of her double shifts at the hospital.

He pictured her reaction. She'd be dumbstruck. He couldn't imagine Katie scrambling for something to say, but there was a first time for everything.

When the shit hit the fan, though, when he'd been to the police and had the woman who'd kidnapped him arrested, he'd not find anyone more supportive than Katie. She was rock solid; he'd draw on her strength and maybe some of it would seep into him, giving him the courage to get through this. Let's face it, Daniel, his inner voice mocked, emotional stuff isn't your forte.

He was learning, though. With Katie's help, he might even get good at it one day.

He didn't doubt what lay ahead would prove challenging; his visit to the police would start an inescapable chain of events. They'd arrest Laura Bateman and perhaps he'd find out what had motivated her to steal him from his family. God knows he needed answers on that score.

He'd meet his biological parents as well. What sort of people were they? Would he be able to re-establish a relationship with them, after being wrenched away so many years ago? There would be that moment, that pivotal moment, when he'd stand before his mother, claiming her as the woman from his memories, as the shadowy figure beside his childhood bed. He'd also be reunited with Howard Cordwell, the father he'd never had.

From out of nowhere doubt struck him. What if he didn't measure up to the image of him they held in their minds? To be judged and found lacking by his true parents would be a blow too far. His hands clenched into fists, his palms sweaty with fear.

Don't get your hopes up, he warned himself. Odds were he was setting himself up for a major disappointment. What guarantee did he have of finding in them the elusive something for which he'd always searched? OK, so he got those warm fuzzy feelings whenever he brought his mother to mind. They might be springing from the idealism of his four-year-old self, though. He had no real concept of what she'd be like. As for his father, he was even more of an unknown quantity.

Katie seemed the only constant in his life he could count on. Her wide smile breezed into his mind, pushing away his dark thoughts, transforming his glass from half empty to half full. Optimism for the future washed over him, a sense of something out of kilter finally clicking into place. Thank God for Katie, the best thing ever to happen in his messed-up life. With her beside him, he'd get through this.

He pushed back his chair. He needed to find a way to forget, for one night at least, the weirdness in his head. He'd go back to the flat, crack open a beer, and try to make sense of things. He might even raise a toast to the forthcoming reunion with his parents. And another to Katie and their future together. Why the hell not? His glass was half full, after all.

Damn the demons in his head. He might be able to outrun them after all.

15

SHATTERING ICE

I didn't sleep the night following my baby's burial. I sat in an armchair asking myself over and over why the hand I'd been dealt was such a shitty one. I'd had a few months of contentment with Gran and my baby, no more, and it didn't seem fair when the rest of my life had been so crap. Not that I believed in a higher power dealing out happiness as a reward to the deserving. To me, life seemed like a giant lottery and some people pulled out a dud ticket. I was obviously one of them.

The temptation of suicide danced in front of me, its allure soft and seductive. I thought about finding rope to hang myself with, swallowing a bottle of sleeping pills or taking a sharp knife to my wrists.

The numbness stopped me killing myself, Daniel. Like some primitive survival mechanism, a self-generated version of Valium took over, leaving me in a state of frozen unresponsiveness. Choosing between rope, pills or a kitchen knife required more effort than I was able to manage. No, I'd stick with the decisions I'd already made, starting with leaving this house as soon as possible. I made a pact with myself. I would try to find some way of dealing with my baby's death. I'd give myself six months in Bristol, no longer. Suicide would be my release if, at any time during those six months, I returned to the agony I'd endured before the numbness set in. I couldn't survive pain as intense again; the torment would crush me and I'd end up swallowing a bottle of pills or slashing my wrists.

So Bristol it would be. I'd go there, I would mourn my baby, and attempt to come to terms with the devastation of his loss. If I never did – well, one day my landlord would knock on the door, and he'd find my body, like my mother so long ago, and beside it a note.

I don't know if you can grasp how things were for me back then, Daniel; what it was like, wanting to end my seemingly pointless life. I can't think you've ever suffered anything bad enough to make you want to kill yourself, and I pray you never do. I'm not sure how to describe it so you'll understand. It's as if I'd retreated into a dark world, where all that existed was unhappiness and despair and unending misery, my existence narrowed down to a bleak tunnel going on and on. I didn't believe there would ever be any light at the end, or even that an end existed. I think once someone like me finds herself in such a place, the idea of suicide becomes the light, a beacon pointing the way out.

The next day I packed what few possessions I owned: clothes, photos of Daniel and Gran, her jewellery. I placed Daniel's birth certificate, proof he was still alive under the sapling, on top of everything. My entire life fitted into one canvas suitcase. Then I boarded the next train for Bristol.

I picked the first guesthouse I found in Yellow Pages after I arrived at the station, and took a taxi there. After unpacking, I bought the local paper, hoping to find myself a cheap bedsit. The next day was spent making phone calls; I took the first available place. The room smelled of the dirt in the shaggy carpet, which might once have been cream but was now grime-coloured, of stale cigarette smoke mixed with a whiff of drains. It was vile, shabby and ugly and exactly what I wanted. No beauty existed in my life right then and my scruffy bedsit reflected the desolation of my frozen psyche. We made a good match.

I spent most of the first few weeks in Bristol in my room, only going out to get food or to use the payphone to sort Gran's estate and then scuttling back to my bolthole. I signed over power of attorney for my solicitor to sell the house; besides him, I spoke to nobody unless I had to. I slept as much as possible, finding sleep a welcome oblivion. When I was awake, I'd shower, dress, eat my food, and for the rest of the time I'd lie on my bed staring at the stains on the ceiling, my mind a sanctuary of inertia. Weeks went by like that; I had no notion of time or dates. Nothing mattered anymore.

I never thought I should be doing something, getting a job, exploring Bristol. The city was alien to me apart from the busy road on which I lived. Every time I went out I passed people of all skin colours, women wearing strange and exotic clothes, heard languages I couldn't identify. At night, looking out of the window, I'd see girls in tight short skirts, hanging around in doorways, smoking cigarettes. The city pulsed with life around me without touching me in any way. I had no thoughts, no feelings. I never let myself think about the event that had shattered my life.

God knows what a psychiatrist would have made of me back then. Shrinks have visited me so many times since I've been in this place, Daniel; they all think they can unlock my tongue and get inside my head. They haven't a clue. Seems to me the human brain is more complex and far more multi-dimensional than any psychiatrist can ever gauge. Oh, they have their theories, which change according to the latest so-called expert, and they try to categorise people's behaviour to match some arbitrary set of rules, but I don't think our depths are so easy to reach, Daniel. Can one person ever fathom what goes on in another person's head, really get to grips with what drives them? Probably not.

One day I dragged myself off the bed and walked to the corner shop to get some eggs. A new assistant, one I'd never seen before, a middle-aged woman, stood behind the counter.

'Morning, sweetheart!' I glanced up, startled. 'You need a bag, love?'

'No,' I mumbled.

'Well, haven't you got the prettiest blue eyes?' My face flushed. I looked at her.

Our eyes met, and she knew some awful thing had broken me, because she was one of those people who connected easily with her fellow human beings. She could read me because she'd studied people all her life. A woman who understood others, this one. She'd reached right in and got straight to the core of me, with no more than a look.

The ice around my soul melted a little as her warmth touched me.

'Thanks,' I muttered. I grabbed the eggs and walked out.

The next day, I needed milk.

She was there again, the same warm smile, the same look of knowing.

'Morning, my love!' She rang up the milk. 'You moved in round here, have you?'

'I live in one of the bedsits above the launderette.' It was more words in one go than I'd uttered at any time in the last few weeks.

She laughed. 'I know your landlord! We went to school together. My, that takes me back. He asked me out once, but I had too big a crush on the head boy to notice Barry. We laugh about it now.' She handed me my change, her fingers skimming my palm briefly, and the warmth of her touch melted my icy shell a bit more.

'You get any trouble with Barry, you tell him Emma Carter will come and sort him out. That'll put the fear of God into him.' She laughed again, showing a gap where a molar should have been.

'If you need anything – anything at all – you get yourself over here. You take care of yourself, sweetheart.' She patted my arm as she spoke, and the ice melted a little more.

Well, I found myself going into that shop every day. The prices were higher than the supermarkets, but I didn't care. Emma's innate empathy reached out to my frozen soul; I craved those few moments of warmth each day. I guess we all need human contact and I was no exception, Daniel, even when I still felt so dead inside.

The numbness lessened a little each time Emma greeted me, though. After a few weeks of her soft smile warming me each day, I took out the box containing Gran's photos, and I managed to look at them without crying. I still missed her and thought of her every day but the pain of her death was no longer as raw, as fresh. I traced my fingers over her beloved face and realised how lucky I'd been to have her in my life. I might not have received much maternal love, but I'd experienced Gran's warmth and understanding instead and with her I got quality rather than quantity. I'd been blessed, all right, and I realised I'd had the first thought in weeks that held a nugget of positivity.

I found I was no longer spending every day lying on my bed. The grime and whiff of my bedsit had started to get to me. My inner housewife took over; I went to the shop and bought lots of cleaning products. Well, I did say I was the homebody type. Before, the state of my bedsit hadn't mattered. Now I figured I might as well spend my self-imposed sentence somewhere clean that didn't smell bad. My real motivation was Emma Carter. I wanted her to think well of me, to believe I had some pride; I dreaded what would go through her head should she ever see the ugliness in which I lived.

It took a long time. That bedsit probably hadn't been cleaned in years. The smell of bleach and – according to the label on the all-purpose cleaner – summer meadow freshness filled the small space. I buffed the windows and stuffed the net curtains, grey with dirt, into my laundry bag. The ancient cooker got a thorough scrubbing as I coaxed solidified grease from it. I squirted polish on the wardrobe, rubbing the battered wood to a semblance of a shine. Next I wiped bleach inside the old fridge and chipped away at the thick ice around the tiny freezer compartment.

At the end of what seemed like forever, I had somewhere to live that didn't smell bad, with clean windows, where the once stained furniture now shone. My arms ached, but my inner housewife was satisfied. The place looked unrecognisable from the squalid hovel I'd moved into a couple of months before. It was still cramped and there wasn't much I could do about that, but it was clean now, and I intended to keep it that way.

My mood continued to lift, albeit slowly. I began reading, scouring the library for books to lose myself in. One weekend I bought one of the Sunday newspapers, the type that came with a thick supplement aimed at women. I scanned through the recipes, skipped the fashion advice, before turning the page to an article that made me draw in a sharp breath. It was titled 'Taken Young: How I Dealt with the Loss of my Child' by a woman called Mariette Sinclair.

I didn't read the article at first. I couldn't. Something compelled me to start reading eventually, though, and I didn't stop until the last word.

Mariette Sinclair might have been telling my own story. The raw pain shining through her writing was my pain too. We'd never met, we never would, yet the shared agony of holding a dead child in our arms bound us together. Like me, Mariette had thought cot death always happened to other people; like me, one morning she woke up with the same deep sensation of dread. She rushed into her baby's nursery and found her daughter limp and lifeless. This woman understood the agony of finding a baby cold and dead, when before there had been a warm body and flailing limbs. Probably she had screamed out her despair in the same way I did. Perhaps she had pounded the floor in anguish as well. She admitted she'd contemplated suicide, like me.

She told how, even with a husband who shared her grief, her sorrow isolated her. She shut him out, walling herself off, describing how she imprisoned herself in her own mind. I guess her mental jail was her equivalent of my frozen heart. Same thing, semantics the only difference.

I read how she got to grips with her pain at last. It seemed impossible at first and every tiny step forward she took was beyond difficult. She began with tearing down the wall shutting her off from her husband. She talked to him and realised their shared grief was a column of support to cling to in her misery. He encouraged her to call a friend who had lost a baby to cot death and she wrote about how valuable she found it to talk to someone who had experienced a similar tragedy. The same friend introduced her to the idea of getting grief counselling, which she did, eventually retraining as a psychotherapist.

The article touched me with incredible intensity; Mariette Sinclair's words were the catalyst for my brain to unfreeze at last. I'd been bottling everything up, Daniel. Well, not bottling things up, as that suggested I'd suffered grief over the death of my baby, but thanks to the pervading numbness, I hadn't felt anything these past few months. My baby's death was still a no-go area, the ice still solid around the place inside me where he lived.

I finished reading, curled up on my bed, my knees hugged to my chest, and it was then the frozen wasteland around my heart started to crack. Big shards splintered off, exposing the raw devastation beneath. My baby had died. The awful reality of his death rolled over me in one huge agonising wave, my sobs choking me as I broke down. Instead of the floor this time, I pounded the bed with my fists, furious denials tearing from my throat. The pain, the terrible crushing agony I had experienced while cradling my dead child in my arms, returned full force, smashing its way into my heart and mind. My beloved baby, my soul and very existence, had died. How could I ever heal such overwhelming despair?

The idea of taking a sharp knife to my wrists flashed across my mind again in that moment, Daniel, the thought bright and shimmering and showing me the end of the tunnel. Only for a moment, though.

Through my tears, I caught sight of Mariette Sinclair's article on the bed beside me. This woman had experienced the same agony as I had, and she had survived. Somehow, she found a way to deal with her grief.

Perhaps a way existed for me too. I had no idea what it might be. Mariette Sinclair had been married, with a husband and friends to support her. I had neither. She'd also attended counselling. No way would I be doing that. Impossible to talk to somebody who hadn't herself known the searing grief of finding a beloved child dead. There must, of course, be counsellors, like Mariette, who had. Other than sharing a common experience, though, how would that help? Would a counselling session breathe air into my dead baby's lungs? Would I have to listen to futile questions about how I was coping with my child's death? I'd need to lie about his burial, about the makeshift grave under the sapling. I could never have explained how I'd thought if I didn't tell anyone, my baby's death wouldn't become a reality.

Somehow, though, the agony wasn't as crushing as before. Perhaps time, such a tired cliché, had helped a little. Despite the pain, I knew I wasn't going to commit suicide. That article, written by my sister sufferer, had spoken to me, snuffing out my desire to kill myself. Mariette Sinclair had survived; so would I.

She'd been lucky in having people around her to support her, though, Daniel. I didn't.

It sank into me then how very alone I was.

16

HAMMER BLOW

Daniel dragged himself awake late the following morning, head pounding, mouth parched and tasting foul. The whole situation, already thoroughly screwed up, now came with the mother of all hangovers. Not that he regretted his session on the sauce, although he'd never intended to sink so many beers.

He sent Katie a text, suggesting he should come over early afternoon, asking her to text back yes or no. Within two minutes, he got a yes response and switched off his mobile. He popped a paracetamol, then forced himself to take the hottest shower he could withstand, willing the water to wash away his hangover. He caught sight of his face in the mirror as he brushed stale booze from his breath. Half-moons inked under his lower lids. Eyes sporting a lattice of red veins. Pasty skin, dark with stubble. Not a pretty sight.

He glanced at his watch. Half past eleven. He figured he'd go round to Katie's after he'd caught up on some more sleep, about two o'clock.

He woke up again early afternoon, head still throbbing but definitely better. Time to set off for Katie's flat in Putney. He hadn't a clue how to tell her what he'd discovered without it sounding like a bizarre joke.

She answered the doorbell immediately, all curves and spice in her trademark tight jeans and figure-hugging top, and pulled him straight into a fierce kiss. The silk of her hair swung against his cheek, her skin soft against his. All thoughts of what he'd come to tell her vanished from his mind, his only thought the sensations she provoked in his groin. God, he yearned to take her to bed, their passion denoting a fresh start. Not yet, though. They needed to talk first.

He pulled her into the living room, sitting beside her on the sofa.

'Katie . . .' His hands reached out and grabbed hers. 'I've got some news. Incredible news. You won't believe what I've found out.'

'About your real mother?' Excited impatience sprang from Katie. 'Did Laura Bateman tell you the truth when you confronted her?'

'She didn't tell me anything. Same old story of denial. No surprise there.'

'What, then?' Puzzlement clouded her face. 'Did you tackle your stepfather instead? Did he reveal something to you?'

Daniel snorted. 'I haven't seen the bastard in years and even if I did there's no way he'd say or do anything to help me. Found it all out myself, Katie. I've discovered who I am, where I come from, my real parents, everything.'

'How?' Bemusement drew her forehead into lines, endearing puckers Daniel longed to smooth away. He ached to sink into the comfort only she could give, bathe in her reassurances that he wouldn't disappoint his new-found parents. As well as her cool common sense concerning Laura Bateman's motives. He pictured Katie's reaction to his news, the way he'd done a hundred times already. Disbelief first, probably, then shock and amazement once he convinced her he wasn't bullshitting. Then a hundred eager questions, prising every detail out of him.

'The British Library. That's how I found out the truth. Checking through the newspaper archives.' He drew in a breath, savouring the moment. 'I was kidnapped, Katie. My real name is Daniel James Cordwell.'

She gasped, the sound strangling itself in her throat. Taken aback, he checked her face, gauging her reaction.

Not what he was expecting. Shock, definitely shock, but the incredulous response he'd anticipated was missing. Instead – what was he seeing? Anguish, although he had no idea why. Katie's expression spoke to him of denial, of wanting to crawl as far away as possible from what he was saying. His self-belief plummeted several notches, making him stumble over his next words, uncertain as to what her reaction signified.

'Katie . . . what is it? What's wrong?'

He'd never seen her so pale. This woman wasn't his confident sassy girlfriend. Something in her expression reminded him of how she looked when talking about her sister. He didn't like it, didn't understand it, but something told him not to press her, to wait for her to speak.

'Oh, God, Dan. Please, no.' Agony reigned in Katie's expression, before anger took over. 'This is crazy. You're talking bullshit.'

He didn't answer, not trusting himself to reply.

'What's happened? Why are you saying this?' Suddenly she burst into tears and walked quickly from the room into the kitchen, returning with a handful of paper towels. She wiped her face, blew her nose.

'You're not making any sense.' A sob came from her. 'OK, so your mother isn't your mother and you need to find out what's behind all that, but you being kidnapped?' She shook her head in confusion and denial, more tears running down her face. He'd never seen her cry before. He still had no idea what lay behind her reaction.

'Katie.' She wouldn't look at him. His hopes of getting reassurance from her were withering like autumn leaves, pain at her response replacing them. He continued anyway, because what choice did he have? 'Katie, I read the newspaper reports of the kidnap. I saw the picture of my mother and I recognised her as the woman who used to sit beside my bed. The girl I remember, the girl with the dark hair – she was my nanny.'

'No.' Katie shook her head. 'No, I don't believe this.' Her voice rose in pitch. 'It's all coincidence. Just because you find out your mother isn't your mother – it doesn't follow you were kidnapped. You have no proof whatsoever.' She dabbed at her face with a paper towel. 'You should have thought this through before barging in here, spouting such crap. I can't believe it. I won't believe it.'

Betrayal, sharp and painful, shot through Daniel. Where was the support, the love, he'd counted on? Her insensitivity seemed so out of character. 'Katie . . .'

'Don't do this to me, Dan.'

In order to convince her, he undid his belt, pulled down his jeans and boxers a few inches and twisted his body towards her. 'Look, Katie.' He pointed at his hip. 'The newspaper article said Daniel James Cordwell had no distinguishing characteristics, apart from a mole on his right hip. You've seen it often enough. There's your proof.'

She didn't look at his pointing finger. She didn't need to.

'Oh, God,' she said. 'Oh, my God. It's true, then.'

'Yes. Katie, what's wrong? Why are you reacting this way?'

The air hung thickly between them, laced with desperation on his part, anguish on hers.

'Katie, talk to me.'

After what seemed like forever, her eyes met his. Pain struck him at the torment in them.

'Christ, Daniel, I wish to God there was an easy way to tell you this. The woman in the newspaper article, the one you recognised as your mother. Her name's Sarah, isn't it? Sarah Cordwell.'

Confusion pushed aside pain. 'How the hell did you know . . . ?'

She dropped her gaze before delivering the hammer blow.

'She's my sister, Daniel.'

Then she was on her feet, running from the room into the hallway towards the bathroom. The door slammed behind her. Loud choking sobs hit Daniel's ears.

He sat in stunned silence.

His mind flew back to being in bed with Katie, when she'd talked about her family. Oh, God. It couldn't be. It couldn't possibly be.

Sarah Cordwell. He'd never known the surname of Katie's married sister. He was her son, Daniel James Cordwell. Katie was his aunt. His blood relative. His kidnap by Laura Covey must have been the skeleton in the family closet she'd mentioned.

He'd have laughed at the irony of the situation, if he hadn't been so utterly distraught, if his guts weren't twisting themselves into a double helix, the double helix of the DNA he shared with Katie.

He'd gone looking for an aunt, expecting her to be the sister of Laura Covey.

Well, he'd found an aunt all right. The problem was – she'd been sharing his bed for the last few weeks.

And holy shit, he'd always wanted to be part of a different family, a happy, united one that didn't include Ian Bateman. He'd envied Katie her family set-up, with the devoted parents and the adoring sister. And there lay the irony. Turned out he belonged to it and always had done.

The only problem being – he was the loud, rattling skeleton in the family closet. A bad case of be careful what you wish for.

He rubbed his hand over his face, forcing down the emotions blocking his throat. He'd met the one woman capable of turning Daniel Bateman, consummate player, into Mr Faithful, the only girl he'd ever thought he could fall in love with, and she turned out to be his aunt. An aunt whose penchant for sculpture had drawn her into the shop where he worked, the conversation they'd had about Balinese carvings sparking their mutual attraction. The sense he'd had when he first met Katie of already knowing her must have been déjà vu waving a red flag at him.

Christ. He'd told her this was a big can of worms, but he'd been wrong. The whole sorry mess was an almighty can of maggots, and now he'd opened it, they were crawling everywhere, smearing filth over his life and his relationship with Katie. There was no way to stuff them inside and seal it up again either.

Katie, oh, Katie. Would he turn back the clock, if it meant being able to continue with her, never knowing his real family, both of them oblivious to their blood relationship? Would he suppress the memories, accept Laura Bateman as the only family he had, if he could keep the woman he loved?

No. In order for him to be reunited with his parents, and even for Katie's sake, he wouldn't deny himself, or them, that reunion, what they'd forged would have to end. His identity, or rather the fact he'd always felt as if he didn't have one, meant too much to him. And he was certain he'd have got to the truth anyway. Katie would have told him eventually about the kidnap and his doubts would only have grown stronger. He'd have met her sister, his mother, at some point and his intuition would have flagged up to him their shared genes, as it had when he read the newspaper article. Then, when the truth came out, Sarah Cordwell would have to endure knowing her son had slept with his aunt, a bombshell powerful enough to blast his new family into the stratosphere.

Dear God. He and Katie were over; they had to be. The pain of her loss cleaved him in two. He loved this woman, had dreamed of a life with her, yet their relationship had proved a mirage, their hopes built on sand rather than rock. How he'd handle seeing her in the future, he had no idea. They'd have to ensure they didn't meet for as long as possible, to take the heat out of the situation, until the passion between them had died. Their relationship had to remain a secret too; no one must ever know they'd dated, slept together, fallen in love. Her family didn't need another skeleton in the closet. He was about to release the one they already had, and he wasn't going to replace it with another.

He shook his head in disbelief. Several good parts did exist in what he'd unearthed. He'd had his instincts confirmed, he'd identified the two women for whom he'd pined for years, and he'd found his birth family. His discovery would have seemed almost miraculous if it hadn't been for the inevitable break-up with Katie. That was the bad part. Finding the truth had come with an expensive price tag.

He realised he should go to her. He walked to the bathroom, pounding on the door, calling her name into the silence stretching before him.

Eventually the door opened and she pushed past him, her eyes refusing to meet his. He followed her into the living room, forcing himself to say something, anything, to cut the tension.

'Christ, Katie.' He ran his hand through his hair in frustration. 'This whole thing is so incredibly messed up. There must be some mistake, has to be. Your sister is my mother? We're related?'

She carried on avoiding his eyes. 'God knows I wish it wasn't true. I've prayed every day for your safe return. Our whole family were desperate to get you back.' The heartbreak in her tone shattered Daniel. 'But I never thought . . . never imagined my prayers would be answered like this.'

'I can't wrap my head around it.' Daniel's voice shook with emotion.

'I can hardly believe it either.' Her words were still thick with tears. 'I mean . . . we used to play together as kids, endless games of hide and seek. Sarah and Howard would bring you up from Bristol at weekends. You don't remember?'

'No. I was four years old, Katie. I remember my mother and the nanny . . . nothing else from back then.'

'I was only six myself. My memories are pretty hazy too. I certainly don't recall you having a mole on your hip.' She was calmer now, her face still pale with shock, though. 'What I do remember is knowing something terrible had happened to my sister. To you as well. Oh, Mum and Dad did their best to explain it to me.' The tears started to flow again.

'I remember them telling me how you had been taken away by somebody bad, very bad, but everyone would do all they could to bring you home safely. Mum told me how terribly upset Sarah and Howard were they'd lost you.' She shook her head. 'I remember crying and Mum comforting me. Sarah looked so heartbroken, so distraught. I'd ask every day when you were coming home, when Sarah would laugh again as she used to. She was never the same after you'd been abducted; she'd still play with me, but didn't smile anymore. Later on, Mum told me she'd become ill, seriously unwell, but they hoped she'd recover.'

'Did she have a breakdown?'

'Suicide attempt. About a year after you'd been abducted.'

Christ. This didn't get any better. Whoever said the hard way always got easier was completely off-beam. 'What happened?'

'She cut her wrists in the bath. Howard came home early from work, thank God. Seems he had a feeling something wasn't right. She'd lost a fair bit of blood but he got to her in time. Back then, all Mum said was that Sarah had been rushed to hospital, but she would be all right. I don't remember what she told me was wrong with her. Anyway, Sarah needed loads of help for a long time after they discharged her. Counselling, therapy, that sort of thing. I didn't find out until I was a lot older, when I asked Mum about the scars on Sarah's wrists. Howard helped her pull through. He'd not realised how bad she'd got before the suicide attempt but afterwards . . . well, Mum says he was incredibly supportive. I think it would have killed him to lose Sarah. He'd already lost you, remember.'

'They must have given up hope I'd ever be found.'

'I think they did. Nobody ever actually said so, of course, especially around me. The story was always that you'd be found, and soon, and the bad person who had taken you would be punished. The police didn't find any solid leads, though. Mum told me that after a while, as time went on and you remained missing, everyone's worst fear, that some perverted monster had taken you, seemed increasingly likely. Everyone thought you had to be dead if that were the case. She also told me they actually hoped you were dead, rather than alive with a paedophile, which they found too awful to think about.'

She paused. 'That was why I never made the connection when you told me your doubts about your parentage or when the DNA results came back negative. Never once did I consider you might be my nephew. When I was old enough to think about things properly, I decided you must be long dead. I believed whoever took you must have killed you. The odds of you being alive . . . they didn't seem good. Far more likely you'd been murdered by a sexual predator, as much as I hated to think about such a thing.'

Daniel shook his head. 'I can't even begin to imagine what that must have been like. For my parents. For you.'

'Both Mum and Sarah have told me everyone went through sheer hell. Howard and Sarah loved you so much, you see. Well, we all did. Mum and Dad lost their adored only grandchild. Me a playmate. You can understand why it all got too much for Sarah. She blamed herself. She still does.'

'Why?'

'The way she sees things, she was your mother and that meant she should have protected you from harm. She felt guilty because she'd been a working mother and had a nanny; she condemned herself for not spending more time with you. The thing was, Howard and Sarah simply wanted a night out by themselves, as couples do. She was never to blame, as far as I can see, but she obviously didn't think so.'

'No, she wasn't the one to blame. Only one person's guilty here. Laura Bateman. Or Covey, as she was then.'

'Don't forget the nanny. You were four years old. She left you in the flat alone.'

'I suppose so. She'd put me to bed, though. She'd checked on me before she went out, or so the newspaper report said. She must have thought there wasn't any risk. How was she to know some strange woman would snatch me, for whatever weird reason?'

'No excuses, Dan. Sarah hired her to be your nanny and, as such, she should have stayed with you. If she got hungry, she should have raided the fridge or phoned for home delivery.' Katie's face grew grim. 'Sarah couldn't bear to see her afterwards. Nobody has a clue what happened to her. I don't think anyone cared.'

'I'm going to the police tomorrow, Katie.'

'Of course. You'll need to tell them as soon as possible. I presume they'll do another DNA test, a proper legal one this time.'

'Yes. They'll arrest Laura Bateman as well. The bitch. What reason did she have to wreck so many lives? I want to find out why she did it, Katie.'

'We all do.' Katie's voice shook. 'I'm not going to say anything, to Mum and Dad, or to Sarah and Howard. I can't anyway, not without revealing our relationship. The police will have to tell them. Sarah and Howard . . . I can't begin to think how ecstatic they'll be. Mum and Dad too. My head's a total mess, though. I'm glad you're alive, that you weren't murdered by a paedophile, of course I am. Am I being selfish, though, Dan? I lose you as a boyfriend, if you're my nephew. I forfeit what we had, what we were building.' The tears started again. 'I can't help it. This whole thing rips me to shreds.' She choked back a sob. 'I fell in love with you, Dan. Hard.'

Daniel's emotions churned at the paradox of her timing. He pulled her in tight to him.

'Me too, Katie.' The familiarity of her body crushed against his reminded him of what he would never experience with her again, a loss almost too much to bear. 'Things are going to be, well, more than awkward when all this comes out in the open. You and me . . . family get-togethers and all that . . . how's it going to work?'

Katie pulled away.

'Simple truth is – it won't. We can't see each other again. At least not for a long time. I wouldn't be able to bear being around you.' She blew her nose. 'Thank God I never told Mum and Dad much about you. Nobody must know about our relationship. Ever.'

'I'll never tell them, I swear.'

'I'm going to Australia, Dan.'

He reeled at the finality of her words. 'You sure?' He didn't really need to ask.

'Yes. I was planning to go anyway, remember, even before we met. We need to put distance between us. It's the obvious thing to do.' She pushed him even further away. 'I'll start making arrangements. I already have the visa. I can rent out my flat, give a month's notice at the hospital. I should be able to go straight away after I finish work. In the meantime, I'll make whatever excuses I can think of if Sarah tries to arrange some sort of reunion between us.'

The finality of her words smashed through the last of Daniel's defences.

'I should go,' he said.

'Yes. You should. Leave, Dan. Please.' She didn't need to say it again.

17

FISH SUPPER

The next day I realised I wasn't so alone after all. I did have somebody to turn to. I walked to the shop and went straight up to Emma.

'Would you come over and have a cup of tea with me sometime?' I blurted out.

'Of course I will, my love! I'd like that.' She looked surprised, but pleased. 'When would suit you, sweetheart?'

'This evening?'

'I'll come over straight after work, love. Tell you what.' Her face lit up. 'I'll nip into the chippie and get us two of their huge portions of cod and chips. My treat. We'll have ourselves a right feast, and a good old chat. What do you say?'

'Sounds lovely. Thank you.' I hadn't eaten fish and chips since Gran was alive, and my mouth watered at the thought of thick-cut chips and chunks of white cod encased in crispy batter. I didn't realise at the time I'd said yes to more than a meal together. I'd also taken my first step towards the light at the end of my tunnel.

The hours until Emma was due to arrive dragged by that afternoon. I was glad I'd bothered to clean my bedsit so thoroughly; I could look forward to her visit without embarrassment. I scrubbed everywhere again, made sure I had enough tea, bread and butter, checked the plates and cutlery to ensure they were sparkling. We'd have to eat perched on my bed, the way I always did, but I didn't think Emma would care about such things.

The smell of the fish hit my nose as I opened the door to Emma that evening. I waved her inside.

We sat on my bed to eat. Neither of us spoke as we cleared our plates, stuffing vinegary chips and chunks of cod into our mouths. I wondered how best to bring up the subject of my baby's death. Despite all the tears I'd cried the day before, I could still hardly bear to think about Daniel, let alone talk about him.

Maybe some of my churning emotions showed in my face. Emma Carter had realised from the start I'd been badly damaged by life, and she wasn't one to ignore somebody in need.

When we'd finished eating, she put her plate on the floor and moved closer.

'Nice little place you have here, Laura, my love, and you keep everything spotless, you do.' She laid her hand on my arm. 'But I don't see any photos, sweetheart. Do you have any family? You're not originally from around here, are you? It's the accent, my love. Gives the game away.'

I shook my head. 'No. All my family are dead.' My tears were already starting. 'I used to live with my wonderful gran. I loved her so much. She died, though. Not long ago.'

'Your mum, sweetheart? Your dad?'

'Mum never knew who my father was.' There didn't seem any way to make the truth sound less stark. 'She died when I was fourteen. Drank herself to death.'

'Oh, my love. I'm sorry. That must have been hard on you.'

'I didn't know any different. I was an only child and in the end, I needed to take care of her, rather than the other way round. She . . . well, she didn't want to live, not with all the pain she carried inside her. She got worse, drank more and more. I ended up in foster care, and eventually she died.'

'You went to live with your granny afterwards, my love?'

'Yes.' I saw no reason to tell her what had forced me to run to Gran. I needed to talk about my baby instead, and we were edging dangerously close. Hot tears warmed my eyelids and slid down my cheeks. I wiped uselessly at my face with my sleeve.

'Here, my love. Always carry a packet of these with me. Never know when they'll come in handy.' She pulled a travel pack of Kleenex from her bag and handed me a tissue.

I scrubbed off the tears and went over to the wardrobe. Words seemed impossible. A photo would have to tell the story for me.

I opened the canvas suitcase and took out my favourite photo of me with Daniel, taken a month after his birth. A happier version of me stood smiling into the camera, holding my baby in my arms. I'd just fed him and he was sated and contented, his tiny mouth looking as if he were smiling along with me.

I handed Emma the photo. I sat back on the bed, grief choking me at the thought of his fat arms and legs wriggling while Gran fussed around with the camera. I could almost feel the weight of him; the memory rushed back, gloriously painful, of how wonderful it had been to stroke his soft dimpled skin with my fingers.

I sensed Emma laying the photo carefully down and then she wound her arms around me while I soaked her with tears and shook with the pain. I eventually hiccupped to a halt, completely wrung out.

'Sorry,' I muttered as I pulled away to grab another tissue.

'Your baby, my love?'

'Yes.' I blew my nose. 'But he . . . he . . .' I didn't say the words, for that would make his death real. 'I went to check on him one morning, and he . . .' I didn't need to say any more. Emma understood.

'I wanted to be the best mum ever.' Sobs choked me. 'Be the sort of mother I never had myself. Gran said she'd help me, but she died, and it was just him and me. We were doing all right. But then it happened.' I surrendered to a fresh wave of pain.

'I had to get away afterwards. Somewhere different. That's why I'm here.' I didn't mention my trek through the woods with my dead baby in my arms. Neither did I tell Emma about the birth certificate in my suitcase, without its counterpart, the death certificate I had never obtained.

'I understand, Laura, my love. I know exactly what you're going through.' The pain in her voice pierced my self-absorption. I realised she meant it. This woman beside me – she had also endured the agony of losing a child. Her world had been ripped in two as well.

I stared at her through the tears. 'You too, Emma? You lost a baby?'

'Not like you, my love. My Jamie was seven when he died.'

'What happened?'

'A drunk driver. Jamie was walking home from football practice; the man in the car had been drinking all afternoon and he still got behind the wheel and drove.' She paused. 'He was overwhelmed with guilt afterwards. Hanged himself. I'm ashamed to say this now, but at the time I was glad. I hated him so much.'

I didn't know what to say. Emma had been a mother for far longer than I had. She'd gone through seven years of loving her son, of being his mother, only to have him ripped from her. Could what she'd endured have been even more agonising than what I'd gone through?

'Jamie didn't die straight away, my love. He'd been terribly hurt, though, and he only lasted a few hours. The thought of my beautiful boy suffering, being in pain – it tore me up, sweetheart. I didn't deal with his death at all well.' Tears trembled in her voice. 'Coming to terms with such a tragedy seemed impossible. My husband was as devastated as I was, but I shut him out. I locked myself in my own world, along with the pain and the grief.'

Echoes of Mariette Sinclair. 'What happened? How did you get through it?'

'My bossy older sister came to stay with me. She sat me down, and boy, did she ever talk straight to me. No nonsense with her. She said I had to get my act together; my husband needed me and if I'd let him, he'd support me in my grief. She acknowledged that yes, Jamie's death had been terrible; no, it wasn't fair, but neither was life. She told me if I expected anything else, then I was naïve and a fool. See what I mean about the straight talking?' She laughed.

'Did it work? Her saying those things?'

'Yes, because she really did understand, my love. She revealed how, years ago, she'd suffered a miscarriage at ten weeks. She'd never told me that before. She had tears in her eyes – my big sister, who I'd not seen cry since she was eight years old. She spoke of her anguish, how losing a child at any age is a tragedy, even if the child is never born. The pain never goes away, not ever.'

'No.' I couldn't imagine not experiencing that raw devastation.

'But it does get easier to cope with, my love. Eventually you make peace with it. The pain becomes part of you. The awfulness of what's happened begins to fade, a little at first, and then a bit more. You start to remember the one you've lost without crying, and you find yourself smiling when you think of them.'

'Yes.' She was right. 'That's how it's been with Gran. Her death was terrible at first. We were so close, you see, and she only died recently. The other day, though – I looked at her picture, and I found myself smiling. Just as you said.'

'That's how it works, Laura sweetheart. You lost your granny, and your baby, in such a short space of time, and you so young. Life can be very cruel, my love. Things do get better, though. They have to. Nobody can go on suffering that intensity, that amount of grief, forever. The wound starts to close over, given time.' She laughed. 'A cliché, sure, but it's true. Time really is a great healer, although it's awful to hear people say it.'

'It does get better, then? It is possible to . . . live with it, somehow?' I didn't quite believe it yet, but both Mariette Sinclair and Emma Carter were still here. Their grief hadn't drowned them, in the way I thought mine would, if I ever allowed myself to think about Daniel.

'Yes. Part of the healing is acknowledging what's happened. I think, sweetheart, you've been keeping all this bottled up and that's not healthy.' I nodded. 'What was your baby's name, Laura?'

I didn't answer right away.

'Daniel,' I eventually managed.

'Do you have any more pictures of him, my love?'

I took out the rest of the photos of Daniel from the wardrobe, and together we looked at them. I remembered his gummy smile, and the way he wriggled around as I changed his nappy, and the snuffling sounds he made as he slept. I remembered, and I cried, and the agony softened into something I thought I might be able to deal with, in time.

I hugged Emma fiercely. 'Thank you,' I whispered.

I allowed the pain to come to the surface after she left, releasing as much as I dared, hot tears stinging my face as I looked through the photos of Daniel again. I read Mariette Sinclair's article once more and I thought about what Emma had said, and about her sister too. All three women had been through the same agony I had experienced, and all had come through it. Eventually.

I might be able to get through it as well. Wasn't that the decision I'd come to anyway, when I realised I was no longer contemplating suicide? I could survive this. I might not manage to be happy, but I didn't want to slash my wrists and let my life drain away in a pool of blood anymore.

It didn't happen overnight. I did a lot more crying, spent hours looking at Daniel's photos, more evenings soaking up Emma's warmth and understanding. I didn't stop once I started. I spent less time reliving the agony of his death and more in remembering the joy of being his mother. He had graced my life for a very short space of time, but what an incredible blessing he had been. My beautiful, beloved baby. My Daniel.

I was right. Happiness eluded me, but the frozen numbness had gone for good. The pain of his death still sliced through me every day but not in the old agonising way. It was bearable. The more I cried, the more I slowly healed and came back to life.

I bought a copy of the local paper one day and browsed the job vacancies. I had no training for anything, but some job must exist for me in this city and I didn't care what I did.

Time to start some sort of living again.

18

WHEELS IN MOTION

On his return home, Daniel slumped on the sofa, not even bothering to take off his jacket. He curled on his side, knees to chin, arms around his shins. When Tim came in some time after ten o'clock, he found Daniel in the same position, the lights off, the room cold.

'What are you doing sitting in the dark?'

Daniel stirred. He'd lost track of time since getting back from Katie's flat.

'Mate? You OK?' Tim sat beside him on the sofa. 'Has something happened with Katie?'

From somewhere he found his voice. 'We split up.' Such bald words, ones that choked him up, almost unbearably.

'What? But I thought . . .' Daniel heard genuine regret in his flatmate's voice. 'How come? Wasn't everything going great between you two?'

'Something's happened, Tim. I need time to get it all sorted, and right now I can't deal with a full-time relationship.' He stood up. 'I'll grab us both a beer. This may take some time.'

Within half an hour he'd told an incredulous Tim what he'd found out, omitting any mention of Katie. The pain of their blood tie must remain a secret.

'So that's why you were suddenly so interested in family history websites?'

'Yeah. That was the first avenue I went down. Proved a dead end, but after the DNA test showed she wasn't my mother, well, I became a bit obsessed. Then I got the notion she might have kidnapped me. It seemed an insane idea, but I had to follow it up. I did some digging in the old newspaper archives and then things moved pretty quickly.'

'You're not joking, mate. But what about Katie – this is going to be a weird time for you once you go to the police – don't you think you'd be better off sticking with her, getting some support?'

'Tim, I don't know who I am anymore. One minute I'm Daniel Bateman, son of Laura Bateman, and the next I'm Daniel Cordwell, son of Sarah and Howard Cordwell, people who are my parents but who are almost strangers. I have grandparents I had no idea existed. I need to get my head round all that and right now I have nothing to offer Katie.' Definitely better than telling Tim that as well as parents and grandparents, he also had an aunt he'd been bedding every chance he got for the past few weeks.

Don't go there, he warned himself. He stood up, draining his beer.

'Look, mate, today's been one big rollercoaster so far. I need to get some sleep. Going to the police tomorrow.' He gave a wry grin. 'That'll be a wagon-load of fun. Can't be every day someone turns up claiming they're a long-lost kidnap victim.'

'I'll be thinking of you, mate. You're going to need all the luck you can get.'

'Amen to that.'

Daniel's brain shot into overdrive the next morning as he went through the motions of forcing breakfast down himself. He yearned to text Katie, find out if she felt as crap as he did. He resisted the urge. A clean break was the only solution. Right now, though, he ached for her; her loss had ripped a gaping hole in him and he hadn't a clue how to deal with the pain. At some point he'd have to meet his grandparents, Katie's parents, and hear everyone talk about her, see photos of her; he didn't know how to recover from her loss when she'd still be all around him. The hard way continued to get harder, not easier.

Tim came into the kitchen and looked at the dark shadows under his flatmate's eyes. 'You OK? Still planning to go to the police?'

'No point in putting things off. I tell you, Tim – I'm not looking forward to this.' He slammed his coffee mug down. 'The shit is going to hit the fan and I haven't a frigging clue how to deal with it. I mean . . .' He shook his head. 'How weird is it going to be, meeting my real parents? It's been twenty-two years, for God's sake. I don't remember a single thing about my father. What on earth will we say to each other?'

A stupid question. As if Tim could give him the answer. He'd have to figure things out as he went along.

He'd already decided he'd go to New Scotland Yard; there seemed little point in asking the local police to deal with something like this. OK, so his kidnapping had taken place in Bristol, but his kidnapper, damn the bitch, lived here in London.

'Better get going. See you later.' New Scotland Yard was calling. No point in further delay. He grabbed his jacket and keys and headed for the Tube.

Eventually Daniel stood outside, his feet rooted to the pavement. Crunch time. No going back once he entered the building. He breathed in deeply, willing the cool morning air to dissolve the rock in his chest. It didn't help, but neither would postponing the inevitable.

A good half-hour was needed to get his brain in gear before he walked in, heading towards the front-office clerk at the main desk. 'I need to talk to somebody about a child abduction.' He cleared his bone-dry throat, which felt as if it were closing over. 'I believe I was the one who was kidnapped.'

He'd done it. He'd said the words, clocked the look on the man's face. And, boy, did he get everyone's attention pretty damn quick. He ended up being ushered into a room, with two police officers, one male, one female, who listened as he told his story.

He kicked off with his memories of the girl and the woman, how he'd never believed Laura Bateman was his mother, and he saw the disbelief in their faces. The younger of the two officers, the woman, did little to conceal her impatience with someone she clearly thought was some kind of weirdo or time-waster. The disbelief faded a little when he mentioned the eye colour thing, and how genetics had fuelled his suspicions.

He told them about the DNA test and the results, and watched the raised eyebrows when he admitted falsifying the consent form. Well, what the hell; he had to tell them the whole story anyway. Leaving anything out would be pointless and he doubted they'd be too concerned with such details when they had a genuine kidnap victim, alive and well, in front of them. More interest than disbelief was now coming from their side of the table, or so he hoped. Was it his imagination, or was the room getting hotter?

Next he described the ugly scene when he confronted Laura Bateman. Then the visit to the British Library, finding the story about the kidnap. He gave them his age, how it fitted with him being Daniel Cordwell.

Finally, he told them about the birthmark mentioned in the newspaper article, pulling down his jeans to reveal his hip. He fell silent then. He'd done his bit.

Questions were fired at him, lots of them, many repeated until Daniel nearly exploded with frustration, his conviction that he'd nailed the truth of the matter chafing against the apparent cynicism still coming from the other side of the table. The scepticism dissipated as the questions went on and Daniel wondered whether he'd managed to convince them he wasn't a time-waster or loony tune.

'Christ. Not every day we get someone like you walk in here, that's for sure.' The more senior officer looked like he'd seen an ugly thing or two in his time. Daniel could sense the man's barely leashed anticipation of solving such an important cold case. 'We'll need you to come back tomorrow and provide a full statement. It'll mean taking a day off work. Giving a statement and all that goes with it isn't something we're going to get through quickly – be prepared to be here for several hours.'

Dear God. He'd hoped to get this over with today. Nothing he could do except go with what he'd started, though.

'Fine. Just tell me what you need from me.'

'Obviously we won't say anything to Sarah and Howard Cordwell until we have conclusive proof you're their son. Don't want to raise their hopes unnecessarily. It'll be easy enough to prove, one way or another. There'll be DNA from Daniel Cordwell, obtained at the time when the case was fresh. You'll give us a sample of yours tomorrow and we'll check if they match.'

'I'll give you my DNA. Whatever you want.' Relief flooded through Daniel. He'd done the hard part. The rest was up to the police.

There was paperwork, form-filling, a mountain of migraine-inducing details to wade through, before Daniel was allowed to leave. Back at the flat, he spent the evening with a six-pack of beer, downing enough to take the edge off his churning emotions without getting drunk. A clear head would be needed the following day and he didn't intend to screw it up by arriving with a hangover.

He ended up being right about that. If he'd thought the initial police interview hard-going, the second one proved ten times worse. Not in all ways, he'd give them that. Once convinced there was a case to investigate, the scepticism had disappeared, being replaced by a brisk determination to handle a potential kidnap victim with the right degree of sensitivity. The questions were hell, though; they probed every aspect of those hazy first memories, his childhood, how Laura Bateman had treated him, asking the same thing in different ways, turning him inside out. 'What makes you think . . . ?' 'How can you be sure . . . ?' He'd wanted to scream with frustration but steeled himself to stay calm, in control.

The worst had been when they started on about his stepfather. He'd had no option but to fudge the facts, telling them truthfully he didn't have a close relationship with Ian Bateman but clamping down on revealing anything that would lead them too far down that path. Not so hard, really; he'd had years of suppressing his hatred of the bastard. So what if he didn't tell them everything? It had no bearing on the fact Laura Bateman had kidnapped him, which was the whole reason behind being at New Scotland Yard anyway.

The day ground on and on, but eventually his ordeal ended. He signed the statement, had his cheek swabbed to provide a DNA sample and was told they'd let him know when the results came through. The wheels were in motion, turning faster and faster. No stopping them now.

He walked out into the cool evening air, a jackhammer pounding in his head. Satisfaction, smug and triumphant, washed over him, shitty day notwithstanding. The process he'd started meant that Laura Bateman, damn her, would soon be arrested and charged with his kidnap. For some twisted reason, she had stolen him from his parents. She'd taken him from a loving family in which he could have grown up with a father as well as a mother, with grandparents, and a little girl called Katie who would always have been simply an aunt. Above all, he would never have suffered Ian Bateman.

Yeah, payback would be sweet. The woman was going to get what she deserved, and then some.

A voice whispered inside Daniel's head, reminding him Laura Bateman loved him, always had. Despite the anger, the hurt, he'd never doubted her feelings for him. He shoved the thought aside. Right now, anger was an emotional crutch, one he needed to get through this mess.

He got drunk that night once home, hammering the beer, drowning out the questions, the memories, washing them away on a tide of alcohol. After his sixth beer, Tim quietly suggested he should ease up on the booze, Daniel responding by yelling at him to leave him the hell alone. His flatmate ended up going out in an obvious attempt to avoid further confrontation. Fine by Daniel. He needed solitude, time alone to nurse his bitterness.

The next evening was a repeat performance. He didn't get drunk on the third night, though. Booze wouldn't have cut it for him that evening; his dark fury was too overwhelming. Because on the third day he came home to a message from Ian Bateman on the flat's answering machine.

No niceties. Straight to the point. Typical of the arsehole.

'You shit. You goddamn little shit. Your mother's having one of her turns, but this time she's a hell of a lot worse than before. Won't say a word, just sits there holding a photo of you, staring at your stupid face. If I find out you've upset her . . .' There was a pause. 'I'll make you regret it.' The click as he hung up echoed in Daniel's head.

The years melted away, transporting him back to his teenage years, when a look from the man was enough to cow him, and that was when he grabbed his workout kit, heading for the gym. The punch bag got the stuffing pounded out of it, his obvious fury concerning Len the trainer. The leather ball became his bastard stepfather's face, but somehow his fists could never hit it hard enough, and that had been when Len had dragged him away, sweating and still full of fury.

All he could do now was wait to hear from the police. In the meantime, he resisted the temptation to go hunting for an easy lay. Roll on getting the DNA results, he thought. At least whatever happened from then on should kick out all thoughts of that prick Ian Bateman.

19

OBSESSION

I ended up getting a job waitressing in a little café near The Triangle. Each day I buttered bread, poured coffee and came back to life a little more. I wasn't happy; the loss of my Daniel was still too recent, too raw, and I had no idea, and didn't care, if I'd ever be happy again. It was sufficient to know I'd decided to live, whatever such a choice might mean.

Restlessness kicked in after a year of waitressing; I decided to train for something better paid, with the aim of affording somewhere nicer to live. I ended up doing an evening course in bookkeeping, carrying on with my job in the café during the day. My marks were high and I considered browsing the job vacancies after I completed the course. Something, though, perhaps lack of confidence or unwillingness to tempt fate by changing the status quo, held me back. I carried on waitressing and promised myself I'd search for a suitable bookkeeping job soon. No hurry, I told myself.

Emma Carter and I remained friends, sharing regular fish suppers, until one day she told me she was retiring to Devon with her husband. Her going inevitably left a big gap for me; by now, though, I'd forged enough of a life for myself to ensure I'd still have people around me. The manager of the café was something of a mother hen and I got on well with the other staff.

Time slipped by, bringing with it my Daniel's fourth birthday, had he lived.

I took the day off work and spent the time crying over photos of him, remembering the bittersweet delight of being his mother, of being able to cherish him for such a short time. The pain of his loss hit me even more acutely that year, probably because I didn't have Emma around. I tried to picture what he'd be like now. The vision of a healthy four-year-old, all dark hair and big eyes, rose up to torture me; I ended up on my knees, begging a God I didn't believe in to let me have my Daniel back.

I've never put any credence in such things, but fate seemed to be stepping in when a young girl walked into the café the next day and ordered a cappuccino for herself along with juice for the little boy clutching her hand. Enchantment at his beauty washed over me. He was dark, chubby and utterly gorgeous, and so like how I'd pictured my Daniel would be. Everything about the child pierced me through the heart, wringing it out with longing. The concept of fate stretches beyond all logic, I know. I couldn't shake off the sense, though, that my desperate pleas the night before had been answered.

I brought over the coffee and juice, and leaned down to give the carton to the child, angling the straw towards his smiling mouth.

'Aren't you gorgeous?' I said. The girl with him laughed.

'He's going to be a heartbreaker when he grows up.' Pride shone in her face. 'Everyone thinks he's adorable – which, of course, he is.'

'How old is he?' He had to be about the same age as my Daniel.

'He's almost four. Got his birthday in March, and the party's already being planned.'

I couldn't take my eyes off him. I had to find out more.

'You don't seem old enough to be this little darling's mother. Are you his sister? I'm sorry,' I said as the girl smiled. 'I can't help it, I'm afraid. I'm incurably nosy.'

She laughed again. 'You're right. He's not mine. I'm his nanny. Both his parents work. I mind him during the day until they get home.'

I didn't try to fight it. Yes, it was judgemental. No, it was none of my business. I'd been smitten by the child's dark hair and big eyes, though, and a wave of anger swamped me. This beautiful boy had two parents, yet both of them worked and hired a girl fresh out of college to be his nanny. I would never have abandoned such a gorgeous child to anyone else had he been mine. I'd have loved and treasured him, no matter how tight money became or how much I wanted a career.

'Doesn't his mummy miss him? I would, if I had a little boy as adorable as this one.'

'Yes. She's always calling me during the day. Hugs him like crazy when she gets home. She's determined to have it all: the job – she's something high up in sales – the company car, the child.' She laughed. 'She's lovely. Well, they both are, although I don't see much of the father. I've been lucky. They're great to work for, and this little cutie, well, he's every nanny's dream.'

I bent down level with the child, and looked straight into those beautiful eyes.

'What's your name, sweetheart?' I asked.

He beamed at me, his smile twisting my heart again. 'Daniel,' he said solemnly.

It's a common enough name. There must be lots of Daniels around, and yes, some of them are going to be four years old, like my boy would have been, and with dark hair. Those undeniable facts didn't matter as Daniel's smile met my own. I stared at that beautiful child and something wonderful swelled and came back to life in my heart; I recognised the sensation as happiness, absent from my life for too long. My emotions overflowed almost as they'd done when my newly born Daniel was placed in my arms, all red and screaming and utterly adorable. I could only marvel at what had brought this child into my life, exactly at the time I needed him.

'Daniel,' I repeated. 'What a lovely name.' I forced myself to move away, back to the counter, where I busied myself wiping things down, stealing as many glances as I could at the two of them.

The girl didn't notice me staring, thank God. She kept her eyes on the child, giving him the occasional tickle, making him laugh with delight and causing waves of dark jealousy to torture me.

I moved back over once I saw her drain her cup and set it down.

'Does his family live around here?' I forced a laugh, willing her to tell me more. 'Sorry, I'm being nosy again. It's just – well, I've worked here for a long time, and I've never seen you in here before.'

'I'm new to the job,' the girl said. 'Only been looking after him for a couple of weeks.' She laughed. 'I've been prowling around Clifton and The Triangle, searching for the perfect cappuccino. I reckon I might have found it here.'

'You'll have to come in again, then.'

'I'll be back. Every day, probably. I get a generous allowance – Sarah's well aware of my coffee and cake addictions – and it would be a shame not to spend it all. Come on, handsome boy. Time for your nap.' She smiled goodbye and headed towards the door, taking that beautiful child, so utterly gorgeous, so like my Daniel, and yet not mine, with her.

I couldn't stop thinking about him afterwards. I remembered holding my baby in my arms, his limbs thrashing around, and then imagined his four-year-old self, laughing and slurping juice. I wondered about the years in between, and I visualised Daniel crawling, then trying to stand, taking his first steps and falling over. I heard him speak his first word, saw him smile as he managed to say 'Mummy'. And that Daniel merged into the laughing Daniel in the café, the two becoming one and the same in my head. Somehow this beautiful child had entered my life and I prayed again after I got home, for more, much more, all there was to have of him, dear God, please.

I think I recognised from that day the possibility of what I'd end up doing.

I didn't think about it consciously at first. All the signs were there, though.

They showed in the way I always chatted with the girl when she came in, but maintained a certain distance, so she'd not think my behaviour was unusual. I took care not to reveal my name and she never asked. It would have made things more personal if she'd known who I was. Most likely she never gave me a second thought once she left the café. That was how I wanted it: nothing concrete to connect Daniel with the busy waitress who served coffee to his nanny.

My eyes would stray constantly to my beautiful Daniel whenever I thought nobody would notice. I'd stare at him, drinking in his dark beauty and creamy skin and big eyes and it was all I could do to stop myself snatching him up and hugging him tight and never letting him go.

My obsession grew stronger daily. I lived for the half-hour or so each afternoon when I'd glance up and the girl would be in the doorway, holding Daniel's hand; each time I'd devour him with my eyes, hardly able to contain the love consuming me.

I'd never really accepted Daniel's death, despite my talks with Emma and all the tears I'd shed. How could I? He was kept alive by the oak tree growing skyward with his tiny body held fast in its roots. By me not having a certificate saying he'd died. By my passionate love for him, the adoration of a young girl who had given her entire being to a baby that died. Over the last four years, my love for my son had had nowhere to go. Now it had found an outlet at last.

I picked up things during the scraps of conversation I had with Daniel's nanny.

His parents went to the cinema every Friday night, and on those evenings, his nanny did extra duty, looking after Daniel until their return.

'Isn't that a long day for you?' I asked.

'I don't mind. It doesn't seem like work. I play all day with my gorgeous boy here and we have fun, and doing a few more hours on top doesn't matter.'

Jealousy hit me again. This girl had everything I yearned for. She spent her days caring for Daniel and I craved that so badly it hurt. Anger welled up in me alongside the envy. It wasn't enough for his parents to spend all day away from their precious son; they also left him at night. What did his mother have of this child except for snatched moments in the morning and at bedtime? Perhaps she did call during the day, as the nanny had said, but how were phone calls any substitute for real mothering? For being there with her child?

Neither of them realised what a treasure they possessed. They didn't deserve the role of parents, if they passed such an important responsibility onto an inexperienced girl.

One day the nanny mentioned the road in Clifton where they lived, describing how the flat was on the corner, not far from the fish and chip shop. I already knew they owned a garden flat; the girl had talked about playing ball with Daniel on the lawn.

The next day was Saturday; the nanny's role was weekdays only so she never brought Daniel to the café at weekends. I finished my shift and instead of walking home, I turned towards Clifton. I found what I thought was Daniel's home easily enough. The big bay window was hung with nets so I couldn't see in. I noticed the steps down to the narrow side passage leading to the front door, along with the thick overhanging branches of the trees planted on the pavement next to the wall. They would make the passageway dark at night, I thought. Anyone could slip down it and probably not be observed.

Then a woman came up the steps from the flat, and she had Daniel, my Daniel, with her. I pretended to be searching in my bag for something but she never even glanced at me. She was in her twenties, tall, slim and dark-haired, but I didn't register much else. This must be his so-called mother. Bitter hostility mixed with jealousy hit me once more. She was busy adjusting my boy's jacket before breaking off a square of chocolate from the bar in her hand, pressing it into his eager mouth. He was too enthralled with the chocolate to notice anything else and both of them moved away without even seeing me.

When I got home, I curled up on the bed and thought of that beautiful child, of how badly I wanted him.

He should be with me, not with that dark-haired woman who abandoned him so often, her casual attitude robbing her of the right to be a mother. He shouldn't be with the young nanny either. What could she possibly know about motherhood?

He should be with me.

20

FLESH AND BLOOD

Daniel was in the living room of his flat, sitting opposite one of the officers from New Scotland Yard.

'We've got the DNA findings back from the lab. They prove you are indeed Daniel James Cordwell, son of Sarah and Howard Cordwell.'

Twenty-two years had led to this unreal moment. He'd been right all along; he wasn't as weird or as screwed up as he'd once thought. No false memory syndrome had been playing tricks on his mind. He'd never have to force down his gut feelings again or deny the woman beside his bed was anyone but his mother. Daniel Bateman would officially end today and Daniel Cordwell would begin.

'What happens now?' Christ, he wished his voice didn't sound so shaky.

'We'll send an officer over to speak with your parents. Assuming we can get hold of both of them, and depending on how they take the news – this will obviously come as a huge shock – it's possible you might be reunited with them today.'

'My God.' He'd not anticipated seeing his family so soon; the idea both thrilled and terrified him. 'I didn't think things would move so quickly.'

'Remember, they've been waiting twenty-two years. I don't imagine they've ever given up hope. I wouldn't if one of my kids disappeared. No matter how many years it took.'

'How will I see them again? I'd rather it wasn't at New Scotland Yard.'

'I get that. We'll check out what your parents think, how they want to play things. Could be we take you to their house, or something along those lines. But no, it doesn't have to be at the station.'

Thank God for that. Meeting his parents again in the sterile surroundings of a police station held little appeal, not for a reunion as emotional as this one promised to be.

'We'll call after we've spoken with them. We'll also be picking Laura Bateman up and bringing her in for questioning. But for now – all you can do is wait.'

Daniel let the police officer out and threw himself down on the sofa. His head pounded as if he'd shoved it into a blender, but through all the mental chaos he felt buoyant, almost good. The news had managed to push his break-up with Katie into the background. Maybe the world was returning to how it was meant to be, before Laura Covey had stolen him; perhaps now he'd lose the sense of not belonging he'd always carried. The thought of experiencing life in a real family at last, with his parents and grandparents, was overwhelming. Dear God, he had to hope they were nothing like the sham set-up into which Laura Bateman had forced him. Given how Katie had described them, he didn't think he had cause to worry, but insecurity still nagged at him. What if he didn't measure up to their expectations?

The ringing of his mobile, shortly after four o'clock, jolted him out of his thoughts. He listened to the family liaison officer on the other end.

'We've been able to reach your parents. First by phone, then we sent an officer over. Understandably, they're in shock. Asking whether we'd identified you properly, questioning if it's really you. It took a while to convince them we'd found their long-lost son at last. But we got there in the end, I'm pleased to say. Predictably enough, they're ecstatic.'

'Do I get to see them today, like you said?'

'You do. They want to be reunited with you as soon as possible, at their house. I'm to take you there but I won't be present afterwards; they want the meeting to be private.'

Daniel concurred; the reunion would be intensely personal, not something to share with strangers.

'I'll be at your flat within the hour to collect you if that's the way you want to play it as well.'

The police car didn't arrive for fifty agonising minutes. On the way to his parents' house, the liaison officer told him Howard and Sarah Cordwell lived in Richmond, having moved to London after the kidnap to be closer to Sarah's parents. Not surprising with such a tight-knit family, Daniel supposed. There was Sarah Cordwell's suicide attempt, for one thing. He remembered Katie telling him about his mother's descent into despair. He pictured her, anguish drowning out hope in her brain, the knife slicing through her veins, turning her bath water crimson. A devastating thought; he'd been through some god-awful moments in his twenty-six years, but he didn't think any of them would top what his mother had suffered. Laura Bateman deserved to burn in hell. Given half a chance, he'd stoke up the fires himself.

The battle through the rush-hour traffic did nothing to ease Daniel's shredded nerves; the turmoil in his head only increased when the car pulled up outside his parents' house. Dear God. Hazy dreams were about to become reality; he'd see his mother again, and how the hell would that feel? Because this was it, the moment when the blurred face of the woman beside his bed would become real. Would he get the usual sense of security he experienced on recalling the mother of his memories? What about his father, a man of whom he had absolutely no recollection? How would they greet each other? A manly handshake, macho slaps on the back? It hardly seemed appropriate but he couldn't think how else to visualise it.

The place was typically Richmond, a large detached affair with trees in the front garden and a Jaguar in the drive, but Daniel barely had time to take in any details. Nor did he care about them.

He stared instead at the woman running through the open door of the house, down the drive towards the police car, as he stepped out. The breath stilled in his chest, tightening his lungs with terror. His whole life rested on this moment.

She stopped in front of him. Tears were welling in her eyes, running down her face. The elation, the undisguised utter delight in her expression, caused an answering leap of joy in his own heart. He recognised this woman as the missing piece of his life's jigsaw. She slotted into place perfectly and the old sense of knowing stirred within. This was his mother. Their reunion must be as intense for her, of course. They'd bonded once, when he was fresh out of the womb, and she recognised him, her son, through the strength of their connection.

Neither spoke. Instead, they stared at each other for what felt like hours but which must have been only a second or two. Then his mother pulled him towards her, her hug fierce and possessive, ecstatic sobs shuddering through her body. Daniel breathed in her perfume, filling his lungs with her, the world reduced to the two of them. His emotions swam up, thick and overpowering. A sense of justice overwhelmed him; he belonged to this woman, and something that had been wrong for a long time had finally been set right.

He became aware she was saying something. 'Daniel. My precious baby.'

She pulled back, looking at him, her smile shaky. Her fingers reached up, wiping tears from Daniel's face. 'My darling boy. I thought

I'd lost you forever.' She shook her head. 'They say miracles don't happen, but they do. I've got you back.'

Over her shoulder, he saw a man standing in the doorway of the house. As reluctant as he was to pull away from his mother, the need within drew him towards this man, his long-forgotten father. He moved towards the doorway, his mother's arm tight around him.

The two men stared at each other, Daniel looking at the father denied to him for twenty-two years. He retained no conscious memory of him, and yet he felt a sense of recognition that hadn't existed when he'd looked at his photograph. Not as deep, not as strong, as with his mother, yet undeniably there. Another missing piece of the puzzle of his life slotted neatly into its appointed place.

Then his father strode out from the doorway and pulled him into a fierce hug. 'My son. You're home.' Howard Cordwell drew back and brought his wife close to him with one arm, still holding Daniel with the other. He guided them into the house.

The three of them sat on the front room couch, Sarah's hand clasping his. Tears flowed down her cheeks, not that she attempted to staunch them. Instead, his mother stared at him, joy evident in her expression. On his other side, Howard's face mirrored his wife's. The apprehension Daniel had harboured vanished, snuffed out forever.

'I couldn't believe it when I got the phone call. I'd almost given up hope over the years. I didn't think you could still be alive.' Sarah wiped tears from her face. Daniel's gut clenched at the scar slashed across her raised wrist.

His mother went on. 'They told me on the phone about that woman. Did she treat you well, Daniel? Were you happy?'

He closed his eyes, yearning to unburden himself to this woman who had always represented comfort and safety, but he couldn't. He'd conceal the wretchedness of his childhood from her. She deserved that.

'Yes. She was good to me.' No lie needed there, anyway. Right now it scarcely seemed to matter he'd not been happy.

A hand squeezed his arm, and Daniel glanced up. His father gave him a slight nod, a reassuring smile. It warmed Daniel right through to his heart, this unspoken approval. He also grasped that Howard understood what his son had left unvoiced. Like him, his father wanted to shield Sarah from additional hurt, the same way he'd protected her after he'd found her limp and bloodied in her bath.

How was such a sense of collusion possible when they'd never really known each other? Probably something inexplicable, a quirk of unspoken communication between their genes.

He gazed at the older man's face, seeking similarities with his own besides the green eyes. Howard must once have had hair as dark as Daniel's own, although now his father sported a lot more grey than brown. His skin had started to fold into the lines of middle age, his neck somewhat slack, pouches forming under his eyes. He shared Daniel's full mouth but the lopsided smile was all his own. His father's face: unremarkable physically, but something in it spoke of the man's underlying strength.

He stared at his mother. Thank God, he couldn't see much of a resemblance to Katie. The heart shape of her face was similar, her smile reminiscent of her sister but other than that, he wouldn't have thought the two of them were related. Sarah's hair was a lighter brown, mixed now with a few strands of grey. Her mouth was more regular than Katie's was. She had little in her mannerisms to remind him of her either. Perhaps once she'd had the same bullish poise as her sister, but having a child abducted then surviving a suicide attempt doubtless knocked the stuffing out of a person.

His mother was speaking again. 'Thank God. You've no idea the relief it is, hearing she took care of you. Tell me, my love. About your life, I mean. Where did you go to school? What do you do for a living? Do you have a girlfriend?' Sarah's words tumbled forth, joy and eagerness in every one, Daniel wincing at being asked about his love life. To keep thoughts of Katie at bay, he concentrated on satisfying his mother's curiosity. Howard smiled encouragingly on learning about his son's employment. Katie had been right, they weren't snobs, just ordinary people – oh, dear God. So much for not thinking about her.

'Your grandparents will be coming over later. They said they'd give us some time to ourselves first. They couldn't believe it when I phoned and told them; Mum was laughing and crying and absolutely beside herself. Do you remember them at all, Daniel?'

'No. I do remember you, though. My nanny too.'

His mother's expression hardened, but she didn't say anything. Daniel continued, 'What became of her?'

'I have no idea. We had no contact with her after it happened. I couldn't bear to see her.' Sarah's voice began to rise. 'She abandoned you. She left you in the flat all alone.' Anger dripped from her words. 'We trusted her to look after you. It should never have happened. Never.'

What could he say? He supposed she had a point, but for him, the one to blame had to be Laura Covey. Probably because his nanny had always been there, in his memories, and he remembered her as the laughing girl who played with him in the garden, and for that he retained a certain fondness for her, affection for her smile and her swinging dark hair. He didn't blame her; she'd not been the one to kidnap him, after all.

His mother got up and walked across the room, pulling a thick photo album from the bookcase. The leather cover was worn, the edges battered; the photos it contained had obviously been looked through often. He stared at the old pictures, saw himself as a baby, as a toddler. His mother's voice was proud, adoring, as she turned the pages. 'You were such a beautiful baby, Daniel.' She pointed to a photo of two small children. 'Look. There's you, with Katie, my little sister, your aunt, in our back garden when we lived in Bristol. Mum and Dad would bring her with them from London to stay at least once a month. Wasn't she pretty?' She laughed. 'She still is, of course.'

The younger version of Katie smiled at Daniel from the photograph, a miniature version of the woman with whom he'd fallen in love, and it hurt. A knife to his heart, in fact.

'Do you remember her, Daniel?'

Daniel shook his head, unable to speak.

'You used to play together. There's only two years between you, after all. I called her at her flat, but she wasn't home, so I left a message. Seemed so wrong, somehow, speaking into an answerphone about something as wonderful as this.' His mother laughed. 'You'll love her. She's so warm, so caring. A doctor.' She sighed. 'I wish she wasn't, odd as that sounds. She told us, only yesterday, she's emigrating from the UK to Australia. We knew they'd granted her the visa. Thing is, we all hoped she'd decide to stay in England. Especially as she'd found herself a boyfriend she seemed crazy about. Never did find out his name. They've broken up, however, although she wouldn't discuss the details. Anyway, what with the mess the NHS is in, I can't blame her. I just wish Australia wasn't so far away.'

'She'll come back to visit, love. We can fly out to see her too.' Howard reached over to grasp his wife's hand. 'Daniel, we'll make sure you two get together again before she goes, don't worry.'

He forced himself to speak. 'When will she be off?'

'Eighteenth of next month, she said. We'll have a leaving party for her, of course. It can be a joint one. A send-off for Katie and a celebration of having you back.'

Dear God. There would be no getting out of it. He had no option but to agree, because if he didn't, he risked hurting his mother and the rest of his newly found family; far better for him to take the hurt. He glanced again at the scars on his mother's wrists. She shouldn't have to suffer another unhappy day in her life.

'Your grandparents will be here soon, my love.' His mother looked at the clock on the wall. 'They adored you, Daniel. Their first grandchild.'

'I can't wait to meet them.' He had no conscious memory of them, but they formed part of his new-found identity. He'd paint over the blank spaces in his life with fresh, vibrant colours, and in a short while he'd get to fill in the hues where his grandparents should be.

His grandmother definitely exuded the colour of melted chocolate, he decided, when half an hour later he gazed into her brown eyes, so evocative of Katie. She was an older version of her daughter, all wide mouth and sassy confidence. 'My lovely grandson. I can't believe it.' She stepped back from the tight hug she'd wrapped Daniel in to look at him. 'Do you remember us? No?' she said, as Daniel shook his head. 'Well, you were so young, it's not surprising. My God, look at you! So tall. So handsome.'

India Trebasco stepped back to allow his grandfather to pull him into an embrace. He heard Richard Trebasco speaking, his breath warm against his ear, his voice hoarse with emotion. 'Welcome home, Daniel. None of us are ever going to let you go again.'

'No way.' His mother's voice shook with tears. 'We have an awful lot of catching up to do.'

'Yes. I know so little about you all. You're my family, but I don't remember much, being so young when that woman took me.' He found it impossible to say kidnapped; the word was too brutal.

'They must have arrested her by now,' Howard said.

'I hope they throw her in jail for the rest of her miserable life,' Sarah replied. 'I wonder if they'll find out why she abducted Daniel. She can't ever have been a mother herself. I wish to God she knew the agony of losing a child.'

'Perhaps she was mentally ill,' his father suggested.

'I don't care, Howard. I wouldn't be able to trust myself if I came face to face with her. There's no excuse for what she put us all through. None whatsoever.' She burst into fresh tears.

'I never believed she was my mother. Never. Even though she took good care of me, did all the motherly stuff you'd expect.' His protective urge surfaced again; Daniel was mindful of the need to convince Sarah he'd been happy with Laura Bateman. 'I had memories, you see. I always thought something wasn't right.'

'Was it just that, Daniel? You didn't think of her as your mother and you needed to find out the truth?'

'Not only that, no. Someone told me it was unusual for me to have green eyes, with parents like mine.' Daniel was careful not to let his emotions about Katie bleed into his words. 'Laura Bateman has blue eyes. Thing was, though, she'd always told me my father – she said he'd died when she was pregnant – had brown eyes. Anyway, the eye colour thing made me think. I ended up doing a DNA test, with some of her hair, and the results proved she wasn't my mother. That led me to check out old kidnap cases and . . .' Daniel smiled. 'Here I am.'

His mother stroked her fingers down his cheek, her gesture almost unbearable in its tenderness for Daniel. She'd been waiting twenty-two years to touch him again and she didn't intend to stop any time soon. 'Indeed you are. Welcome home, my darling.'

21

BREAKING POINT

A couple of weeks after my visit to the flat, I went to clear the table after the nanny and Daniel had left, and there, on the red plastic of the bench seat, was a set of keys. There were several on the ring; at least one would be for the garden flat in Clifton, where my Daniel lived.

I glanced around. The other waitresses were all busy; nobody noticed me with the keys. I picked them up.

'I'm going to take my break early, if you don't mind,' I called out to Kathy, the manager.

'You go, love. You've hardly stopped since you got here.'

I grabbed my coat and walked as fast as possible to the key-cutting shop nearby.

'One copy of each of these. Quickly, please. I don't have much time.'

I left the shop with a duplicate of all the keys on the nanny's ring. I walked back to the café, checking my watch; I'd been away for twenty minutes. I figured it would take the nanny fifteen minutes to walk to the flat, longer if she stopped along the way, and the same again to walk back once she realised she didn't have her keys. I tried to slow down my breathing, to appear calm. Despite my efforts, sweat prickled the back of my neck.

I pushed open the door to the café, and put the original set of keys behind the counter.

'Kathy? I forgot to tell you before I went on my break. The dark-haired girl who comes in with the child left her keys behind. I've put them here, for when she comes back.'

Ten minutes later, the nanny rushed through the door, Daniel in tow. My breathing quickened; I thought of the duplicate keys, safe in my coat pocket. I was clearing tables at the back of the café, so it was Kathy, not me, who returned the original set, thank God. I wasn't sure I'd be able to behave normally around the girl.

My shoulders sagged in relief after she'd left. I had got away with it.

Thinking about it afterwards, I couldn't say why I'd made a copy of the keys. At that point, I had no conscious thought of taking Daniel. It was as though they possessed magical powers, transforming me into his mother. Those keys fuelled my fantasies every time I ran my fingers over their cool metal. I imagined myself walking down the side passage, unlocking the front door with one hand, the other one wrapped tight around Daniel's palm. My heart would swell with happiness every time.

Now, with the hindsight born from long hours spent alone since my arrest, I'm able to admit the real reason behind copying those keys. My growing desperation to claim Daniel as my own was the driving force, of course. An omen, had I stopped to take notice, foretelling what I'd end up doing.

Daily life at the café went on as usual. The nanny still brought Daniel in, but not as often. I got panicky on the days I didn't see him; he had become essential to my wellbeing and I lived for those brief half-hours when he came into the café.

I mentioned it in a joking way one day, asking if she'd found some-where that did better chocolate cake than we did, and she said yes, she'd started going to a little café in Redland some days where they did excellent brownies, something we didn't do.

'I'll ask the manager if we can add those to the menu,' I said, my forced smile hiding the anxiety threatening to choke me.

The only link I had to my boy was through the café, a tenuous connection that could be snapped at any time. Any number of things could break it. The nanny getting another job. Daniel's so-called parents deciding to move away. Daniel was four as well and at some point soon he'd be starting school.

My fear grew daily. I spent most of my time thinking about Daniel and the idea of not seeing him was unbearable. It wasn't enough any longer to look and not touch. I yearned for more, to cuddle him, play with him, hold him on my lap and read to him.

I had no idea how to achieve my dream, though.

A month or so after the keys incident, the nanny let slip his parents intended taking Daniel to London for the coming weekend to visit his grandparents.

I'd not seen a lot of him during the week; I think I simply wanted to be close to him. My desire prompted me to go to the flat where he lived on Saturday afternoon after my shift. I walked up to Clifton, the duplicate set of keys in my pocket.

I turned the corner into the road where Daniel lived, and slipped quickly down the side passageway. Nobody was around. My trembling fingers closed around the keys and I pulled them out. The door had two locks, a Yale and a Chubb, and I tried one of the Chubb keys on the ring. It worked. The second Yale key I tried fitted as well, and I pushed the door open, getting ready to slam it shut and run if I heard the warning screech of an alarm.

Only silence greeted me.

I went into the hallway. It ran down the right side of the flat, with the rooms off to the left, the doors all closed. My heart pounded hard against my ribcage; I was petrified Daniel's parents might have cancelled the London trip and still be in the flat.

After a couple of minutes, I heard only my breathing.

I wrapped my sleeve around my hand so I'd leave no trace of my fingerprints, took hold of the handle of the door in front of me and turned it, pushing as I did so.

I stood in the living room, which was big enough to swallow my bedsit completely. The thick plush carpet underfoot felt so different to the threadbare rug in my tiny room. Several photos were lined up on the mantelpiece, mounted in heavy silver frames. I looked at the woman who claimed to be Daniel's mother, holding a much younger Daniel, probably about eighteen months old, in her arms. He was all dark curls and angelic smile, and an overwhelming surge of love washed over me. Adoration mixed with anger about being deprived of that stage of his life; so much of his development, such as his first words and steps, had been denied to me.

The next room was the kitchen, a small galley affair, with saucepans hung from racks and a multitude of cookbooks and potted plants; I wondered when Daniel's mother ever bothered to cook, considering she couldn't even make time to look after her son.

The next room I looked in was obviously the master bedroom, with a huge sleigh bed and matching heavy furniture. More family photos, all with Daniel in. The wardrobe door stood open and I saw women's clothes, clearly for an office environment. She must get dressed here each morning, I thought, putting on those soulless suits in order to abandon her beautiful son and go into the world of work she so obviously preferred.

I clenched my fists. The bitch. She didn't deserve to be a mother.

The second bedroom at the far end made me want to sink to the floor and cry. It was my Daniel's room. Tears stung my eyes as I stood where he slept every night, drinking in the essence of him.

It was a little boy's room all right. The walls had been painted pale blue, apart from one done in a darker shade to resemble the night sky, with a silver crescent moon and a spaceship hurtling towards the ceiling. I stared at the small bed, picking up the pillow and holding it close to my face, inhaling the scent of talcum powder. I ached for Daniel, to hold him, love him and never let him go.

A large plastic box stood in one corner, full of toys. I went over to them, picking them up carefully, my sleeve still wrapped over my hand. I held a red building brick in my palm, a letter on each side of the plastic cube, and pictured myself sprawled on the thick carpet, Daniel beside me, while we formed the word mummy out of bricks.

Several more plastic crates full of toys stood stacked along one wall: wooden trains, a plush chocolate-brown puppy, more building blocks. I lost myself in fantasies. In one, Daniel and I sat on the floor among the scattered toys. His fingers stroked the soft fabric of the puppy while I built him a tower with the bricks. Every time, as soon as it reached a certain height, he'd laughingly knock it down, dispatching shafts of love deep into my heart.

In another scenario, I picked up a wooden xylophone, and this time we were making music together, something I had no ability for in real life. We laughed as he banged the keys, the perfect mother and son, secure in the cocoon of my imagination. In my fantasies, measles and scabbed knees and night terrors didn't exist; we lived in a perfect world where Daniel and I played and laughed and loved and never stopped.

I stood in his bedroom for a long time, absorbing his essence, breathing him in, before dragging myself away. Once outside, I pulled the front door shut behind me. Nobody would ever know I'd been at the flat.

I didn't sleep that night.

About a week afterwards, the nanny said the words that hit me hard in my gut and made me grateful I had my back to her so she couldn't see my reaction.

'Won't be able to come in for much longer. I'll miss the chocolate cake, for sure. Not half so much as I'll miss this little darling, though.' I breathed deep and long, forcing down the shock caused by her words. I managed to exert some control over my emotions and turned to face her.

'Oh? How come?'

'The family's moving up to London. Daniel's daddy, he's a banker; he's landed a promotion, and his mummy's got herself a job up there as well. So I need to find myself a new poppet to look after.'

'When do they go?' Tension knotted my stomach.

'Not for another three months or so. They'll be putting the flat up for sale next month. The rest of the family live in London and they'd like Daniel to grow up closer to his grandparents and Sarah's little sister. Katie's only two years older than Daniel and they're great playmates. Even though it means I'm out of a job, I can't help but think it's the right thing for everyone.'

London. They were taking Daniel to London, away from me.

No. God, no. That mustn't happen.

I'd already lost him once. I couldn't lose him again.

My obsession took over; I thought of nothing else. He'd become my whole world and in three short months he'd be taken from me and I'd have nothing left. Life was screwing with me once more, intending to snatch my beautiful baby all over again. I swore I wouldn't let that happen.

The answer didn't come to me for a while. I'd been turning things over in my mind and getting nowhere, my desperation growing all the time. I considered moving to London, but I had no guarantee of getting a job or a place to live that would enable me to see my boy. I had no idea what his future nanny would do on a daily basis that would mean I'd get to spend time with him.

His nanny. They'd be palming him off on some new woman. She might be the strict type. At the thought of somebody smacking Daniel, I reached breaking point.

No. Enough was enough.

The idea came to me then, and took root and grew.

The details could come later. I didn't know how I'd accomplish what I'd decided. It was the only solution, though.

Daniel deserved a loving mother and I would give that to him. I'd take him away from Bristol and let the huge anonymity of London swallow us up.

Yes, Daniel would be going to London.

He wouldn't be going with his undeserving parents, though.

He'd be going with me.

22

BANGLES AND BITTERNESS

'These ones are set with turquoise. Those, they're with amber. I prefer silver to work with. I like its coolness.' Sarah Cordwell held up the bangle she'd been working on, its chunkiness a sharp reminder of Katie. Daniel remembered she'd told him she'd got a lot of her jewellery from her sister, but he'd assumed she'd meant they'd been bought as presents. Now, standing in his mother's workshop the day after their reunion, he realised where they'd come from.

He rubbed his thumb over the stones. 'It seems I have a very talented lady for a mother.'

Sarah laughed. 'We're a creative family. Your father – well, he'll show you later. Woodwork's his thing. Not much he can't do with those old hand tools he insists beat modern ones any day. He made that big kitchen table and the matching chairs – yes, he did,' she added, on seeing Daniel's look of disbelief. 'Katie, well, she's pretty artistic too, at least until she started her doctor training. Then she didn't have time for anything apart from studying.' His mother smiled fondly. 'She took sculpture classes and found she loved working with stone. Turned out some lovely pieces, mostly heads and figures, as I recall.'

Daniel thought of the small reclining nude on top of Katie's bookcase, of the cool caress and simple lines of the stone. He'd intended asking her once where she'd bought it, but then she'd come in looking delicious enough to eat and the question went out of his head. Now he realised she had probably carved the piece herself. The family's creative genes had delivered Katie to him on a sacrificial platter the day she came to browse through the Balinese sculptures in his shop. A woman who turned out to be forbidden territory, all because of their shared DNA.

He'd emailed her the night before, mentioning the proposed joint party, and saying he didn't think they'd be able to avoid meeting again.

Her reply had been brief and to the point. 'I agree.'

Then another email, five minutes later. 'I miss you like crazy. We're doing the right thing, though.'

His mother was talking again. 'I started doing this a couple of years after it happened, as a hobby at first, and then as a part-time business. I had to give up work after your abduction. No way could I carry on. I'd been such a career woman, so sure I'd end up as the best sales manager in the company. Looking back, I can't think why I ever believed that was important. Nothing else mattered after you were taken.' Her voice shook.

'I can't imagine what my kidnap must have been like for you.' His hand squeezed her arm, making her pain his own.

'Both your father and I endured sheer hell. Time went on and the leads didn't go anywhere. I could see in the eyes of the police officers dealing with the case that they were losing hope. I don't blame them. They worked themselves into the ground trying to find you, but without clues or witnesses it all seemed impossible. The guilt ate away at me, all day, every day.'

She wiped away a tear. 'Logically I knew Howard and I should be able to enjoy an evening out together – God above, what with his career and mine we didn't spend a great deal of time with each other – but I still thought myself the worst mother in the world. I gave myself an incredibly hard time for not being more thorough with choosing a nanny. She was so young, but she really took to you and you to her. I thought everything would be fine. I hated her for what happened but I loathed myself even more.'

Daniel flinched at the raw emotion in her voice. 'It wasn't your fault. You decided to enjoy an evening out, and why not? I don't doubt the nanny has suffered huge guilt herself. She'll find out what's happened soon enough, anyway. The story's made the papers already. Front page news. Spotted the headlines when I bought those flowers for you.'

'Did you read what the papers said?' His mother's rising voice betrayed her concern. 'I hope the police are right and that the media will respect our privacy. Last thing I want is some tabloid hack pounding on the door, asking inane questions about how I feel about getting my son back. Like I'd be able to put something so miraculous into words.'

'I didn't read what they said, no. The police liaison officer told me he'd emphasised very strongly to them the need to stay away, at least at first. We may need to give a press conference soon, though, to keep them off our backs. Listen, none of what happened was your fault.'

'I've never allowed myself to believe that, in spite of what your father's always told me. I didn't think I'd ever experience happiness again. Everything else in my life, the job, the company car, seemed so pointless. I was walled around with grief and unable to let Howard in, even though I wanted to.'

Emotion rose in Daniel's throat. Would he ever get used to having Sarah Cordwell in his life, this woman whose love had left such a deep imprint on his psyche? He sensed they were leading up to the bad place in his mother's life, where she'd grown so desperate that letting her blood drain into a bath of hot water became a blessed release. Her despair mirrored how his life had turned into hell for him as a teenager, how he'd nearly succumbed to the seduction of killing himself. Suicide had beckoned him, its appeal being the freedom it promised. A time he'd spent years trying to move past, without success. Empathy moved him to take hold of her wrists and trace his fingers over the scars.

'I went into a very dark place, Daniel. Wasn't able to find my way back.' Her voice trailed off for a while and she wiped away her tears. 'Your father hadn't realised how low I'd sunk. Afterwards, though . . . well, he was so strong, and when I got better, I tried to give something back to him. He was hurting too; he'd lost you and nearly ended up without me as well, yet he still found the strength to help me with my grief. I felt humbled when I understood what kind of a husband I'd married. I always knew him to be a good, solid man, but he proved it beyond all doubt in the months after I was hospitalised. We're lucky to have him in our lives, my love.'

'I can't wait to get to know him.'

'No time like the present. He's down the bottom of the garden in what used to be one of the garages. We converted the second one into a workshop for him years ago. He'd spend days in there, sawing and sanding, if I didn't rescue him with food and cups of tea from time to time.' His mother laughed. 'You go and check on him. I want to call Mum and Katie anyway.'

Fine grains of sawdust tickled Daniel's nose as he entered his father's workshop. Howard was smoothing some wood, his hands working the sandpaper slowly and rhythmically.

'Decided to take a look at what I do to relax? I'm surprised your mother let you go.' His voice teased Daniel. 'She's – well, I don't think I've ever seen her happier, apart from the day you were born.'

'That reminds me. When's my birthday?' It sounded a strange question once he'd asked it. 'The birth certificate I have, well, it's obviously not mine, so neither is the date.'

'March 3rd. Best day of my life too.'

'Wow.' Daniel shook his head. Not only did he have a new name, but he was also three months younger than he'd always believed. 'It's going to take a while to wrap my head around all this.'

'It will for all of us, Daniel. We have time, though. You're back with us now, and that's like a miracle for your mother and me.' He squeezed Daniel's shoulder. 'I thought so often, over the years, of getting that phone call, of the police saying you'd been found alive and well. I never believed it would really happen. And then when Sarah called me at work, told me the police had phoned and were on their way over, I could hardly grasp what she was saying; she was laughing and crying and not making sense.'

'I missed having a father growing up. A real father, something my stepfather never was. The woman who took me . . . I wonder. Did she ever think of the devastation she caused?' Daniel remembered the scars on his mother's wrists. He thought back to the dark time of his teenage years. 'Why did she abduct me? The need to know goes round and round in my head. It's driving me mad.'

His father shook his head. 'We may never find out. While you were with your mother in her workshop – she's got an amazing talent, don't you think? – I took a call from the family liaison officer. He said Laura Bateman isn't talking. Not at all, not to the police, her lawyer, or even her husband. They're bringing in psychiatrists to assess her mental state.'

Daniel snorted. He'd not allow the bitch the slightest leeway on this. 'She always did suffer some issues that way, whether genuine or not, I can't say. Probably all an act. She'll ramp up the mentally disordered bit, so she can get off more lightly.' Daniel heard the bitterness in his voice. 'She kidnapped me when I was tiny and kept me from my family all these years. She lied to me about who my father was, who I was, everything. She's an evil woman and she won't hesitate to do whatever's necessary to protect herself.'

'Are you so sure, son?' The empathy in his father's expression surprised him. 'Your mother says the same as you, but I'm not so certain. Think, Daniel. She took you as a small child, raising you as her own. To me, her actions indicate she had to be healing some hurt in her own life. There's the birth certificate, the one that isn't yours. What happened to her child? Did she lose a son and try to replace him with you?' Howard took hold of Daniel by the arms, forcing him to return his gaze. 'Perhaps she deserves our sympathy, not our judgement.'

Daniel looked away, unable to comprehend his father's compassion. 'She kidnapped me. Took me away from my family. To say I didn't have an easy time growing up is an understatement. Think about Mum too. I've seen the scars, heard her talk about how awful it was for her. I can't forgive that woman. There's no reason good enough to explain, or excuse, what she did. None.'

His father moved away, running his hand over the smooth wood lying on the workbench. 'Well, you might think differently one day. Now, let me show you what I'm working on here.'

Daniel spent the rest of the morning with his father, wrapped up in the heady experience of being with the man who had given him half his DNA. His grandparents came over again in the afternoon, the warm ebullience of India Trebasco stabbing him once more with poignant reminders of Katie. He dragged himself away late in the evening, mindful of work the next day, his mother's reluctance to part with him evident in her final hug.

Tim was still up when he got home. They hadn't seen each other for a couple of days, his flatmate having been away with work. Daniel had texted him the afternoon before to tell him the DNA results and about the imminent reunion with his family.

'Dan! Been waiting for you, mate. How did you get on meeting your parents?'

Daniel sat opposite him, exhaling deeply before replying. 'My family – they're great, Tim. Laura Bateman – I always felt she smothered me. With my real mother, though – I can't get enough of her.'

'I'm pleased for you, mate. Can't tell you how much.'

'Mum and Dad are everything I'd hoped they'd be. I've met my grandparents too, and they're wonderful as well.'

His tone of voice didn't match his words; besides, he'd shared a flat with Tim for too long to fool him. 'I'm sensing a fly lurking in the ointment, Dan?'

'Yeah. Sort of.'

'Which is?'

'They're all so talented. You should see what my father does with wood. He turns out furniture, incredible pieces, just perfect. Mum too – she makes amazing jewellery. Got her own workshop.'

'And that would be a problem – why?'

'Because I can't help thinking how different my life would have been if I'd never been taken from them. I'm talking about my art.'

'You mean you'd have got more encouragement?'

'Yes. Exactly. If I'd grown up with them, I'd have attended art college the first chance I got. Instead, I got saddled with a stepfather who despised anything creative. Got told art was for no-hopers. He denied me the chance to go to college, when painting was all I'd ever wanted to do.'

'I can understand that must rankle.'

'Yeah, it does. I can't tell you how fantastic it is to be with my family again, but I'm bitter. Why did this happen to me? I might be putting on gallery exhibitions and making my living as an artist if I'd never been kidnapped. Instead I landed a job in a shop peddling marble Buddhas.'

'Being resentful won't help, Dan. OK, so you'd probably have gone to college, as you always wanted, I grant you. Does anyone make a living from art these days, though? Don't kid yourself. Perhaps you'd have still ended up with the marble Buddhas.'

'Yeah, well. Like you say, who knows?' The truth behind Tim's words grated. He stood up. 'I'm going to take a shower, hit the clubs. Check out who I can pull.' No need to mention he'd be targeting men.

'Thought you'd given up on all the screwing around.'

'So did I. Looks like we were both wrong.'

23

HATCHING PLANS

I had the keys to the flat. Now I had to find the right opportunity.

I needed to arrange my new life in London as well, which meant finding a place to rent for Daniel and myself.

The next time I had a day off, I took the bus to London. Thankfully, I had the cushion of money from the sale of Gran's house to tide me over for a while. My lack of income, until I got a part-time bookkeeping job, bothered me. I wouldn't be able to afford much at London prices; I'd probably end up living somewhere run down, like my bedsit, a place few people would want to rent. Well, that didn't matter; I'd learned some DIY skills while living with Gran, and hard work didn't scare me.

I found nothing that day.

I went up again on my next available day off. This time I widened my search, starting with the London train map – not being able to drive, living close to transport links was essential. The plan was to find somewhere further out, where I hoped the prices would be more affordable. I found myself getting off the train at Bromley South.

It didn't appear too bad a place. I looked in the estate agents' windows. The prices still seemed high, but they were more in line with what I wanted. One possibility stood out. The flat was small, and above a fish and chip shop, but I didn't mind that. It had the necessary two bedrooms and the rent was cheap.

I went inside, telling the woman behind the desk I'd found a job nearby and planned to move to the area in the near future. I deliberately made no mention of Daniel; she had to think I wanted the flat for myself only.

'The landlord's allowed the place to get a little run down,' she said. 'We can go over and view it straight away, if you want.'

She wasn't wrong; the flat was certainly shabby. Like my bedsit when I first moved in, I doubted anyone had got to work with any cleaning materials for a while, and the decor and furniture were tired and old-fashioned. Strong whiffs of fried fish assaulted my nostrils as I walked through the cramped rooms. No wonder the rent was so cheap; few people would choose to live in such a dump. None of that mattered to me. I didn't care about the colour of the walls, and I'd scrub everything else with bleach and disinfectant. It was affordable and being within walking distance of the local primary school and Bromley South train station made the flat perfect for my purposes.

'I'll take it,' I told the woman.

I returned the following week, paid the deposit and first month's rent and got the keys. I also took as many of my belongings as possible, my photos of Daniel and Gran, her jewellery, my clothes and books. I left just enough stuff in the bedsit that would fit into a large rucksack. I wanted to travel light when the time came.

I considered my options about where Daniel lived. My only chance of getting my boy would be to slip unnoticed down the side passage, open the door and snatch him from his bedroom when whoever might be in the flat was elsewhere. I remembered what the nanny had told me about how his parents went out every Friday night, leaving her to babysit.

I figured if I opened the front door a fraction, I'd get enough of a view to see whether I could slip undetected down the hallway. The nanny would probably have the door to the front room closed if she was watching television or listening to music. I'd go into Daniel's room, take him and go back out again in a couple of minutes. I'd have to hope he'd be sufficiently sleepy and familiar with my face that he wouldn't be frightened. Several weeks had passed since I'd copied the keys and I figured the nanny would have totally forgotten the incident. My ease of access to the flat would almost certainly be blamed on the front door not being shut properly. One less thing to lead back to me. I'd need luck to pull it off but the payoff would be worth the gamble. My Daniel's happiness was at stake.

I carried on making preparations. I bought a dark-coloured jacket with a hood large enough to cover most of my face and some cheap soft-soled shoes. I found a child's battered pushchair at a car boot sale. At four, Daniel was too old for one of those but for what I had planned, I daren't risk taking a taxi and it would be too far for him to walk.

I bought clothes for my boy as well, scouring the local charity shops for cute little trousers and miniature rugby shirts as well as toys and games and anything else he might need. My maternal instinct, suppressed for so long, revelled in every minute and I filled the small closet in his soon-to-be bedroom with my purchases.

I told Kathy at work I'd be leaving, and hugged her when she told me how hard I'd be to replace. Not wanting anyone to make the connection between me and London, I said I'd landed a bookkeeping job in Bath, and would be moving there. I spun my landlord the same tale. I only needed to give a week's notice, so I'd be able to leave within a few days if all went as planned. If Daniel's parents went to the cinema as usual this Friday, I planned to snatch him then.

I never thought what I intended to do was wrong. Why would I? Instead, I congratulated myself, certain I was doing the right thing for a neglected child's welfare. I'd love Daniel far more than his birth parents ever would, and wasn't that all that mattered?

The next time the nanny came into the café I made casual conversation as I brought her coffee.

'Any exciting plans for the rest of the week?' I asked.

She shrugged. 'Looking after Daniel on Friday evening, when his parents are at the cinema. Not much else.'

'Sounds good. What are they going to see?' I had to find out what time they'd be leaving the flat. I'd be able to check the times if I knew what film they'd be watching.

She named some obscure art house flick playing at the Arnolfini. I made a mental note of the name.

'Not my kind of thing,' the nanny said.

'Not mine either. How's the job-hunting coming along?'

'I've found a new nanny position. I start right after Daniel's parents leave for London.'

'I've got a new job as well.' I kept my tone deliberately casual. 'Over in Bath. This is my final week working here. So I guess,' I said, kneeling in front of Daniel, 'this may be the last time I see this cutie-pie.'

I bought the *Evening Post* later on. The film started at seven in the evening, so I figured Daniel's parents would leave by half past six at the latest. Then the nanny might take a while putting Daniel to bed. I decided I'd attempt to enter the flat just after eight o'clock.

That day was Wednesday. Before long I'd take Daniel away from his unfit parents to give him a new life, to love him and cherish him, as he had never been before. I had two days, two long, drawn-out days, to wait.

On the Friday, after my final day at work, I walked back to my shabby bedsit for the last time, nerves tearing away at me. What I was intending to pull off was risky, incredibly so.

I had to do it, though.

Because, if it worked, I'd be getting back the part of my life that had been missing ever since I found my baby dead. The Daniel-shaped hole in my heart would be filled. I never doubted I'd be able to get him to accept me as his mummy. He'd seen me enough times, after all. He barely knew his real mother, and he was young enough to adapt. Soon he'd call me Mummy. I couldn't wait for the moment when my beautiful boy smiled at me and called me that for the first time.

I glanced at my watch. Time to get going.

I took one last look around my cramped bedsit, now almost empty of my possessions. The place had served its purpose, providing a refuge when I needed one, but I wasn't the same girl who'd fled to Bristol four years ago.

I grabbed my rucksack from the wardrobe, and slung into it some clothes for Daniel, a warm blanket and the cheap shoes I'd bought.

I put on the dark-coloured jacket and pulled the hood over my face. Finally, I grabbed the pushchair and threw my rucksack into it. I was ready.

24

STRAIGHT TALKING

Daniel smashed his hand down on the alarm button, cutting off the shrillness slicing through his hangover. Pain spiked behind his eyes. He'd forgotten to turn the damn thing off, having got to bed barely four hours ago.

He'd not been able to escape the hell of last night. No getting out of the joint party his parents had organised to bid farewell to Katie and to celebrate his return. He'd had to be in the same room as her again for the first time since they'd broken up.

Up to then they'd managed to avoid each other; she'd not been over to his parents' house or that of his grandparents. He'd heard his mother mention how the hospital had been overburdening her with double shifts; she'd been sorting out packing, etc.

He was on his second beer by the time Katie walked in, tight jeans squeezing her bottom and a clingy top hugging her breasts. She wore some jewellery he'd not seen before, obviously made by his mother. The familiar waft of her perfume, all musk and memories, drifted in with her, and his stomach dropped as their eyes met. Mirrored in her face was the same hell he was going through. Their shared past rose up between them: every kiss, every caress. Then she turned away to hug her sister and her parents and the moment was over. He released the pent-up breath hammering against his ribs.

He poured himself another drink. Alcohol would serve as his crutch tonight and boy, did he need every drop of help it offered.

'Daniel, Daniel! Katie's here!' From across the room, his mother's voice halted his brooding. 'Come and give her a hug and say sorry for cheating at hide-and-seek all those years ago.'

The last thing he needed was for them to touch, not that he had any choice. He turned, forcing his arms around his former girlfriend, their bodies tense. Those tight jeans made her arse look smoking-hot, he thought, before clamping down, hard, on his venture into forbidden territory. Force of habit, he reasoned; finding out Katie was his aunt hadn't dampened his feelings. They were both trying to do the right thing here, but sexual passion of the intensity that had flared between them didn't die overnight.

Christ. There were at least another three hours of this hell to endure. Katie had been right. Her going to Australia was the only solution to this nightmare.

He made some banal comment about her forthcoming departure.

'Yes, bad timing, isn't it?' He detected the faked jollity, her voice too high-pitched like his own. 'Life's been manic at the hospital – lots of double shifts – otherwise I'd have been over before. Not every day your long-lost nephew gets found, safe and well.' Her gaze shifted to her sister. 'Sarah was ecstatic when we finally spoke on the phone and she told me the incredible news. I was so delighted. I've always hoped this would happen.' Her voice cracked a little.

'The miracle I'd been praying for every second of the last twenty-two years,' Sarah said. 'Let me get you something to eat, Katie. I've made those cheesy canapés you like.' She steered her sister towards the food table.

Daniel spent the rest of the night fielding enquiries about his kidnap from the other partygoers, grateful for the diversion, however painful the questions. Katie floated past from time to time, clutching an ever-full wine glass. Most of her friends were there, though, meaning she had plenty of other people with whom to occupy herself. He'd not met any of them, thank God; nobody could rat on him as being Katie's former boyfriend. They'd been too wrapped up in each other during those intense first weeks.

He carried on with the beer. The alcohol sanded the edge off his pain, although a fierce pang stabbed him at the end of the party when Katie, her coat on and ready to leave, leaned towards him for a hug.

'Be happy, Dan. Take care of Sarah for me.' Her voice ran a forbidden caress over his cock and he'd needed to down a finger of whisky in one after the door closed behind her. At that point, the room started to swim around him.

He'd insisted on getting a cab home, despite his mother's pleas for him to sleep off the booze upstairs. Fresh guilt hit him at her disappointment; he promised himself he'd make it up to her, and soon. Right now, though, he craved solitude. Katie's perfume still hung in his nostrils; he remembered the warmth of her breath against his ear. Better to suffer the inevitable hangover at home.

In bed the next morning, his head pounding, he thought how surreal the last few weeks had been. The reunion with his family had been an experience beyond words. He'd spent as much time as possible with his mother, letting her spoil him, cook for him, delighting in her joy. In contrast to Laura Bateman's fussing, Sarah Cordwell's love never grated, but felt exactly right. As for Howard Cordwell, he'd watched his father as he sawed and planed in his workshop, getting to know the man who was as solid as the furniture he created. His grandparents had been over frequently as well. It had all been damn good, no denying that.

Only two obstacles prevented him from being happy.

One was Katie, and she was leaving the country the following week; he'd be able to move on with his life then. Her loss was raw, but he'd deal with it.

The other was the resentment that seared through him as he watched his mother turn silver and stones into jewellery and his father carve wood into furniture.

He knew he'd sounded childish when he'd mouthed off at Tim. He was human, though, with all the flaws that entailed and, God, the loss of his art pissed him off. He had no doubt he'd have studied it at degree level if he'd not been abducted.

OK, so Tim had a point; college might not have guaranteed him a successful career as an artist. He'd have had a far better chance, though.

He'd not painted anything for weeks. He knew the reason; he'd never been one to lie to himself. Every time he looked at his paints, at the canvasses stacked against the wall, bitterness overwhelmed him and he couldn't bring himself to pick up a brush. He didn't see the potential in a blank canvas anymore; he saw the barrenness of his life with Laura and Ian Bateman.

His stepfather's contemptuous voice rang in his head frequently during those weeks.

Decision time; he'd go out tonight and bag himself a hot lay, despite not having touched a woman since Katie. Instead, a good hard shag of a good hard man was needed. Sunday nights were quiet for pick-ups, but he'd find someone. He'd been intending to try a new bar nearby; a mixed place, so he'd heard, gay, straight and lesbian, and he was tired of his usual hard-core male meat markets. Something more low-key was called for tonight.

In the meantime, he'd sleep off his hangover.

Or so he thought. A few hours later, the ringing of the doorbell carved through his head. Daniel peered at his alarm clock; one in the afternoon. His mouth was still parched although his headache had sub-sided. He contemplated ignoring whoever was at the door, going back to sleep, but the bell rang again. Cursing, he struggled out of bed, heading into the hallway.

'You look rough, son,' Howard Cordwell said after Daniel opened the door.

When he didn't reply, his father continued, 'Can I come in?'

'Of course. Sorry. My brain's a bit fried.' Daniel stood back to allow him to pass. Despite his hangover, a surge of happiness hit him. Denied a father for so long, now he couldn't imagine life without this man.

'I'll make coffee,' he said. He could use a cup, no doubt about that. 'Make yourself comfortable.' He gestured towards the living room.

When he returned from the kitchen with two steaming mugs, his father smiled at him. 'How's your head?'

'Bad. I'll live, though.' Daniel sipped his coffee. They chatted for a while – *how's Mum? She's fine, working on her jewellery* – before Howard set his mug on the table.

'I get why you drank so much last night, son,' he said. 'Finding out your life's been a lie must be tough. That's why I came. I wanted you to know your family's here for you.'

Daniel found himself unable to reply. His father's words hit the spot, though.

'It won't all be plain sailing, of course,' Howard continued. 'The hole in our lives will take time to mend. We all love you, though.'

Daniel stood up, intending to demonstrate what words couldn't convey. 'Come with me, Dad. Got something I'd like you to see.' He moved towards the door, his father following.

In his bedroom, he headed towards the stack of canvasses in one corner, pulling out the painting of the woman, girl and child. 'See this? I never forgot, not really. My family stayed with me. In my head, I mean.'

His father's eyes roved over the fluid shapes, the hazy colours, for what seemed a lifetime.

'It's beautiful, son.' Howard's voice held pride. A sweet moment.

His next words were even sweeter. 'Why don't you give it to your mother?'

What a perfect idea. Daniel smiled. 'I'll do that. Can't wait to see her face.'

Howard traced his fingers over the girl in the painting. Daniel's mind travelled back to the sound of her laughter. To her hair, dark, shiny and swinging.

'Alison Souter,' his father said. 'She must know you're safe and well, what with it being all over the news.'

In his head, a ball curved through the air, tiny hands stretching to catch it, the memory poignant.

'Your mother wouldn't want me to find her. Someone should, though.' Howard's eyes flashed a message. 'Besides the media, I mean.'

His next words shocked his son. 'The woman who took you. Have you considered visiting her?'

Disbelief, laced with hurt, hit Daniel. How could his father suggest such a thing? 'No way,' he managed. 'Not going to happen.'

'Hear me out, son. It's my belief you need to forgive her.'

'You don't know what you're asking.'

'All I'm suggesting,' his father replied, 'is that you think about it. Nothing more.'

Daniel's silence spoke for him. After an awkward pause, Howard said, his voice strained, 'How about more coffee?'

For the rest of the afternoon, they avoided all mention of Laura Bateman. Dad's a good man, Daniel decided, but he doesn't understand the impossibility of forgiving that woman. Visiting her? Equally a no-no. The best panacea was sex, not giving his kidnapper a get out of jail card.

He arrived at the bar just after ten that night; the place was almost empty when he entered. He glanced around. A couple of good-looking guys were playing pool at one end. Two women held hands on one of the sofas. An older guy, mid-thirties, dark, toned, caught his eye with an obvious come-on, but the man had dominant top written all over him, which didn't gel with Daniel's preference when it came to men. He turned to the bar. He'd stay for one drink and see if anyone half decent came in; if not, well, there were plenty of other places.

'Scotch on the rocks.' He stared at the barmaid. Not his type at all. Early thirties. Mousy hair, decent enough eyes. As for her nose, someone kind would call it interesting; an unkind person would label it hooked. She had good skin, but was otherwise unremarkable.

No, she wasn't his type.

Something about her held his interest, though. A haunted look lurked in her eyes, as if happiness hadn't come her way in a long time. Her expression reminded him, in a way he didn't need, of Laura Bateman during one of her depressive phases.

Shit. The last thing he wanted was a reminder of *her*. He almost walked out. He didn't, though, because the barmaid's haunted face echoed his own bleakness. For that, he stayed. He didn't know how or why, but they were the same, he and this beak-nosed woman. Life had damaged both of them, and badly.

Force of habit led him to give her arse the once-over as she stood with her back to him, glass held tight against the optic. Not bad, he thought, and the black trousers she wore hugged the curves underneath nicely. She turned with his drink, and clocked he'd been staring at her. She didn't seem offended.

'I guess I should ask if you come here often, but on the one hand such a question would be clichéd, and on the other, seeing as I've worked here all three nights since this place opened, I know you've not been in before.' Her voice didn't match the plainness of her face; low, melting and distinctive, it would have earned her a fortune on a sex chat line. Daniel thought whoever owned this place had probably turned her down for the job the minute they saw her, and seconds later changed their mind after hearing those husky tones.

She poured peanuts into a bowl and pushed them towards Daniel. 'Enough ice in that Scotch for you?'

'It's fine.' Daniel downed a mouthful. He decided to play along and make small talk with her. It would help pass the time until anyone promising came along. He shifted his stool in order to survey the door better. It was still early; he'd give it half an hour, or until he'd finished chatting to the barmaid. She grinned at him.

'You've picked a good spot there. What are you after tonight? The guy in the leather trousers keeps giving you the eye. Not sure you're his type, though.' She laughed. 'Think he needs someone a little more, shall we say, pliant.'

Daniel should have resented her plain speaking, but he didn't. He drained his whisky. 'I'll have another of those when you're ready.' He checked out her arse again as she refilled his glass. Yep, nice and tight. He had no intention of coming onto her, though, and he doubted whether she'd go for him anyway. Something about her haunted look told him this woman had walled herself off emotionally, although, as he knew from experience, that didn't necessarily include physically as well.

He decided to carry on the small talk. 'So how do you like working here?'

'It's a job. Pays me a wage, which was what I needed. Wasn't fussy what I did.' She shrugged. 'I'll stick with it. For now.' She had that clouded expression on her face again.

'Going to tell me your name?'

'Annie.'

'My name's Daniel.'

'Daniel.' She gave an approving quirk of her lips. 'Good old-fashioned biblical name. The way you're sinking your Scotch makes me think you've spent some time in the lion's den lately.' She leaned towards him. 'Am I right, Daniel?'

This woman was definitely smart. Maybe she'd clocked the same thing about him as he had about her. Like recognising like on some underlying primitive level. He drained his second glass. 'Yeah. Just about sums the last few weeks up.'

'Want to share?'

'Yes. No. Hell, I don't know. Can I buy you a drink?'

She shook her head. 'Manager's rule. We're not allowed to accept drinks off the customers.'

'Is the manager around? Is he going to find out? Go on. Join me in a lemonade and lime. I need to ease off the hard stuff, anyway. It's not as if I'm tempting you to anything alcoholic and therefore sinful.'

'I will, then. We're hardly madly busy tonight; I've time to spare.' She occupied herself pouring her drink. 'Go on. I'm curious. Tell me about life in the lion's den.'

'You read the papers?'

'I get one of the tabloids for an elderly neighbour who can't get out. Always check the lurid headlines before I hand it to her.' She laughed. 'So do I have a media celebrity sitting at my bar?'

Daniel pulled out his wallet and fished for his new driving licence, handing it to her. Her expression turned into one of bemusement. 'Daniel Cordwell. Why do I recognise that name?'

'Kidnap case with a rare happy ending. Splashed all over the news a few weeks back.'

She whistled under her breath. 'And you're really him?' She stared down at the photograph. 'Guess you are.'

'Definitely feels like I've been in the lion's den.'

'I'll bet. So what are your family like? I take it you've met them by now?'

'They're great. Spend as much time as I can with them. We've got twenty-two years to catch up on, remember.' Daniel laughed. 'My mother doesn't ever really let go of me. Keeps calling me her miracle reborn. Not that I mind.'

'So what's the problem?' She leaned towards him. 'Because don't tell me there isn't one. Something's brought you in here tonight, angling for a pick-up and looking like someone pissed on your pizza.'

'Christ. Are you always this blunt?' Daniel drained his drink. 'You're right. There's a catch. I feel so damned furious about the whole thing. Part of it is the fact my family's so great. The woman who kidnapped me deprived me of twenty-two years of being with them. My mother went through hell because of what happened. And the life I got thrust into – well, let's say it wasn't always the proverbial rose bed.'

'She treated you badly? The woman who took you?'

'No. She didn't. My stepfather was a total prick, however. Plus, I lost my girlfriend when the truth came out.'

'Listen.' Annie's tone was firm. 'Don't get me wrong. I have no idea what happened between you and your stepfather and I'm sorry you broke up with your girlfriend. I'm not going to mince words here, though. Girlfriends come and go. If you split up over this . . .' She shrugged. 'Perhaps it wasn't meant to be. As for your stepfather, well, all the Scotch and screwing around in the world can't change that. It's in the past, and you have to find a way to deal with things.'

'Ouch.' Daniel gave her a pained smile. 'You were right. You don't mince your words, do you?'

Annie slammed her glass down. 'You had something precious taken from you. Now you have it back. So don't dwell on the other stuff. Focus on what you do have.' She leaned in closer. 'Some people lose what matters most to them, and they're never given the chance to get it back. You're one of the lucky ones, believe me.'

25

MUMMY'S HERE

The walk up to Clifton took less time than I'd anticipated; in my desperation to take Daniel, I walked faster than usual, arriving hot and sweating outside the flat. I held on to the wall, taking deep breaths. My mouth was desert-dry from nerves, and I yearned for some water.

I walked around the block to regain some measure of control, doing my best to avoid other people. I crossed the road if I saw anybody and I stuck to tree-lined streets that offered more concealment. I didn't hurry; I wanted to appear calm in case anyone did see me. In my jeans and hooded jacket, I looked nondescript anyway; no one would be able to give an accurate description of me, or so I hoped.

By the time I arrived back at the flat, I'd managed to get a grip on myself. My mouth was still dry, but my legs didn't shake as much; I felt better about what I intended to do. I walked slowly past and round the corner, where I could see the door of the flat through the trees overhanging the passageway.

I stood for a while, waiting, and then I got handed my chance.

The door opened, and the nanny came out, shutting it behind her. She walked up the passageway and turned right, towards the rank of shops. To my amazement, she didn't have Daniel with her.

Anger welled in me. She must have left my little boy all alone in the flat, while she went out for God knows what. Wrong, so wrong. My duty was clear; taking Daniel from such a neglectful environment would be the right thing, the only thing, to do. The nanny's negligence had dispelled all fear, all worries. My nerves had never been steadier, all tension gone. I was ready.

I was sure no one else would be in the flat; she'd never mentioned bringing a friend when she babysat and she'd told me she didn't have a boyfriend. Besides, I'd do what I'd already planned. I'd open the door a fraction, and check out the flat before I entered, in case anyone was there.

I figured the nanny had probably gone to get a takeaway, meaning I didn't have much time. I went round to the steps leading down to the passageway, slipped off my shoes, and put on the cheap ones I'd bought. I daren't risk any footprints from my trainers; I'd switch them later and ditch the other ones. I padded softly down the steps, taking the rucksack with me and leaving the pushchair hidden behind the rubbish bin.

I walked to the front door, keys in hand. I took a final deep breath, and inserted the Chubb key in the lock, carefully turning it.

Next, the Yale one. I edged the door open, slowly, just enough to peer into the flat.

All the doors were closed, and the flat felt empty. Nobody was there, except for my Daniel. I went inside.

I pushed open the door to Daniel's room, and there he was, asleep and looking adorable, and I moved swiftly to the side of the bed. I didn't want to frighten him in any way, counting on my face already being familiar. I dug under the duvet, scooping my hands underneath him, lifting him up and wrapping the blanket from the rucksack around him, just as he started to come awake.

'Everything's all right, darling. Mummy's here,' I whispered in his ear, his hair soft and wonderful against my cheek. He smelled of bubble bath, shampoo and sleep and I held him to me, revelling in cuddling him for the very first time.

I moved quickly, striding down the hallway, through the front door and into the evening air with my precious bundle heavy in my arms. I deliberately left the door open to give the impression the nanny had left it that way. Daniel had hardly stirred and he lay, still half-asleep, with his head against my shoulder. I dragged out the pushchair, pulling it open with one hand and carefully lowering him into it. I pulled the blanket around him, tucking his feet in and making him as warm as possible. He relaxed into the pushchair, asleep again.

Time to get as far away as possible. I slung the rucksack onto my back, hauled the pushchair up the steps and rounded the corner. I strode towards The Triangle, my destination the bus station in Marlborough Street. I'd decided Daniel and I would travel to London by bus. Not only would it cost less, but also Bristol's bus station was run-down and grimy; I figured the chances of working security cameras would be low, if they even existed. I had my nondescript clothing and big hood to conceal my identity as well.

Before long, I arrived at the bus station, hot and breathless again. My first priority had to be getting Daniel dressed properly; I didn't dare take the risk of anyone noticing he still wore his pyjamas, even under the blanket. I found the toilets and prayed I could do this. It meant waking Daniel up, and that worried me.

'Come on, sweetheart. Let's get you dressed. We're going on a big adventure, you and me.' I pulled him gently upwards, and watched his eyes open, still thick with sleep. He stared at me, his gaze unfocused. I stroked his hair reassuringly.

'You know me, darling, don't you?' I smiled lovingly at him.

He nodded. 'Lady who brings me juice. I like you.'

I pulled the clothes I'd brought for him out of the rucksack, and gently stood him on his feet. He balled his fists and rubbed his eyes, and he was so utterly endearing; I reached for him and pulled him against me, hugging him tight.

'My boy. My beautiful Daniel,' I murmured into his ear. My words seemed to reassure him. He had no fear in his eyes as he looked up at me. I couldn't have borne it if I'd seen distress in his face. My Daniel had nothing to be frightened of with me. I started to pull off his pyjamas. He didn't resist as I put on his clothes and shoes. I got him to use the toilet; then he let me sit him in the pushchair and strap him in.

We were ready.

I wheeled him back out onto the concourse. It was now ten past nine. The next bus left at nine twenty. Perfect. I bought the tickets, along with sandwiches and juice for both of us. Hunger was gnawing at me; I'd not eaten since lunchtime, what with nerves knotting my stomach and having to get everything ready.

I pushed Daniel over to a seat, pulled the plastic wrapper off one of the sandwiches and broke off a piece. 'Here, my love,' I said, proffering it towards Daniel. He put it in his mouth, smearing egg mayonnaise around his lips, and the sight was simply wonderful. I smiled adoringly at him as I ate my own sandwich.

'Where're we going?' he lisped at me through a mouthful of food.

'On a big adventure, darling. Isn't that exciting?' The trust implicit in his solemn nod tore at my love for him.

I stowed the pushchair, boarded the bus and took the first two available seats. Nine twenty had already come and gone. The bus driver was in his seat, messing with some paperwork, and I prayed for him to get a move on. Every minute counted, every second took Daniel and me closer to the flat in Bromley, to our new life. By now, the nanny would have returned and found Daniel missing. She would have alerted the police straight away. I had no pity for her. She'd gone out and left a four-year-old child alone and I figured she deserved every moment of the anguish she must be suffering right now.

We were so nearly there. Once the bus rolled out of the station, I'd be able to relax.

At nine twenty-five, the driver started the engine, and began to reverse from the concourse. We were London-bound at last.

I let out the breath I'd been holding. Daniel was asleep again, small snuffles escaping his lips, his noises reminding me of the sounds my sleeping baby made all those years ago.

Fate, if it did exist, was definitely on my side that night. Not many passengers had chosen such a late departure, which meant fewer potential witnesses. Daniel slept most of the time, waking up occasionally to eat more of his sandwich, but never doing anything that would draw attention to us, thank God. I even managed to doze along the way, my eyes lulled shut by the dull scenery of the M4 corridor, lit by the glare of the motorway lights.

We arrived at Victoria right on time. I undid my own and Daniel's seat belts and pulled his unresisting body, warm from sleep, into my arms.

'We're here, darling. And there's more of the adventure to come.' It was now after midnight. I grabbed the pushchair from the hold, and sat Daniel in it, strapping him in. Chocolate might be a good idea. There was a vending machine nearby, and I bought a bar of Dairy Milk, breaking off a piece for Daniel and taking a chunk for myself.

Time to pull my hood up again. I walked out of Victoria Coach Station into the cold London night, heading towards the train station. I broke off more pieces of chocolate as I hurried along, leaning down into the pushchair to press them into Daniel's eager fingers.

I hated every minute of the journey, but Daniel, bless him, was a little angel, sleeping as the train hurtled towards Bromley, faint smears of chocolate around his lips. I kept my gaze on the grimy floor, avoiding eye contact with the other passengers, praying for the driver to go faster.

Eventually we arrived. After leaving the train station, I pushed Daniel's chair as quickly as possible, my body getting hot under my jacket, the growing heat contrasting with the cool night air as I strode along. We went past the school where I intended to enrol him as my son Daniel Mark Covey, using the birth certificate, safe in my rucksack, as proof to the world he was mine.

At last we got to the door of the flat. I took the keys from my pocket, hands trembling, and fumbled for the lock. Then we were inside. I was desperate for sleep, warm and safe with Daniel in my arms.

'Come on, darling. Let's get you into bed.' I stripped him quickly out of his clothes, replacing them with his pyjamas. He sat on the edge of the bed, rubbing his eyes, a bewildered look on his face. I knelt down in front of him, my fingers stroking his arms through the soft fabric.

'It's all right, darling. You know who I am, don't you? You're safe with me.' I gathered him close. 'Mummy's here, my love.' I pulled back to look at him. I hated the confusion on his face. He was young, I told myself. He'd forget what he'd known before, and get used to me, and we'd be so happy. I had my Daniel with me again, and everything was now perfect in my world. Maybe I did believe in fate after all.

'Come on, sweetie-pie. Let's clean your teeth.' I was tempted to crawl straight into bed with him, but a responsible mother wouldn't send her son to bed with chocolate on his teeth.

Daniel brushed his teeth like a good boy, and I did my own, and washed my face, then led my beautiful son back into the bedroom.

'You're going to sleep with Mummy tonight, darling,' I told him. 'Just for one night, and then you'll have your very own room. I've made everything as nice as I can for you. I'll show you tomorrow, and we'll play together, with all the lovely toys I've bought.' I leaned over and kissed him.

He gazed at me, still with an expression of bewilderment on his face.

'Mummy?' His voice sounded shaky, unsure. 'I want my mummy.'

'Mummy's here, sweetheart.' I hugged him tightly. 'I love you, Daniel. And I'm never going to leave you. Never.'

26

TYING UP LOOSE ENDS

'Don't dwell on the other stuff. Focus on what you do have.' Annie's words, thrown at him with such conviction, had stuck in Daniel's mind, after he'd left the bar without the pick-up he went for. Sassy, that Annie woman, he thought, not short on plain speaking. To his surprise, he found himself doing what she'd advised. He spent far fewer sessions on the booze, less time obsessing over his anger concerning the loss of Katie, being denied his art. He was elbowing self-absorption out of his life, he realised, passing his free hours outside work with his parents and grandparents, soaking up the novelty of being with his family. Yeah. Concentrating on what he did have was good. Annie, bless her, had been right.

One thing was missing, though. A lost piece to slot into place. The need to find it had brought him to Bristol today. To this particular house.

He checked the time. Two o'clock, almost certainly too early. A small park opposite had a few benches on which to wait. From there, he had a clear view of the house in case anybody turned up. Specifically, Alison Souter. His nanny with the swinging dark hair.

He'd never harboured any resentment towards her, despite what both Katie and his mother thought. OK, she shouldn't have left him alone, but in the part of his memory where she lived, forever young and laughing and tossing a ball to him, he retained a deep affection for her. No way did he hate his former nanny. Instead, he felt driven to find her, especially after his father had planted the idea in his head. Alison Souter was a loose end he needed to tie up.

Nobody knew what had become of her after the kidnapping. Daniel did the necessary digging, without telling anyone at first what he planned to do, not even his father. His findings had led him to this shabby house in a run-down area of Bristol.

He wondered what life had been like for her after the kidnap. She hadn't been much more than a kid, after all, and she must have taken a lot of criticism from all sides. His mother had experienced guilt strong enough to make her slash her wrists; what dark emotions had Alison Souter endured, once she understood the role she'd played in enabling Laura Covey to snatch him?

The wait ended up stretching to over three hours; she must be at work, he decided. Eventually he spotted a woman walking down the street towards the house. A petite woman with dark hair who appeared in her early forties, the age Alison Souter would be. She unlocked the door and went inside.

Daniel strode over and rang the bell. Seconds later, the door opened; he looked into the face of his former nanny, and another piece of the jigsaw clicked into place. The same certainty as he'd experienced when reunited with his mother struck him once more.

'Do you know who I am?' he asked.

She didn't speak, staring at him with an expression he couldn't fathom. Then she nodded.

Daniel stepped past her into the hall and then the front room. Alison Souter followed him, and they gazed at each other for a moment. Then Daniel held out his arms and she ran towards him.

He pulled back to look at her, as she fumbled in her coat pocket for a tissue. Her expression spoke of unhappiness. Still the same dark hair, cut in a shoulder-length bob, greying now at the sides; her features were less familiar, her face in his memory being too indistinct. She'd been pretty, no doubt about that, and still was, in a way, but an air of self-neglect clung to her. Bare skin devoid of make-up, baggy clothes in dull don't-notice-me shades, no jewellery. A stab of sadness twisted in him at the contrast between this woman before him and the carefree girl of so long ago.

She wiped her eyes. 'I heard about it on the television. Not to mention a few reporters sniffing around. They said you'd been found safe and well. Such incredible news. I'd always hoped . . . I wondered whether I'd be able to see you. I didn't know how to get in touch with you, though, or if you'd want anything to do with me, after what I did.'

'I needed to come. I've never forgotten you. You've always been part of my life, even when I didn't remember exactly who you were.'

'How did you find me?'

'Electoral register. Not difficult, once I managed to get your full name. I could have asked the police family liaison officer to help, I suppose, but to be honest I preferred not to. He's been great, especially with Mum, but I wanted to track you down myself.'

'I imagine I wouldn't be hard to find. I've never married or moved away from Bristol.'

'Even if you had, I'd have found you somehow. I needed to see you again.'

'I've searched for you every day since.' She gulped, choking back twenty-two years of heartache. 'That's why I've never left Bristol. I thought perhaps, if you were alive, you might still be here. I used to

stare into young boys' faces, hoping one day to see yours. I wanted to
be the one who found you, to help put right the terrible wrong I did.'

'I've never blamed you for what happened. No, really,' Daniel continued, seeing the look of disbelief on her face. 'You're one of my earliest
memories, and one that helped lead me to the truth. I remember you
in the back garden playing ball with me. I can still picture how your
hair used to swing about as you moved. It's a distant memory, but I've
always carried it with me. Always treasured it.'

'I remember.' She gave him a fleeting smile. 'You used to love playing ball. I was so excited when I got the job looking after you. I'd not
long finished college. Your parents seemed lovely, and I took to you
right away. It didn't seem like work. We'd play, and I'd feed you, and
we'd have such fun. I couldn't be a nanny anymore after you were taken.'
Her voice shook. 'I decided never to have children. Didn't trust myself.
Your mother blamed me. She was right.'

'Did you find things tough? Afterwards?'

She nodded. 'I got death threats, hate mail; you wouldn't believe
the poison in those letters. Nothing I didn't deserve, though. The police
arrested me, you see. I became the prime suspect, at least initially. They
obviously thought I was covering up some terrible accident. They grilled
me repeatedly, the same questions, until I thought I'd go mad.'

'Oh, Alison. I'm so sorry.' He pulled her close again. She'd suffered
more than he'd realised, what with being a suspect in his possible murder or manslaughter. Not to mention the death threats.

'Must have been hell for you.' How inadequate his words sounded.

'Worse than hell. For anyone to think I'd be capable of hurting
you . . . I adored you. Eventually, they grasped I hadn't done anything
awful, but the guilt was still unbearable. I was the worst person in the
world, or so I thought. I've always hated myself for what happened
that night.'

Echoes of what his mother had said. 'No. You had no reason to
know what that woman had planned.'

'I'd been hired to take care of you, though, and I didn't. I was so stupid. Your mother was always good to me. She usually left plenty of my favourite foods in the fridge. I had this craving for fish and chips, though. It wouldn't go away, and I told myself I'd only be gone five minutes. I'd tucked you up safely in bed, or so I thought. I was as much to blame, even though you don't seem to think so. I still don't understand how that woman managed to get in. I guess I left the door unlocked.'

'The police are looking into all that. She's not talking. Gone mute. Being held in a psychiatric facility. They sectioned her after she went berserk during the police interview.'

'Who was she?' He realised this was a very old question for her. 'I've always wondered. Thought about it endlessly after it happened, went through everything repeatedly in my head. Who it might be. All they said on the news was that a woman was being held for questioning.'

'Her name's Laura Bateman. Laura Covey, as she was then. Does that name mean anything to you?'

'No. Not a thing.'

'The police have told me she lived in a bedsit in the Stapleton Road area. Worked as a waitress in a little café near The Triangle. Don't know if either of those facts helps.'

'I remember.' Her voice betrayed her surprise. 'The girl in the coffee shop. Never did get her name. Small, blonde. Always pleasant and friendly, but she never showed any particular interest in us, other than to make small talk. I can hardly believe it.'

'You never suspected her?'

'No. She'd serve us when we went in, chat politely, nothing more. I've always tortured myself, you see. I thought some vile pervert had taken you. To find out it was someone like her . . . I can only thank God. Was she good to you, Daniel?'

The second time he'd faced that question in recent weeks, and he still wasn't sure how to reply. The safe option seemed the kindest one, as it had before.

'Yes. She was good to me.'

'I wonder why she did it.' She paused. 'I can only think perhaps she'd lost her own child.'

'That doesn't excuse her taking someone else's.'

'No; but it does make it understandable. Imagine the suffering she must have endured. To lose a child must be a parent's worst nightmare. Even though you weren't my own, your abduction shattered my life. I've never married, never had children, because of it. Your mother – I wasn't in touch with her afterwards, but she must have gone through hell.'

He thought of the jagged lines scored across his mother's wrists. She'd gone through hell all right.

'Emotions like that – they can overwhelm someone. I'm not making excuses for what this Laura woman did. I'm saying, if she ever chooses to talk, she may reveal a tragic story behind what happened.'

'Perhaps.'

'Do you think . . . ?' She took a deep breath. 'Now you're back . . . that your parents . . . that they might forgive me someday? I realise I've no right to expect such a thing. You, though – you don't hate me for what I did. I can't tell you how much it means to me, you coming here. And if your mother, if one day . . .'

Daniel looked at her. The events of twenty-two years ago had ravaged her as much as everyone else. She'd carried the burden of a moment of thoughtlessness all her life, hating herself, denying herself a family because of her guilt. His mother bore the signs of her damaged psyche on her wrists. The scars for his father and grandparents were hidden better, not so obvious, but they still existed. Katie – well, he knew the damage this had inflicted on her.

Perhaps, to some extent, they all needed to find a way to move on. He remembered that his father, although he had suffered as much as anyone through Laura Covey's actions, didn't hold a grudge against her. Nor against Alison Souter. His mother – well, she'd made it plain what she thought about her former nanny. Perhaps, given time, her anger might soften.

'I'll do my best. I can't promise anything. I'll talk to her, though. I told her I intended to come here today, but she wasn't as unhappy about it as I thought she'd be. Besides, I have a trump card to play.' He laughed.

'What's that?'

'I don't think she can refuse me anything I ask. Her only child, returned safely to her – I'm not sure there's anything she wouldn't do for me.'

'If you could talk to her . . . and your father too . . . if I had the chance to tell them how sorry I've always been, and if they could find it in themselves not to hate me, I wouldn't ask for anything else. I've been so unhappy over the years, you see. The guilt. It would mean so much to me.'

'I'll talk to them when I get a chance. I'll visit you again too. If that's all right?'

'You can't imagine how happy that would make me.'

'Got any paper?'

She handed him a pad of Post-It notes. He wrote down his address and contact details. 'Here. You can call any time. I hope you will.' He did too. 'You've meant something very important to me over the years.'

'You'll get fed up of me calling.'

'Will you promise me something?'

'Anything.' She laughed. 'Guess I'm like your mother. I don't think I'm capable of saying no to anything you ask. Look at you. You've grown up so tall. So handsome. The way I always imagined you would.'

He grasped her shoulders, forcing her to meet his gaze. He needed her to absorb his words into her heart as well as her head. 'I want you to stop punishing yourself. Go and live your life, really live it. Nothing would make me happier than for you to tell me you'd found someone to marry, even got pregnant. It's not too late,' he said, as she shook her head. 'But whatever you do, stop blaming yourself. Will you promise me?'

She didn't reply at first. Twenty-two years of guilt and self-hatred were eating away at her, not something she'd be able to make disappear overnight.

'Please, Alison. Do it for me.' She gave him a slight smile.

'I'll do my best. Won't be easy, but seeing you again has done wonders for me. The guilt became my whole life. I'll need to find something to replace it.'

'How about living well and being happy?'

As he said the words, Annie came to mind again, the soft liquid of her voice sounding in his brain. She'd probably tell him, in her blunt fashion, that he ought to apply such advice to himself. Perhaps she'd have a point.

He'd meant what he'd said to Alison. He'd keep in touch with her, and he'd be on her case if he didn't think she was making good on her promise.

He glanced at his watch. 'We've plenty of time before the last train back. Come on. I'll take you out, buy us a meal.' He tightened his arm around her shoulder. 'It'll be the start of your new happier life. Where's good to eat in Bristol?'

27

A MOTHER AGAIN

We both slept late the next day, exhausted after the night before. I woke up to find Daniel still asleep, and I padded quietly out of bed and took a quick shower. He'd begun to stir by the time I got back.

'Come on, sweetheart. Let's get you washed and dressed, and then you can have some breakfast with Mummy. We'll have hot, buttery toast. Would you like that?' He stared at me blearily, and I pulled him out of bed, setting him down on his feet. I led him by the hand into the bathroom and started to run a bath, tugging off his pyjamas.

'Where's Alison?' he asked. I couldn't think whom he meant at first; then I realised. He must be talking about his nanny. I never did find out her name.

'She's had to go and look after another little boy, darling. I'm here now, Daniel, and I'll be looking after you and loving you. We'll have such fun together. We'll go to the park and play on the swings; we'll watch cartoons together here at home, and we'll be so happy. I think your bath's ready now, my love. In you get.' I started soaping him up, smiling as I ran the sponge over the endearing mole on his right hip.

He was such a good boy, although I wished he would talk more. I stared into his face, seeing the same bewilderment as last night. I stroked my hand through his wet hair, trying to reassure him. 'I think we're done now, darling. Let's dry you off.' I towelled him briskly once I got him out of the bath, and quickly pulled on his clothes. I hugged him close, inhaling the scent of the shampoo I'd used. He smelled delicious and I would have held him forever if I could.

We walked into the kitchen. I slotted bread into the toaster and poured Daniel some juice. He was still silent.

'Where's my mummy?' he eventually asked. I thought quickly. The sooner he realised I was his mummy now, the better; I'd do best to act as if his mother and the nanny were completely out of his life.

'Mummy's here, darling. The other lady – she took care of you until I came along to be your real mummy, the one who's going to love you for ever and ever.' I steered a finger of toast towards his mouth. 'Look, my love. Marmite soldiers. Isn't that nice?'

It took me nearly an hour before I got him to eat any of the toast, coaxing as best I could. No tears or tantrums; instead, Daniel stayed silent, withdrawn.

I tried to reassure myself. Here was a small boy, who'd had a routine in his life, one that had been suddenly interrupted; I simply had to replace it. I made plans. We'd have fun and read together in the mornings and I'd find a local playgroup for the afternoons. I wanted him to be with other children as much as possible, once he became more settled; the nanny had never talked about playgroups, and I suspected Daniel had spent most of his days alone with her. Yet another way in which his new life would be much better. Everything would be fine.

The rest of the day passed quietly, with Daniel docilely doing what I told him but rarely talking. I showed him his bedroom, and he did perk up when he saw the boxes of toys, running over excitedly. My mood lifted a little. We pulled out wooden trains, plastic soldiers and soft toys, and soon the floor became a complete mess, Daniel pushing a toy car back and forth, making vroom-vroom sounds. My fantasies made real at last. I hugged and kissed him as often as he'd allow. I wanted to give him as much physical affection as possible; I knew the nanny had been fond of him, but I didn't know to what extent he'd been cuddled and loved before. His quasi-mother probably hadn't bothered with much of that. Too concerned with her precious career.

When bedtime came, I got him settled in his own room by reading to him, part of our new routine. A good mother would do that anyway, and I intended to be a fantastic mother. After an hour, I thought he'd fallen asleep, but then his eyes opened and he stared at me in the semi-gloom with a bewildered look on his face again.

'Mummy?' His voice quavered, high and uncertain; tears pricked the backs of my eyes and love for my beautiful boy shot through me. I pulled him tight against me, stroking the silk of his hair.

'Yes, darling,' I whispered. 'Mummy's here. I love you, sweetheart.' I rocked him and I could have stayed there forever, Daniel safe and secure in my arms, the word Mummy echoing in my head.

People believe what they want to believe, and I was no exception. The word had come from my Daniel's mouth much sooner than I'd dare hope. He meant me, I thought in a surge of ecstasy, squashing down the voice telling me otherwise. I wouldn't let myself believe he'd been thinking of his other mummy, wanting her instead of me. He was too young to understand how I'd love him far more than she ever had.

I reluctantly lowered him down. 'Goodnight, darling. I'll leave the door open and the light on outside and if you need anything, you call Mummy, and she'll come right away.'

I watched the news on television after putting Daniel to bed. I couldn't help myself; underneath the euphoria at being a mother again lurked fear, dark, insistent and terrible. Had I covered my tracks well enough? Discovery by the police would mean my darling being snatched from me, a thought so unbearable I shoved it instantly away.

A stern-faced police officer was talking into the camera. 'Daniel James Cordwell . . .' Oh, so that was what his name had been. Not that it mattered anymore. He was Daniel Mark Covey now, with the birth certificate to prove it. The policeman carried on. 'Disappeared from his home in Bristol . . . left unattended by his nanny . . . parents distraught . . .'

A reporter thrust himself forward, all big microphone and ego, and asked what leads the police had. 'No solid clues as yet . . . working hard with all available resources . . . doing all we can to reunite Daniel with his parents . . .'

The camera cut to a weeping woman, dark hair falling over her face, and I recognised her as being the one I'd seen with Daniel the first time I'd visited the flat. She was almost incoherent, pleading for whoever had taken her precious child to bring him back safely. I had no sympathy for her. She hadn't deserved the beautiful little boy sleeping in the other room.

I carried on checking the news every night, my fear still riding high. The dark-haired woman – I no longer thought of her as Daniel's mother, I had that role now – didn't feature anymore, the man I'd seen in the photos on the mantelpiece replacing her, with the same futile pleas for his return. What I heard reassured me; the police seemed to have no firm leads.

I'd done well. The hooded jacket had concealed my identity, not that anybody had taken any notice of us, either in Bristol or on the journey to Bromley. There would be no fingerprints or footprints at the flat to lead back to me. I'd already ditched the cheap shoes I'd worn. As for the keys – I'd bet the nanny had totally forgotten she'd left them in the café, and with me leaving the front door open I was counting on her thinking she must have gone out without locking it. Perhaps the assumption would be that Daniel had woken up and wandered outside, only to be snatched by an opportunistic paedophile. Nobody would clock me for a kidnapper; odds were everyone believed some vile sex predator had seized Daniel. I had no immediate neighbours to worry about, what with living above a shop, and nobody in the area seemed interested in me. Being mousy and unworthy of attention had turned out to be a blessing.

Things were still difficult the first week; Daniel never behaved badly but he was still far too withdrawn for my liking. When he did speak, he fretted about the whereabouts of his mother and the nanny; I countered his evident distress by reassuring him I was his mummy now. The bewilderment in his face tore me up every time, even though I'd persuaded my inner critic it was for the best. I reminded myself not to rush him, to give him time to adjust. He'd forget all about them before long.

My confidence grew sufficiently for me to take him out on the fifth day, his hair cropped as short as possible to make him less recognisable. We walked to a nearby park with a playground, and I pushed him back and forth on the swings. He didn't seem unhappy, but then he didn't appear happy either. I remembered the laughing child from the café in Bristol, giggling with delight as his nanny tickled him, and jealousy swamped me.

I sat in the sunshine, trying to dispel my qualms. Give it time, I told myself. Remember what you have here – a beautiful healthy son. I lost myself in watching Daniel clambering up the steps to the slide, enjoying the expression on his face as he whooshed to the bottom. You're a mother again, I reminded myself. I turned those two delicious syllables over in my mind, picturing the years ahead as Daniel grew older, started school, got taller, bigger, a teenager. The grandchildren he'd give me.

My daydream ended when I became aware of a woman staring at Daniel.

All the saliva drained from my mouth. I'd been discovered. She'd recognised Daniel from the picture on the television news, despite his cropped hair. She knew what I'd done, and Daniel would be taken from me and I'd never survive his loss; the pain would be too great. I rushed over to the slide and grabbed him on his way up the steps.

'Come on, darling. Time to go.' I ignored his frustrated protests. 'We'll play at home, my love.' Out of the corner of my eye, I saw the woman approaching.

'Is that your little boy?' she asked. I barely managed to force a reply past my bone-dry mouth.

'Yes. He's called Matthew.' The lie came easily despite the difficulty of speaking.

'He's gorgeous. How old is he? He must be about four, am I right?'

'Yes.' I turned away, pretending to straighten Daniel's clothes. My mind went into overdrive. I'd pack the instant I got back to the flat. We'd get on a bus for Manchester, Leeds, anywhere, put London behind us.

'He reminds me of my little boy when he was that age.' She paused. 'Are you all right? You don't look well.' I stared at her then; I detected no undercurrent of suspicion, no threat, in her voice or her face.

I swallowed hard, fighting to regain control. 'Yes. Sorry, I didn't mean to be rude.' I took refuge in another lie. 'I suffer bad migraines; got one coming on now. Need to get home before it takes hold.'

'You go and put your feet up, love. Take care now, you hear?' My nerves faded. She was just a friendly bystander, a doting mother like me, not the threat to my happiness I'd feared. The sweat on the back of my neck cooled; I broke away from her, satisfied I'd been imagining things. Tension still haunted me for the rest of the day, though, terror that the woman had recognised Daniel and reported the incident. Daniel's case was featured on the news again that night, but I relaxed on hearing the police say they had no progress to report. The whole event had shaken me up, though, and I didn't take Daniel out for another week, after my confidence had returned a little.

It took a month before the case faded from daily media attention; a missing child was serious stuff, no doubt about it, but there were only so many times the police could assure the public they were doing everything possible. After a while, I no longer had such a strong compulsion to watch the news. The tension I'd carried ever since the night I'd taken Daniel eased, a sense of contentment replacing it. I had my boy safe with me, and I was a mother again. Life was good.

After a couple of months, I judged Daniel to be ready for a local playgroup I'd found. It wouldn't be long now until he started nursery school, and the playgroup was important to get him used to other children. We went every afternoon, and, thank God, Daniel took to it straight away. He was still withdrawn a lot of the time at home, which hurt me, so it was good to see him laughing and playing, seemingly carefree.

I'd already put his name down for the nursery class attached to the nearest primary school. The headmaster made comments about how I'd left things very late, and I played the dizzy blonde and murmured yes, so sorry, but I'd only recently moved to the area, and how I'd been so busy sorting everything. The same fear I'd experienced with the woman in the park rose up once more, making me stumble over my words; I prayed he'd put it down to me being the timid type. I needn't have worried; he made no connection between the reserved four-year-old in front of him and the laughing Daniel from the photograph the police had released. As much as I hated his withdrawal on one level, Daniel's behaviour, along with his cropped hair, was helping disguise his identity; the public had imprinted on its mind an image of a smiling, curly-haired Daniel, so unlike how he was now.

I still worried about his reluctance to hug or kiss me. I put his reticence down to him being a little boy; they weren't known for liking that sort of thing, and I figured perhaps Daniel hadn't been used to a lot of physical affection from his parents or the nanny. Me, I'd have hugged and kissed him all day; I thought him delicious and I adored him more and more as time went on.

He never called me Mummy unless I prompted him and I hated having to coax him. I craved to hear him say the word, as if Daniel saying it stamped a seal on the fact I was his mother now. I didn't know what to think; he'd obviously found the abrupt change in his life more of a wrench than I'd anticipated, but at least he wasn't reacting with temper tantrums. I reminded myself he was very young and he'd surely forgotten about his birth mother and his nanny by now. After all, he never mentioned them anymore.

Overall, though, I loved being Daniel's mummy and it had been a long time since happiness had knocked on my door. I figured I deserved what I now had.

Only one thing was missing, besides finding a job when Daniel started school.

I wanted to meet a man. Not for myself, but for Daniel. A man who would give my boy a home and be a father to him. Then I'd finally have what I'd always yearned for. A husband, child and a stable home life.

28

WORTH WAITING FOR

On the day Katie left for Australia, Daniel forced himself to join in the seemingly endless goodbyes at Heathrow, plastering on a smile, his nerves stretched tight. He watched her arrive, taking in her long-legged stride as she walked towards him and the rest of the family, all sass and confidence, an Oscar-deserving performance on her part. Behind the wide smile, she had to be hurting every bit as much as he was. Hell, they'd talked of doing this Australia thing together. This wasn't how it was supposed to play out.

In a way, he thought later, her departure was good, despite hurting like mad. His head was still a mess, but among all the pain he felt relief. They'd done the right thing, awful as it had been. The raw wound called Katie could start to heal. She'd gone, giving them both the chance to move on.

The thought of Annie came into his mind. He needed a dollop of her plain speaking, delivered in that sex-soaked voice of hers. They'd chat, he'd down a few drinks and perhaps the knot of pain in his heart would ease a little. He wanted, if he were honest, to tell Annie about

Katie, how her flying off to the other side of the world had ripped a gaping hole in his life. Probably best not to mention she was his aunt and that they'd been having sex, albeit unknowingly. Despite the fact he could sense she wasn't the type to blab about anything he disclosed in confidence, such a move might be a step too far. Too much information to tell someone who was, after all, a virtual stranger. Besides, he'd sworn to keep it a secret. But what the hell, he needed a sympathetic ear right now. He'd tell her as much as he judged she'd be comfortable with.

The place was half full when he arrived. He pulled out a stool at the bar in front of her. 'Hey, you. Remember me?'

She laughed. 'As if I'd forget such a pretty face. Not every day a celebrity walks in here. What will you have?'

'Whatever the guest beer is. You OK?'

'I'm fine. Things are picking up here.' She held his glass against the pump and pulled. 'Everything going well with your family?'

'Yes. No. It's complicated.' Master of understatement there, he thought.

She handed him his beer. 'Isn't it always, with families? Remember what I told you, though. Enjoy what you've found. Don't dwell on the past or what might have been. A lesson I'm trying to learn myself.'

'Easy enough to say. The past can hold you back at times.'

She leaned across the bar. 'Listen. I don't know why I'm saying this, but anyway. It's busy now, and likely to get busier, so we're not going to be able to chat. Come back to mine for coffee after we close and you can get whatever's bugging you off your chest.' She laughed. 'Don't worry. I won't try to seduce you. I know I'm not the type a pretty boy like you would go for.'

Daniel stared at her. He realised she was talking straight, didn't want or expect sex from him; she was face value, this woman, and he could go to hers and drink coffee and spill out his pain and she'd understand. He'd come here for solace tonight, hadn't he? And she was offering it to him. For that, he was grateful beyond words.

He decided to take her up on her suggestion. There had been a connection established between them the other night, the mutual recognition of some deep past hurt, hence her offer of coffee. He could tell her about Katie, and she wouldn't judge. Perhaps she'd give some hint of what caused the look of pain that crossed her face in unguarded moments.

'Best offer I've had all night. Thanks.'

'It'll be a long wait. I don't finish until two.'

'You're worth waiting for.'

She grinned. 'God, that was bad. Are you always so corny?'

'Sorry.' He smiled apologetically. 'Force of habit around women, I guess. Usually I spin a better line than that. I'm not coming on to you, honest.'

The night passed slowly, Daniel brushing off several attempts to pick him up from both men and women. He wasn't here for sex, not tonight. He didn't mind the time spent at the bar. He reckoned he'd be proved right; Annie would be worth the wait.

At two o'clock, she gestured towards the door. 'Wait for me outside. I'll be five minutes, tops. My flat's just around the corner.'

Daniel stood in the cold night air, hands in his pockets, and then she was beside him, bundled up in a thick coat, her bag slung over her shoulder. 'Come on. This way.'

They walked up the stairs to her flat and she unlocked the door. 'Make yourself at home, if you can find room. Excuse the mess, but I'm not the tidy sort.' She gestured towards a battered sofa, strewn with books and magazines. 'I'll get the coffee perking.'

Daniel tossed aside some books – looked like she was into Gauguin, Matisse and Bertrand Russell – and sat down. He wondered about this woman, who took an interest in art and philosophy and worked nights in a bar, a woman who was nothing to look at but who had read him like the proverbial book.

She brought in two steaming mugs, fragrant with coffee. 'You man-aged to find space among the chaos, then. So tell me. What's been so bad about this week for you?'

'Do you always get straight to the point?'

'Yep. Get used to it.'

'Where do I start?' Daniel sighed. 'My ex-girlfriend flew to Australia yesterday. She's emigrated.'

'Ouch. Was it a painful split?'

'Yes, very. Not what either of us wanted.'

Annie raised an eyebrow. 'You're going to have to explain that one. Why break up, if that was the case?' She paused. 'Was she married?'

He shook his head. 'No. We were both single. Everything had been going great between us. Except for the fact that . . .' He had to tell her; it would make no sense otherwise. He kept his eyes on Annie, willing her to be OK with this. 'We didn't realise, not until I started delving into my past and all the stuff about the kidnap came out . . . I'd been dating my own aunt, Annie.' He dropped his gaze. 'She's the kid sister of my mother, and neither of us had a clue.'

'Shit, Daniel. That's rough. Really rough.' He didn't hear any cen-sure in her voice. 'You loved her?'

'Yes. We hadn't been together long, but Katie was special. Like no other woman I'd ever dated. She'd been planning on going to Australia before we met, but we'd talked about me going with her, and I was up for it.' He drained his coffee. 'She decided to leave anyway once all this shit came out. It would have been too awful for me, seeing her all the time, and she felt the same way. It's a close-knit family, you see.'

'What about your other relatives? Your mum, your dad – that must have torn them up as well.'

'They don't know, and never will. The one good thing I can say about the whole screwed-up mess. She never told them much about me; she liked to tease her mum that way. She was going to tell them, but then we found out about all this.'

'Yup. That's one good thing.'

'It's ironic.' Daniel shook his head. 'She once referred to me being kidnapped as the skeleton in the family closet. Now I've been replaced by a new skeleton – our relationship – and that one's never going to get out. My family's been through enough.'

'Yes. You have too. You've lost your girlfriend, and had to come to terms with a whole new idea of who you are. Can't be easy, Daniel.'

'No. No, it's not.' She didn't know the half of it. Bitterness tinged his voice when he next spoke. 'It would have all been different if that woman hadn't kidnapped me. I love to paint, you see. It's all I ever wanted to do, growing up. Go to college, make a name for myself in the art world. But I couldn't. My stepfather hated me and refused to pay for me to go. I couldn't see how to fund a degree myself; I didn't want huge student loans. Painting's not renowned as being a big money earner for most artists.' God, he hated how petulant he sounded. 'My new family, they're all creative and talented; well off as well. My parents wouldn't have hesitated to send me to college. So I didn't only lose my girlfriend, I lost my art as well.'

'You hate her, don't you? The woman who took you?'

'Yes, I do.'

'Do you know why she abducted you?'

'No one does. She won't talk. Retreated into her own little world and isn't saying anything. I'll probably never find out.' He sounded bitter again, he realised. 'She had a child of her own at some point, so we've been informed, and I ended up with his name and birth certificate. The police are looking into all that. But she's told so many lies; it's hard to tell what's real. I can't ignore how much she loved me, though.'

'Have you thought why she took you and raised you as her son? She must have had a powerful reason to do what she did, Daniel. Did you ever think she might deserve your compassion, rather than your judgement?'

His father's words. Similar to those of Alison. Wrong, both of them, however well intentioned. Anger surged hotly within him. Annie had no idea. He'd been wrong to think she'd understand.

'Hey, don't look so pissed off, mister. I realise you didn't like hearing that. But think about this. You say she won't talk. That's probably a sign she's been badly damaged by life. Suffering heartbreak can send you off the rails. Believe me, I know.' She looked away.

Shame for his petulant behaviour replaced Daniel's anger. 'I'm sorry. You're probably right. She has a history of mental health issues. Bouts of depression, stuff like that. Perhaps she lied about or kept hidden other things as well. My father told me I should think about forgiving her. But I can't.'

'Maybe it's too soon.'

'Or impossible. I hardly know the woman, I suppose, in spite of living with her for so long. I need answers, though. Answers she's not willing to give.' He picked up his empty mug. 'Any chance of a refill? Or have you had enough of my self-pity?'

'Refill coming up.' She took his mug. 'And there's something else you're not telling me. Oh, don't try to deny it,' she said, seeing him shake his head. 'You're hiding something, besides losing your girlfriend and missing out on going to college and all the rest of it. I'll listen, if you want to share. It's your call.' She went out to the kitchen.

She was sharp, this woman, to detect the festering secret he'd hidden for years; she'd sniffed out his shame with unerring precision. Sharp didn't even begin to describe her. He wondered if he could bring himself to confide in her what he'd never told anyone before.

But, he remembered, there had been nobody he trusted enough. Not even Katie.

His intuition was telling him he'd never find a better person than this woman, should he choose to spill the horror of what had happened. Not tonight, though. It was too soon to walk that road and he wasn't sure if he could, not yet anyway. Far easier to bottle everything up, the way he'd done for years. Right now, he needed to deflect this conversation; things were getting too intense, too near the mark. And he wanted to find out more about Annie.

She returned with the refilled coffee mugs. 'So, mister. You care to share your deep, dark secret?'

'Not sure this is the best time. Or whether I'll ever think the time is right. Listen, I've been rattling on about my life, my problems. Enough of me; I want to hear about you. What made you work in a pick-up joint serving beer? When you're into art and . . .' – he picked up a book – '*Forgiveness: A Practical Guide*? Who are you, Annie? What's your story?'

'It's not a pretty one, Daniel. I've never talked to anyone here in London about what happened, not since packing my bags and walking out on my life nearly six months ago. Not sure I'm ready to tell you now.' A tremor in her voice betrayed strong emotions barely under control.

'Then don't. As you said to me, it's your call. If you choose to, though, I'll listen; you'd be doing me a favour. I've been a bit self-absorbed lately. You'll give me something to think about besides my own problems.' He smiled at her. 'Up to you.'

29

THE BIGGER PICTURE

I had no idea how to go about finding a father for Daniel. My daily life was so narrow, centred as it was on my boy; I never met any men, let alone unmarried ones who might be suitable. Joining a dating agency required a degree of confidence I didn't possess. Self-doubt plagued my thoughts. Would anybody want me – timid, mousy, a single parent? I wondered vaguely whether I'd make friends with the other mothers once Daniel started nursery school, women who might be able to set me up with unattached relatives. The thought held little appeal but I didn't have many options available.

I worried all the time during Daniel's first day at nursery school. I hated being apart from my darling, but when I went to pick him up I watched him laughing with the other children and a weight lifted off me. He was happy, I persuaded myself. He was a child, after all; he needed more than his mummy in his life. Friends of the same age were important as well.

He'd be able to paint at nursery school too; his love of art had amazed me over the course of the summer. In fact, it was what he liked to do best; he would get completely absorbed in it, sitting on the floor with his brushes and paints, daubing shapes and colours onto paper, lost in his own world. I'd papered the walls of the flat with his creations. 'My little Picasso,' I called him.

The questions started later that first school day after I'd finished his bedtime story.

'Where's the other lady?' he asked. I hadn't a clue whom he meant.

'The other lady. She used to sit by my bed before I went to sleep.'

Panic hit me. I realised who he must be referring to. I had no idea how to deal with the question, though.

I had only one option: to deny all knowledge of his parents and the nanny. It was for the best, as well as being the kindest thing to do. They were out of his life for good and I intended it should stay that way.

'There's no other lady, darling.' I leaned over and cuddled him. 'Only Mummy. Perhaps you dreamed about this person and she seemed real. It can be like that sometimes.'

'What about the lady who used to play with me? The one with the dark hair?'

'She was a dream too, darling. She's not real either.' I pulled back and met his puzzled look with a smile. 'Nighty-night, Daniel. Sleep tight.'

I persuaded myself I'd handled things well. Any hazy memories Daniel still had of his past life would surely fade soon, buried under the weight of my love. It was simply a matter of time.

I had other things to think about anyway; I'd seen a job advertised in the paper for a part-time accounts clerk at a local construction company. The hours fitted exactly with what I needed; it would work in perfectly with Daniel's schedule at nursery school. I carefully drafted a letter and a summary of my qualifications. A week later, I got a reply inviting me to an interview.

It didn't turn out to be as nerve-wracking as I'd feared. Maria, who interviewed me, seemed friendly and unconcerned about my lack of practical experience. I think she liked the fact I didn't have to give notice anywhere else and she was a mother like me, so when I mentioned Daniel and she talked about her two little boys we immediately established a rapport.

'When can you start?' she asked. I almost leapt over the desk and hugged her.

Things went even better than I'd hoped. Maria was a dream to work for, and I took to the job straight away. Daniel had settled in well at nursery school and I'd started to think again about finding a father for him, still unsure as to how to meet someone suitable.

It turned out to be work that provided the answer.

I came back from lunch one day to find a tall man chatting with Maria. I registered his dark good looks and the way his smile warmed up an otherwise stern face.

Maria introduced us. 'Laura, this is Ian Bateman. He's the financial advisor to the directors here. Ian, this is Laura Covey, my assistant.'

He took my hand with a firm grip. 'Lovely to meet you, Laura.'

My face flushed. I stole a look at the third finger of his left hand. No wedding ring.

Maria laughed once he'd left. 'I think you made quite an impression on him.'

Later that night, Daniel was unusually difficult to settle in bed.

'Would you like some hot milk?' I asked.

He shook his head. 'Been thinking about the lady who used to sit by my bed.'

Anxiety hit me; I had hoped I'd laid that particular ghost to rest. Apparently not.

'The lady you dreamed about? The one I told you wasn't real?' I forced my voice to stay calm.

'Is she really not real?' His disappointment hurt me right the way through.

'No, sweetie, she's a dream. Like the girl with the dark hair.'

'She's not real either?'

'No, my love. Sometimes our dreams can seem very lifelike, but that's all they are. Just dreams.'

He was quiet for a while, and I wondered whether he was falling asleep at last. Then he gazed up at me. To my dismay, I thought my darling boy was going to cry. 'Why don't I have a daddy? Like my friends at school do?'

I had no option apart from another lie.

'Everyone has a daddy at some point, darling.' I chose my words carefully. 'You had one too, like all your friends at school. But yours was special, sweetheart. He got chosen to live with the angels in Heaven.' Even though I had no religious beliefs, I found myself grateful for the weekly Bible class they taught at nursery school. He loved stories about baby Jesus and the angels; I hoped they would help explain things in a way he would understand.

'He's an angel too? In Heaven?'

'Yes, darling. That's why he's special. Mummy and Daddy loved each other very much, and wanted to get married, but Daddy got taken by the angels instead. Mummy got very upset but she knew Daddy was safe and well in Heaven.'

'I'm glad,' he said solemnly. 'I'm glad Daddy's with the angels.'

'They'll take good care of him, darling.' I kissed him. 'Now go to sleep, my love.'

I'd been right; the time had definitely come to find a father for Daniel. Ian Bateman, dark, attractive and hopefully single, came to mind. I thought he was probably about thirty; some people would say too old for me, but I didn't think so. Males my own age held no appeal, based on my experience with Matthew Hancock. Older and presumably wiser sat just fine with me, assuming he liked me. Besides, I wasn't looking for the sweep me off my feet and down the river kind of love. Instead, I'd settle for companionship and a father figure for Daniel. It would be a bonus if the man was attractive, like Ian.

He came into the office again a couple of days later. Maria slipped out of the room at one point, throwing a wink at me, and I found myself alone with him.

We made small talk for a while, with me acting like a gauche teenager, stammering from time to time. The fact he might be marriage material unnerved me; I found myself wondering what he'd be like as a husband. I gave myself a mental shake, forcing myself to concentrate on what he was saying. He carried on the conversation for a few minutes longer before making his move.

'I'd like to take you out on Saturday night,' he said.

I didn't reply. I was too taken by surprise, even though I'd hoped for this. The voice inside my head, the one that frequently belittled me, had done a good job in convincing me Ian Bateman would never be interested in me. He'd want someone smarter, funnier, prettier.

'We'll drive out to a steak restaurant I often go to. I'll pick you up at half seven.'

'Yes,' I managed. 'I'd like that.'

Saturday night. I'd need a babysitter for Daniel, and the idea of leaving him with anyone else was unthinkable, something I'd vowed I'd never do. I thought quickly. I may as well tell Ian about Daniel right now. He had to understand about him and accept the situation or else there was no point.

'Could we meet up Sunday lunchtime instead?' I smiled, willing him to be OK with this. 'It's my little boy, you see. I don't know anyone available to babysit. If you don't mind . . .' Please God, let him not mind. 'If I brought him along . . . maybe we could have lunch or something?'

Perhaps I imagined it, but I thought his face fell slightly. 'You have a child?' he asked.

Maternal love welled up in me. 'Yes. Daniel. He's four years old.' I pulled my purse from my bag, taking out his photo. 'Look. Isn't he adorable?'

I had a twinge of disappointment at his lack of reaction. I decided Ian had a lot to take in. Dating – assuming we did start dating – someone with a young son, a single mother, shouldn't be taken lightly. I must make allowances.

'There's the Royal Oak,' he said. 'They do a good carvery on Sundays, and they have a children's play area. I'll pick you up around twelve-thirty.'

We swapped telephone numbers and he left, saying he'd see me on Sunday.

Lunch at the Royal Oak went well. Ian seemed stiff with Daniel, but from what he told me he'd had very little experience of children. The time flew by. Before I realised it, four o'clock had come and gone. Ian insisted on settling the bill, waving aside any attempt from me to pay my share. As I put away my purse, defeated, he leaned across the table and grasped my hand.

'We'll go out again this coming week,' he said. 'When are you free?'

Bingo, said a small voice in my head.

I gave him a big smile. Playing hard to get wasn't part of my game plan. 'Whenever you are.'

We started dating regularly. Ian's bossiness didn't bother me. I found it easier to fit in with him rather than argue about things I didn't care about anyway. All part of our unspoken bargain. I'd get what I needed from our relationship, and in return I'd do things Ian's way.

To my surprise, he took me to meet his parents on our third date, and they became Daniel's regular babysitters. I hated leaving my darling boy with other people but his parents seemed reliable and Ian obviously considered the matter settled. Besides, we needed to spend time by ourselves if our relationship stood any chance of progressing. There was the sexual aspect, for one thing.

Getting our first time in bed out of the way would be good for me, I decided; it would paper over the vile memory of the rape. I didn't doubt Ian would be a kind lover and if I wanted this to go anywhere, I had to get over this hurdle.

I invited him to the flat for a meal the following Saturday, timed for after Daniel's bedtime. I cooked lamb casserole, a good safe choice, followed by cheesecake, teamed with a decent bottle of wine.

'This is great. You can really cook,' he said, after his second large helping. I laughed, drank some more wine and congratulated myself on how lucky I'd been to have found this man. I saw myself married to him, cooking hearty meals and running his house, being a great mum to Daniel and a good wife as well; Ian would grow to love Daniel and we'd be happy together. I'd finally have the life I'd always wanted.

We polished off half the cheesecake and most of the wine and collapsed laughing on the sofa; Ian kissed me and I realised the time had come. I'd already downed enough alcohol to blunt my fears a little.

'Let's take this somewhere more comfortable,' he said, and pulled me towards my bedroom.

Thankfully, Ian had brought condoms. I forced myself not to think about my rape, but about before, with Matthew Hancock. I'd never particularly enjoyed what he'd done to me, but I was determined to go through with this; all I needed to do was to let go. If I did, everything would be fine. I breathed deeply, willing my rigid body to relax. Large hands explored me in a way Matthew Hancock had never bothered to do and gradually I loosened up. It was easier to allow Ian to take charge, as usual; I had neither the confidence nor the experience to take the lead. I doubted Ian, being the old-fashioned type, would want me to anyway. The sex ended up being better than I'd expected, to my surprise; I realised the thought of our next time in bed didn't seem anything to fear.

Afterwards I lay beside him, cuddled up.

'I'm in love with you,' he said. 'I fell for you the minute I saw you. Those beautiful blue eyes.'

'I love you too.' A lie, but I reminded myself to think of the bigger picture. I'd make a good wife, if Ian proved a good husband. I'd do all the traditional housewifely things like cooking and cleaning, which I loved anyway, thus making life comfortable for him. Quid pro quo, if he was to be a father to Daniel.

Ian told me he wanted us to move in with him not long afterwards. A few months later, I held out my left hand and showed Maria my engagement ring.

I did have the odd moment of worry, though.

Ian didn't pay Daniel much attention or seem particularly interested in him, although I could tell he tried his best, for my sake. But it didn't come naturally and Daniel clearly picked up on his reserve, not interacting much with him. It was the only thing giving me any concern. I'd wanted to give Daniel a father and yet the two of them were awkward and uncommunicative with each other. It wasn't how I'd pictured things in my fantasy.

In the end, I decided to be grateful for what I had. The parenting thing would come to Ian in time; he hadn't been used to children, after all. I simply needed to be more patient.

So one day I stood beside him in the local registry office and made my vows, and I swore to myself I'd uphold them, even if I couldn't do the eternal love bit. Liking would have to suffice, and that day I truly believed it would.

30

WALKING WOUNDED

Daniel meant what he'd said. He'd run his mouth off for long enough; he needed to give Annie her turn. She didn't say anything at first, her expression clouded again. Eventually she spoke.

'Sometimes things happen when you never expect them. Everything gets thrown out of kilter and nothing can ever be the same again. You're not the same person anymore.' She looked at Daniel. 'I guess that's more or less what happened to you. Suddenly you've found your family and lost a girlfriend, and you've had to rethink your whole identity. I can understand why you're angry and confused. But you've gained more than you've lost, Daniel. You have a whole new family, and in time, the pain over your girlfriend will fade, believe me.'

Silence again for a while.

'I was married,' Annie said eventually.

Perhaps that explained the clouded look. The age-old story; she'd been married, and her husband had been unfaithful. Sympathy hit Daniel; he'd not known this woman long but he recognised her warmth, depth and insight. Any man who hadn't done likewise must have been a complete idiot.

'We adored each other. Our marriage turned out to be everything I hoped it would.'

So this husband hadn't been such a fool, then. He waited.

'I met him when I was twenty-two. I'd had one or two boyfriends before, but nothing serious before Andrew. I'd started a job in marketing on the south coast. He worked for one of our client companies. We began dating and realised straight away we were meant for each other. He didn't give a toss about me being nothing to look at. Oh, don't say anything,' she added, as Daniel opened his mouth. 'I'm well aware I'm no beauty. With this nose? Give me a break. But that didn't matter to him. He wasn't anything to look at either. But to me he was the most wonderful man in the world. He had brains, he had a heart and he loved me. So kind too. We got married within a year.'

'Children?'

'No. We talked about them, but the time never seemed right, and I think we were happy just being with each other. It might have happened one day, who knows?' Her face had a shuttered look again.

'I had Andrew for ten years. Ten years that couldn't have been happier, before he was taken from me.' Her eyes filled, and Daniel moved across the sofa to hold her. She pulled away and fumbled in her bag for a tissue.

'Sorry. His loss still gets to me badly. It's not been long, you see. Only six months.'

'What happened?'

'I went to visit my mother one night. Andrew didn't come; he had a bad cold. I kissed him goodbye and told him I'd be back soon.'

She blew her nose and went on. 'The front door was slightly open when I got home, which rang alarm bells with me. I was certain I'd shut it when I left. As for Andrew, he was such a careful man; he wouldn't have done something like that.'

Only one possible outcome to this story, thought Daniel, and a damned ugly one. Dear God.

'I pushed it open and I called his name. No answer. No sounds, not a thing. I went into the hall, still calling his name, ready to run back out if I heard an intruder. Still nothing.' The tears were flowing again. 'I looked down and saw the footprints. Horrible, bloody footprints, leading from the living room towards the front door.' Her voice rose. 'I think I knew then what had happened and I had no idea how to bear it. I pushed open the living room door. And . . . oh, God . . .'

Daniel tightened his hold on her.

'There was so much blood. Everywhere.' The expression on her face tore at his heart; she had a combination of devastation, heartbreak and searing loss written all over her. 'He'd been hit with a hammer. Over and over. Murdered by a crack-head, the one who left the front door open. All for a few pounds stolen from Andrew's wallet. I held him in my arms and I got covered in blood and it was so awful. I thought the whole thing must be a horrible nightmare, and I'd wake up soon, and I'd have my husband back with me, the man who never did anyone any harm, who had always been so kind. But it wasn't a nightmare, it was all too real. Eventually I dialled 999 and I could hardly tell them what had happened, I was shaking and crying so much.'

Shit. If he thought he'd been landed with a crap hand in life, then fate had dealt one a great deal worse to Annie. Guilt stabbed at him when he remembered his whinges about being denied an art degree.

'Sorry,' she whispered against his shoulder.

'Hey, nothing to be sorry for. Nobody should ever have to experience anything so awful.'

'That's life, Daniel. Shit happens, as they say, and it can happen to anyone. Turns out I ended up being the chosen one. Or rather, Andrew did.' She managed a small smile. 'I thank God for every day we spent together. Nothing can ever take them away from me.'

'What did you do? Afterwards?'

'I couldn't cope. Not at all. Everything I'd ever loved had been ripped from me. I still had family, and friends, but I shut them all out. I didn't want to live. Not without Andrew. He'd been such a huge part of me, you see. The hole his murder has left in my life is immense. I don't believe it'll ever heal.'

'You haven't considered talking to someone? Counselling, I mean?'

'No. I'm not sure anyone, even people like the Samaritans, can grasp the agony I'm going through. Talking won't bring Andrew back either, and that's all I want. The doctor prescribed Prozac, but I didn't collect the prescription. Chemicals wouldn't replace my husband and nothing short of oblivion would have helped with the pain, so I ran away.'

'Here, to London?'

'Yes. I had to get away. Couldn't stay living there. They meant well. Family and friends, you know. But I found their pity unbearable and the fact none of them had a clue how to deal with me. What do you say to a woman who finds her husband's body drenched in his own blood and so badly beaten she can't recognise him?'

Daniel had no idea either. Christ, this woman had endured hell he couldn't imagine.

'Like I said, I didn't think I wanted to live. I couldn't picture a life without Andrew; existing without what we'd created didn't seem worthwhile. I packed my bags, drove to London and found this flat. For weeks, I didn't go out apart from buying groceries. I cried and I cursed and I thought over and over about how I could kill myself. There's no great way to commit suicide, and I considered every method possible, believe me. I think taking a dive under a Tube train came out on top.' She smiled faintly at Daniel.

'You still think that way?'

'No. Somehow, those thoughts faded; I remembered Andrew, the kind of man he'd been, and what he would have wanted, which would be for me to carry on living. I tell you, Daniel, I don't have a clue how to be happy again. But I do know he wouldn't want me to commit suicide. That's what I'm trying to figure out now, how to go on. Whatever that might mean.'

'No idea at all?'

'Not the slightest. I took the job in the bar, because I realised I needed to mix with other people, not stay cooped up in this flat twenty-four seven. It's done me some good; I guess I feel more human these days. Even started turning to my old friends, books, for inspiration, as you can see.' She picked up the Bertrand Russell, flicked through the pages affectionately. 'But long term? No idea.'

'But you're not thinking about throwing yourself under a Tube train anymore?'

'No. Those days are past. It's the future I'm not so sure about.' She smiled. 'But I'll work things out. I'll find a way. Just as you will, with dealing with the loss of your girlfriend and your disappointment about art college. And whatever else lies underneath all that, the part you've not told me.'

He rubbed his thumb over her cheek, and she stared at him, eyes still wet with tears, and her suffering made her plain face utterly beautiful to him. He gazed at her and she looked back; the shared grief of their tormented pasts rose up between them and he did what seemed the most natural thing in the world. He leaned in and kissed her, a gesture of understanding and empathy. She didn't push him away and he kissed her again, this time drawing her closer and sliding his tongue into her mouth.

They kissed for a long time and when she eventually pulled back, she was smiling and shaking her head.

'I've not kissed anyone since Andrew. Wasn't sure if I ever would again.'

'It felt right.'

'Yes. Yes, it did.' She smiled again. 'One of those strange things for which there's no explanation. I think perhaps we need this, Daniel.

Right here, right now, you and I can help one another, take comfort together. There must be something about you. Never talked to anyone in London about Andrew before.'

'I've not discussed Katie with anyone else either. Who the hell do you tell you've been sleeping with your aunt by mistake?'

'That's why we're good for each other. We can spill out our darkest secrets. And maybe it will help.'

'I think you might be right.'

Annie stood up and stretched out her hand. 'Bedroom's this way.'

He'd not thought anything sexual would be on the agenda, until he kissed her. But he had a strong need to take this woman to bed, to strengthen their connection, relate to her on some level besides conversation and sharing secrets. He wanted to make love with her and find a deeper solace in her body than he'd ever find in words. He'd submerge himself in the relief she offered, sinking into the comfort of her, this woman who was totally different to any he'd bedded before. Chances were the sex might be the most important he'd ever have.

He was grateful for the condom he always carried in his wallet. They undressed slowly. No frenzied moment of passion, this, but rather two wounded people seeking to heal their hurts with one another. They kissed in between taking off their clothes, Daniel's hands moving over her skin and sliding into her panties. She felt warm and good in his arms and he pushed her down onto the bed, tearing open the condom packet and pulling out the contents.

They carried on kissing for a long time, Annie lying passively under him, not that he minded; this wasn't about passion and never had been. He moved his fingers down to rub and stroke between her legs, savouring her wetness, the touch of her hands rolling the condom on him. Then he was inside her, his cock thrusting hard into the solace she offered; the bitterness and anger receded from his brain as her legs wrapped around him, drawing him further in, her feet pressing against his back. He kissed her and fucked her, a magic formula that sent Katie

Trebasco and Laura Bateman and his stepfather spinning to the outer edges of the universe, and only he and Annie remained, their bodies moving in mutual consolation.

He didn't think he ever wanted the sex to stop, but eventually the pleasure got intense, and he knew he was going to come. Time to slow down, give her a chance to catch up. She gasped, her arms tightening around him, her heels drumming against his spine and then he was coming, white lights sparking behind his eyes, his breath ragged and uneven, sweat running down his face. He was dimly aware of Annie panting under him and calling his name, before he collapsed on top of her, deeply grateful in every cell of his body for what she'd done for him.

He considered rolling off, getting rid of the condom, but he was too relaxed, too comfortable, to care. He kissed her hair. 'You OK?'

'You can't tell?' Her voice teased him. 'I never thought we'd be doing that tonight. When I asked you back for coffee, I meant Kenco and nothing else.'

'I know.'

'Not sure why it ended up being you. Why tonight. No, that's not true. I do know. We're the walking wounded, you and me, and I think we realised that the first night we met.'

'Yes.'

She laughed. 'A comfort fuck's as good as any other. We both needed this, Daniel. Thank you.'

31

FOOL'S PARADISE

I've lost track of how long I've been in here now. I'm still getting daily visits from the doctors who sit in front of me and ask ridiculous questions. What was my childhood like, taking care of a mother who had drinking problems? How did I cope with the death of my grandmother? Why did I take Daniel from his parents? Do they really think they'll ever understand, if they've not been through the pain I've endured?

They've been digging into my life. Well, of course they have. It'll be the police, seeing as they consider a crime has been committed. Perhaps the young officer who stared at me with such judgement in her eyes when I was first arrested. I can picture her now, all quiet efficiency, searching through my past in that small town a lifetime ago. I've never made any attempt to hide my name or how I lived before I came to London. She'll have found it easy enough to trace me back to when I worked in Bristol, and then to my life in Hampshire.

Right now, as I sit here gazing out of the window, they're combing through my past life, and they'll have found the record of my baby's birth and they'll ask themselves the obvious question: what happened to her child?

And the only evidence of my beautiful baby's death is the tree he lies under, my child's only gravestone, in the wood I sobbed my way through so long ago. They don't know about that part, of course. I pray they never find the oak tree under which I buried my baby; I can't bear the thought of his tiny body being disturbed. I hope beyond hope they won't fire more questions at me about his death, although of course they will. I'll blot them out anyway, retreating behind my wall of silence to think about the happy times with my baby. Perhaps then the futile questioning will fade away.

They won't find it hard to work out what happened. Why I ended up with one child no longer around and another woman's son brought up as my own. They'll piece parts of the puzzle together, and perhaps the judgement in the young policewoman's eyes will turn to understanding.

Yes. The records will show the bare bones of my life. They won't show the ugliness of cleaning up after my drunken mother, trying to prevent her choking on her own vomit. They won't explain my terror on discovering I was pregnant by a boy who didn't give a toss about me. They won't reveal the horror of being raped by somebody twice my size and strength. Or the misery of losing my beloved grandmother.

Neither will the records of my life show how the gorgeous four-year-old from the café fused with the memory of my dead baby, so they ended up as one, and how that little boy became my own child in my mind. I had to take him, because a child should be with its mother and Daniel had been palmed off on a nanny who thought nothing of leaving him alone and vulnerable. They can go on labelling what I did a crime but that's black-and-white thinking and sometimes life presents you with shades of grey instead.

The police won't understand about the years I had with my beautiful Daniel, watching him grow into an awkward teenager and then a handsome man who had all the girls after him. About the contentment

I found in my marriage to Ian, who loves me and has always been a good husband. What's more, he did his best with Daniel; he never hit my boy or raised his voice to him. Besides, I can't blame Ian totally for the distance between him and Daniel. My boy was never an affectionate child and the teenage years were hard; he spent hours in his room and sometimes he wouldn't speak to either of us.

I think about my husband. He's bewildered by all this. Ian's always lived in a safe, predictable world, where he went to work five days a week, played golf and came home to a wife and a meal on the table and nothing ever changed.

Now he has to deal with having a kidnapper for a wife and coming home to an empty house and microwave meals.

But he's a good man. He's stuck by me. He comes every couple of days and sits with me and I can tell he hopes he'll be the one who breaks my silence.

The day wears on; I endure more of the questions, and I lie on my bed and long for night to come so sleep can take away my life for a few blessed hours.

And then the miracle I've been praying for happens. The door opens, and a nurse comes in.

'You have a visitor,' she says.

I glance up, expecting Ian, and find Daniel standing in front of me.

I feel exquisite joy for a second, before I register the expression on his face. He has the same look of anger and hatred as before, and my hopes wither.

He takes off his jacket, and slings it down beside me, grabbing a chair, dragging it towards the bed so he can sit opposite me.

One word is all he says, but underneath it are a thousand questions. 'Why?'

I understand he needs answers and I could give them to him, if I chose to speak. Why, he asks. Because I believed it was fate when your four-year-old self came into my life. Because I thought I was doing the right thing. Because I loved you too much to be without you. Because I couldn't think of anything else besides being your mother.

But I don't say any of those things. I can't, not while he has such hatred written all over his face.

I look away, at his jacket lying beside me on the bed, at the pen tucked in the inside pocket, at the spare button that's almost falling off. I itch to do the motherly thing and sew it back on.

He gets up and walks over to the window, deliberately turning his back.

'Do you have any idea what you did to me?' Rage is boiling in his voice. I'm confused. I'd be forced to say no if I were to answer his question. I always did my best for him. What did I do that was so wrong? Yes, I took him from his birth family, but they didn't love him, not as he deserved to be loved. I gave him a home, and a mother who was always there for him, and I even married Ian so my boy could have a male role model.

Why does he hate me so?

'My father suggested I come. He has some ridiculous notion about forgiveness. Not going to happen. I'm here to get answers.'

My eyes travel over my son. Every line of his body holds condemnation.

'They're wonderful. My real family. They're everything I always wanted. My mother adores me and I can't get enough of being with her. I never loved you, not at all. My grandparents are great people too. As for Dad, he's a good man, one I can respect and be proud of.'

I flinch as his words lash against me, every one of them intended to inflict pain and let me know I'm second best to the mother who preferred her career to him.

'Not like the bastard you married,' he continues.

I have no idea what he means. Ian's a good man, if a bit controlling. I'd have left him if I'd ever thought he'd behaved badly towards my boy, no question of it.

'He was the reason I never went to art college, when painting was all I ever wanted to do. Did you realise that?'

His words confuse me. I always thought Daniel would study art and had been surprised when he hadn't. But I thought the choice had been his; I'd assumed he'd decided there were no real career prospects in the art world. It couldn't have had anything to do with Ian.

'He hated me because I was another man's child, because I was always in the way when all he wanted was you. He loathed me and he didn't hold back in telling me so. He told me over and over again how worthless I was, how he wouldn't pay a single penny to put me through art college. I couldn't think of any other way of being able to go.'

He must be making this up to hurt me. What he's saying can't be true.

Daniel has never been a liar, though.

And some small part of my brain, the part where instinct lies, tells me he's speaking the truth.

Now I'm beginning to realise why he hates me. He's been denied his art career, because of the man I chose to be his father. The man whose character I obviously misjudged.

Except I'm wrong. I realise I don't know the half of it. Daniel is speaking again. The strongest intuition hits me of my boy having bottled something up for a long time. How whatever he's been repressing is about to burst free.

'I dreaded you going out, because then he'd start on me. He never did or said anything when you were around. You didn't know, did you?' I can hear the bitterness in his voice. I still don't understand what he means.

'He'd slap and punch me once you'd left.'

Dear God. I am the one being punched, and hard, in my stomach.

But it's nothing compared to what comes next.

'He used to make me suck his prick.'

Shock hits me doubly hard. He didn't say that. He couldn't have said something so awful.

'He'd grab my head and fuck my mouth.'

I can't deal with this. It's too abhorrent, too vile.

'He didn't stop there either. He took it further.'

I pray to God to strike me dead so I can escape such unspeakable horror. I can't believe this can get any worse.

But I'm wrong.

'He'd fuck me as well. You know, fuck me, up my arse, and it hurt like hell, and I'd want to die, it was so awful.'

You and me both. There can't be a God. I know that beyond all doubt now. If He existed, He'd put me out of my misery, and I wouldn't be finding out my husband raped my beloved child. An eternity of torture would be better than hearing Daniel, whom I adore beyond anything, telling me this.

'It went on for years. All the time I was a teenager. Every time it happened, I thought about killing myself. I was scared shitless of him. I kept quiet for you, you see. Thought you'd suffer a complete breakdown if you ever discovered what a bastard you'd married.' He laughs, a bitter quality tainting the sound. 'Ironic, isn't it? I endured years of abuse to protect your sanity. Turns out if it hadn't been for you, I'd never have been in that position anyway. Now do you get why I hate you?'

Yes. Yes, I get it, I really do. For once, I can't bear to look at him, and I'm glad he's still turned away from me.

'So the least you can do is tell me why you kidnapped me. Why you ruined my life.'

My arms reach out, instinct urging me to hug his pain away. Oh, Daniel, my poor darling, I say in my head, but the words never make it to my lips. My tongue is frozen, but this time it's because of the knowledge of how badly I've wronged him. His anger held me silent before. Now, the mental horror inflicted by Daniel's words renders me unable to speak, even though he wants me to.

My arms fall to my side.

'Someone told me I should try to understand. To feel compassion towards you. But I can't. I have no redress, you see. I endured years of abuse and there's nothing I can do to get back at the bastard who hurt me. It all happened years ago and it would be his word against mine. My mother's suffered enough. I don't want her hurt anymore, and if she found out about this, well, I don't think she could handle it. I won't do that to her. I won't, you hear me?' He's shouting now.

He continues to stare out of the window, and I look back at his jacket, at the pen tucked in the pocket, at the spare button hanging by a few threads. It would be so easy to pull it off, and then I'd have a tangible reminder of my beloved Daniel with me, something I don't possess right now. It's not much, but better than nothing.

My fingers stray towards the jacket.

'For God's sake, tell me. You owe me that much. You lied to me for years. You can at least tell me the truth now.'

But I can't. I want to tell him, but I'm too much in shock. I realise I've been existing in a dream world, thinking Daniel would come to me one day, and I'd tell him how it was, and he'd understand, and the hatred would fade from his eyes.

Yes, I've been living in a fool's paradise. I didn't understand the truth before, and now I do.

So I stay silent.

'Fuck you. Guess you're never going to tell me.' With one quick move, he grabs his jacket and bangs on the door, shouting for someone to open it. Then he's gone.

32

ALL SCREWED UP

Daniel peered at Annie's digital clock. He hadn't intended to sleep in so late but then he'd never thought he'd end up back at her flat last night. That had been before the abortive visit to Laura Bateman, though; after he'd stormed out on her, a desperate urge to offload his pent-up fury overwhelmed him. Getting plastered on cheap beer back at the flat held little appeal these days. He'd gone to the bar later in a funk, furious and in need of another comfort fuck, hoping Annie would be working that night. She'd clocked his dark mood immediately but didn't say anything, merely poured him the first of a couple of Scotches before telling him he'd be on soft drinks for the rest of the night. Later, she'd informed him he'd be coming home with her after her shift, her tone not giving him the option of saying no. Not that he would have done. He'd bundled her into the bedroom as soon as they got back to her flat, pulling off her clothes and shagging her as hard as he knew how until both of them collapsed into an exhausted sleep.

She stirred, and he leaned over and dropped a kiss on her forehead. 'Morning, sleepyhead.'

'What time is it?'

'Nearly eleven. Thank God it's my Saturday off.'

She threw back the covers and got out of bed. 'Breakfast coming up. Don't go anywhere.'

Once alone, Daniel's brain looped repeatedly through his visit to Laura Bateman. So much for her alleged love. As well as his father's ideas about forgiveness. The woman could rot in that place, for all he cared.

Twenty minutes later, Annie came back, carrying a piled tray. 'Move over, sunshine. Get some bacon and eggs down you and you'll feel more like talking.'

'About what?'

'About whatever you're not telling me. Something happened yesterday, something that made you walk into the bar last night with a face like a funeral procession and needing to shag me senseless. Not that I'm complaining about the last part.'

'You remind me of my ex. She was like a terrier down a rat-hole when she wanted to prise information out of me.' Daniel shook his head in amusement. 'Are you sure you're not her in another body?'

Annie laughed. 'I'd bet a lorry-load of money my body is very different to hers. With that pretty face of yours, I don't doubt all your exes have been equally good-looking, whether they've been men or women. Oh, don't look at me like that. I saw the way you and that guy checked each other out the first night you came in the bar. You've had your fair share of men and don't you deny it.'

'Guilty as charged.' Daniel held up his hands in mock protest. 'What's my sentence?'

She gestured towards his plate. 'You have to eat all that. Shut up and dig in. You can talk later.'

'Yes, ma'am.'

The silence stretched between them as they ate. His breakfast finished, he put his plate beside the bed, before turning to her. She opened her arms and he pillowed his head on her breasts, relaxing into the comfort of her body. The faint remnants of her perfume lingered from last night and he inhaled the heady scent, turning his mouth to place a kiss on her skin. Her arms wrapped around him, her hands stroked his hair and he recognised the same sense of security he'd always had when he thought of his mother, sitting beside his bed so many years ago.

Annie spoke first.

'I'm here for you if you need to talk. I'll listen. Whatever you want to say.'

Should he really tell Annie about the shit that had smeared itself all over him years ago? After all, he'd never get a better chance to unburden himself. No psychotherapy or counselling for him; he'd never even considered revealing the raw hurt Ian Bateman had inflicted to some stranger, having them prod and poke into his psyche. Something about Annie made him feel relaxed, as though she wouldn't judge him. She'd proved that when he'd told her about his relationship with Katie. She might speak plainly, but she'd understand.

He found himself wanting to unburden his thoughts to her. Not like the frenzied yelling of yesterday, the words spewed out in a torrent of hate and fury. Shouted at a woman who, despite hearing the awful truth she'd condemned him to by her actions, still sat silent and unresponsive, submerged in the enigma of her mind. No, he'd talk to Annie instead, pour all the crap out to her and let her common sense and compassion wash away the pain.

The stopper had been well and truly taken out of the bottle yesterday when he'd confronted Laura Bateman. With Annie holding him, the words started to come.

'I went to visit the woman who kidnapped me yesterday. To demand answers. Why she took me, how she could justify something so terrible.'

Annie nodded. He had an idea she wasn't surprised. 'Did she say anything?'

'Not a thing. She's still not talking. I had plenty to say, though.'

'I'll bet. You probably told her how much you hate her. Did you tell her why, though?'

'Yes.'

'That'll be whatever you've not yet told me. The real reason you're so mad at her.'

'You're right. She's not the issue, though, Annie. She never was, not really. The problem was the bastard she married.'

'Uh-huh.'

'He was an arsehole.' Daniel heard the tremor in his voice, the barely disguised fury.

'Sounds like it, what with not letting you go to college. But there's a whole lot more, right, Daniel?'

'Yes. It's ugly too.'

He clenched a fist around the bed sheet. The walls seemed to be closing in on him; he took a breath, forcing the panic back down.

'I think the way he feels about her was behind the whole thing. He loves her, but I've always thought it's a pretty twisted, controlling type of love. I was part of the package. Like he had to accept me to get her, but he hated me for it. He despised me more and more as the years went on.'

Now he'd started, he found the words, dark streams of hatred, pouring from his mouth.

'He abused me. It wasn't enough him hitting me every time my so-called mother went out, telling me whenever he got the chance how much he hated me. No, he had to take things further.'

Annie's arms tightened around him. 'He touched you?'

'Yes. God, it was vile. It started when I was twelve. She'd gone out one afternoon. I was in my bedroom. He came in and began mouthing off. Told me how worthless I was, how he had to put up with me for the sake of my mother, how he wished I were dead. Then he came towards me. He grabbed me by the arm, yanked me onto my knees. Then . . . oh, God . . .' Revulsion threatened to choke him. 'He pulled down his trousers. He . . . he made me . . . Christ, Annie, it was awful. He held the back of my head, and he fucked my mouth; when I spat out his come he went mad, punching and slapping me. Afterwards he went back downstairs, and I lay on my bed, and I didn't have a clue how to deal with what he'd done.'

'You were twelve. Of course you didn't. You never said anything to the woman who kidnapped you?'

'Never. She was fragile, you see, prone to depression, and while I didn't love her the way she wanted, I couldn't bear to make her realise the man she'd married was a monster. He played on my fears too. Told me she'd suffer a mental breakdown if I ever said anything and I'd be to blame. I believed him.'

'She never suspected?'

'No. He was careful; he never hit my face, never did anything to leave visible marks.'

Her arms tightened further. 'Did it happen often?'

'Every time she left the house, after that first time.'

'How long did it go on for?'

'More or less until I left home. I could have hit back by then. I was already taller than him. But I didn't. He had something about him; he got me completely shit-scared of him. He only had to look at me, and I'd feel utter terror. As I said, he only did it when she left the house. In front of her, you'd never have known how vile he could get.'

'Vile doesn't even begin to describe him. He sounds like a monster.'

'It was just mouth fucking, the first few times. I thought that was bad enough. I'd go through a bottle of mouthwash afterwards, trying to swill the taste of him away. He loved the control, the humiliation, and he got bolder the more scared I got. One day he told me to lose my jeans.'

'Oh, my God. Did he . . . ?'

'He pushed me face down on the bed. He shoved his fingers into me. It hurt like you wouldn't believe. Then he thrust his cock in me. I'd thought his fingers were bad enough but being raped by him was something else. He made me bleed. I wanted to die, I really did.'

He slammed his fist into the bed. In his mind, he was punching Ian Bateman's face, beating it into a bloody mess. 'That only happened a few times. Mostly he'd just do the mouth fucking, and tell me what a little shit I was. In a way, I was lucky. Laura Bateman was a real home bird. Didn't go out much. No friends; he wasn't keen on her having any. So the abuse happened less than it might have done. But still often enough.'

'Daniel, you were just a kid. Now I get why you're so angry about all this.'

'Yeah. It's more than being taken from my family. It's more than the break-up with Katie and the loss of my art. It's what he did to me. My head's all screwed up because of him. Soon as I left home, I started going to the gay clubs. You'd have thought the bastard would have turned me off men, but no.'

'So you like guys as well as girls. Are you ashamed of it? Do you think you shouldn't want men, because of what your stepfather did?'

'No. That's not it. I'm ashamed of the fact I'm perverted, twisted, whatever you want to call it.'

'What do you mean?'

'I go to a particular type of gay club sometimes, Annie. Caters to certain tastes. I pick up a guy and I make it very clear to him who's going to be on top. I go for the ones who I reckon will like their sex pretty rough round the edges. I take them back to their place and I fuck them hard, I fuck them brutal. Every time, it's not them I'm fucking but my stepfather. Every guy I shag, I'm getting revenge for what was done to me.'

'I can understand that.' He didn't detect condemnation in her voice.

'Hell, Annie! If that's not completely screwed up, I don't know what is. I'm as bad as my stepfather.'

'No, you're not. Don't be so hard on yourself.' He didn't think he deserved the compassion in her eyes. 'Stuff like this has to be let out somehow. Otherwise, it festers and turns even more rotten. You say these guys are willing. You've never raped anyone like you were raped. The sex is consensual, Daniel; if they're OK with the whole kink scenario, perhaps it's a good way to blow off steam. Get some of this crap out of you.'

'But it's so incredibly warped. Hardly what you'd call normal behaviour.'

'We've all been screwed over by life, Daniel. It's a question of degree. Take the woman who kidnapped you. People who are happy and stable don't snatch other people's kids. You ever wonder what damaged her so badly she ended up abducting you?'

'Yeah. All the time. No idea if I'll ever get an answer. Like I said, she won't talk. I can't help it, Annie. I've bottled up huge amounts of anger because of what she did.'

Annie nodded. 'I understand. But I reckon there's a tragic story hidden in her past. You say she suffers from depression. She has no friends. A controlling husband. Sounds like she married him for what he could give her. Something must have been badly lacking in her life. Take the way she stole you. She needed a child and didn't have one of her own, assuming she lost the baby whose birth certificate she gave you. Don't think for a minute I'm condoning what she did. But try walking a few steps in her shoes, as the saying goes. You may find you can eventually forgive her.'

His disbelief must have showed on his face. But something compelled him to look in her eyes, and he saw only compassion staring back. 'Think what might have motivated her, Daniel. With your stepfather, it's no mystery – jealousy coupled with a rotten, controlling nature. With her – who knows? But do your best to understand her. It's the first step towards being able to forgive.'

'Like you're able to forgive the crack-head who smashed in your husband's skull? Come on, Annie. That's a load of crap.'

'I'm trying.'

He stared at her. 'Why? What the hell's the point? Where does all this bleeding-heart nonsense get you?'

'It takes some of the pain away. I'm not perfect, believe me; I've not managed to practise what I preach yet. There's no way I can look you in the eye and tell you I've forgiven Andrew's killer. However, I'm trying. In the living room, you'll find books about forgiveness. I'm making an effort to take their message on board, about how hatred keeps the hurt alive. I believe I need to forgive my husband's murderer if I'm to create a meaningful life for myself.'

'You think you can do that? Seriously?'

'Yes. No. I don't know, Daniel. But I do my best.' She shrugged. 'Can't do much else. I think of my husband's killer, and some days I scream and curse and I hate him with every last part of me. But I keep trying.'

Daniel shook his head. 'I don't know if I can ever get past what Laura Bateman did. What I need from her are answers, and I'll probably never get any. As for forgiving my stepfather – the thought seems like sheer impossibility.'

'Maybe it is. Perhaps you'll never forgive him, or her, but instead you'll find a way to deal with what happened, something other than picking up guys to shag. Try to think of what you've gained. A whole new family, one where you can find love and acceptance and perhaps you can do your art, now you're with people who'll be supportive of you.'

'What about you, Annie? Can you find a way to deal with your life? Will things turn out OK for you?'

She gave him a wry smile. 'I don't possess a crystal ball, Daniel. But like I told you, I'm trying.'

33

REDRESS

Sleep is impossible the night after Daniel's visit. I keep hearing his voice, the voice of condemnation, shouting those awful words I'll never be able to tear from my brain.

I reflect on my failure as a mother. I couldn't stop my baby dying in his cot, and I have turned out every bit as bad a mother to my second Daniel. In my arrogance, I believed I was doing the right thing in taking him from his family. I thought I could give him a better home than they had, more love, more attention.

Turns out I was wrong. Unknowingly, I took Daniel into the lion's den, where the place that should have been a loving haven was where he suffered abuse and rape from a man I trusted. The man I chose to be a father to him.

Everything makes sense now. Why Daniel retreated to his room for hours on end as a teenager, something at the time I put down to normal teenage moodiness. Why he hasn't seen Ian for years and always visits the house when he's out.

Ian was dull but safe, I always thought. Now I realise he was anything but safe. I unknowingly brought a snake into the nest I'd made, and snakes always run true to form.

The signs were all there. Why didn't I recognise them? Even before we moved in together, Ian never showed much interest in Daniel and things didn't improve after we got married. I think back over all the excuses I made for him: how he wasn't used to children, how things would get better in time.

Everything else seemed so right back then, you see. He was always so attentive, the sex was better than I'd anticipated, and he appeared to be Mr Reliable. Exactly what I thought I wanted. Be careful what you wish for, as the saying goes.

It's hard to understand, thinking back. I'd have done better to concentrate on what really mattered – how he treated Daniel – rather than his job as a financial advisor and his golf club membership. All the things supposedly making him so suitable. My main objective was to find a father figure for Daniel, so why didn't I make that consideration paramount, instead of turning a blind eye to the fact Ian didn't measure up?

Actually, I do understand my poor choice. Lack of self-love cuts deep. I've never thought very highly of myself, you see. Ian seemed so smitten with me, and so suitable, and I guess I believed I'd never get a better chance. Not many men would take on another man's child, or so I thought. Ian always said how pretty I was but I didn't feel pretty. I thought of myself as mousy little Laura, an easy target for those who wanted to take advantage. Matthew Hancock. My rapist. Ultimately, Ian Bateman.

I think about Ian's motives for raping Daniel. Jealousy must have been the driving factor, along with his overwhelming need for control. He wanted me, only me, and knowing the love of my life was Daniel obviously proved too much for him. I guess he couldn't bear the thought of coming second best to my child. Over the years his antipathy towards Daniel must have turned to hatred. Hatred he was careful to conceal from me and which at some point twisted itself into something sexual, leading him to abuse my innocent boy.

I don't understand how he could have done something so awful, though. However jealous he got, why did it translate into abuse? Why rape a young boy? He knew when he met me I came with a child attached and if he wasn't happy with the situation he should have gone elsewhere. He'd chosen me and he should have damned well done his best with Daniel, instead of raping him whenever he got the chance. Bastard.

No wonder Daniel hates me. Not as much as I loathe myself, though.

I agree with the police now; taking Daniel from his parents was a crime. I am guilty of an appalling injustice against my darling boy, whom I love so much; I am the reason he suffered terrible pain. I should be called to account for my sins; what I've done warrants whatever the British legal system can throw at me. I deserve punishment but somehow I doubt earthly justice, where I'll be locked up yet given food, drink and a bed to sleep in, is going to cut it. I wish I believed in Hell; an eternity of damnation, somewhere hot and fiery, might suffice to atone for what I've done.

I'm not the only one who deserves to be punished, though.

Ian Bateman repeatedly raped and abused my boy. I shudder as I recall the bitterness in Daniel's voice as he shouted at me about lacking redress. He's right. It would be his word against Ian's after so many years, and something tells me that somewhere inside Daniel is still a young boy who's terrified of his stepfather. He's not going to say anything, even now.

I think some more. I could break my silence. I'd tell someone what Daniel told me, and then it would be two against one. Somebody might listen then.

But I quickly realise such a move wouldn't work. There's no actual evidence, and I wouldn't be able to stand up in court and say I'd ever noticed anything untoward between Ian and Daniel, because I never did. Besides, I'm hardly a credible witness, what with all the psychiatric evaluations. I doubt Daniel would want a trial either, as it would mean revealing the vile details to a court. He said as much. I remember what I went through after being raped; there was no way I could have endured hours of police questioning and some hatchet-faced lawyer out to prove I'd been begging for it. My rapist's parting thrust returns full force to mock me: *it'll be your word against mine.* A taunt echoed years later with my husband's cruel violation of my boy.

I wonder what I can do to help Daniel and it seems the answer is nothing. I swore I'd always protect him and I have failed miserably.

Ian's actions will go unpunished, and that's not fair. There will be no justice for Daniel.

I lie here and sob, wondering why my life has been so cursed. I was so naïve, back at that shabby flat in Bromley South; my world seemed finally to be coming right and I thought I was being granted a chance at a happy family life. My naïveté continued for twenty-two years, until the top layer was ripped off the day Daniel stormed in shouting I wasn't his mother.

Now the underlying layer has been torn away too, with the knowledge of my boy's rape at the hands of the man to whom I entrusted him. So now my psyche is raw, exposed, and I don't know how I can deal with this.

Maybe karma does exist. Perhaps I've been as bad in past lives and not learned my lesson. How else to explain my miserable childhood, my rape, the deaths of Gran and my baby, all before I reached nineteen? Now I have to suffer Daniel's hatred, and knowing the man whom I slept beside for so many years is a rapist. Isn't there a limit to what one person is called upon to bear?

Suicide beckons me again. I want to die and then I won't endure such pain. I think about ripping the duvet cover up and knotting the lengths together but of course, they've already thought of such things; there's nowhere to hang an improvised noose from. I could refuse to eat but they'd probably shove a feeding tube in me and there wouldn't be any point.

But there's no point in living either. Everything I ever valued has either been stripped from me or proved worthless and I can see no sense in existing for another forty or fifty years in a room like this, waiting to die.

I'm wrong, though. With intense clarity, the answer snaps into my brain.

It's so obvious. There is a reason, an urgent and compelling one, for me to live. Ian Bateman needs to be punished. I can atone for my sins towards Daniel by getting the redress he doesn't think is possible.

I've been lying to myself all this time, saying there's no way to avenge his abuse.

Since Daniel hurled the vile truth at me, I've known what I must do. I just haven't been able to admit it to myself. Now I can.

It's been a couple of days since my husband last visited me. I'm grateful he's a creature of habit; I can be sure he'll come tomorrow. I lie back and try to sleep. I feel oddly at peace.

The next day, sure enough, I'm told I have a visitor.

Ian is standing before me, asking how I am.

'You look tired,' he comments.

He drags a chair across the room and sits next to me. I'm lying on the bed.

He starts talking about something or other and my mind wanders. I stare at him, and he appears so normal, a family man who sets up pensions and plays golf; nobody would look at him and peg him as the rapist of a young boy. You'd expect someone like that to appear twisted, a bit off-kilter. Then I remember the faces of the murderers and rapists

I've seen on television and most of them seem as ordinary and boring as the rest of us. You can't measure a person's soul by their face. Take me, for example: a petite middle-aged housewife and mother. You wouldn't look at me and guess I was a kidnapper.

Or that I'd be capable of doing what I'm about to do. The time has come to make amends for Daniel. My hand reaches under my mattress. My fingers clutch what I find there.

See, I must have known subconsciously what I was going to do yesterday, when Daniel was shouting at me. When I looked at his jacket and thought how maybe I'd pull off his loose button so I'd have something of him to cherish. And when my fingers strayed towards the jacket.

I did know, because instead of pulling off the button, I reached towards the pen tucked in his inside pocket, drawing it out and hiding it under the mattress. Now my fingers are curled around the barrel, and I prise off the top. I press the point against my palm and I savour the pain as it digs in. It's one of those cheap ballpoints, the ones with the thin ends that write all scratchily.

That's good. That's really good.

I stand up and the pen is in my right hand, and Ian doesn't take much notice of me, lost as he is in some golfing story. I'm a small woman, but as he's sitting down, I'm higher than he is and the difference gives me the advantage. I put my hand on the back of his neck, in what seems like an innocent caress, tightening my grip, to hold his head in place. He looks up at me then and my arm rises into the air and comes down with as much force as I can muster, and the pen is no longer in my hand, but sticking out of his left eye.

And there's blood, and screaming, then the door flies open, and I'm being restrained and all I can stare at is the pen, skewering the eye of my son's rapist and I hope to God what I've done will be sufficient amends for Daniel's abuse. I'd hoped to kill my bastard of a husband, but I might not have hit hard enough and the pen might not be a sufficient weapon. Perhaps he'll just lose his eye. I hope he dies, but I can't do anything to influence that, more's the pity.

My rapist husband, face bloodied, moaning in a way that doesn't sound human, turns to stare at me with his remaining eye. It's the look of a man acknowledging his guilt. I don't doubt he realises why I've done this. That I found out what he did to my boy and how justice, hand in hand with redress for Daniel, is calling him to account for his crimes.

An eye for an eye, they say, except this time it's an eye for a rape, or rather a number of them. Is that a fair exchange? Perhaps. All I can do is hope it will be sufficient for Daniel. He'll hear about what I've done, he'll know why I did it, and maybe that will soften his hatred of me a little. All I've wanted since he found out I wasn't his biological mother was for him to understand, to feel compassion for the eighteen-year-old girl unable to deal with the death of her baby. For him not to hate me. If I can tell myself that my boy thinks of me with some empathy and that he doesn't despise me, then I can bear to stay alive.

Redress tastes sweet. Have I done the right thing for you, Daniel?

34

UNDERSTANDING

Annie put the last of Daniel's paintings back against the stack of canvasses.

'You're good, Daniel. Better than good – this is amazing work. You have a real gift.'

Thank God. Annie wasn't someone to bullshit him. She knew her stuff when it came to paintings, her flat being full of art books and prints, and he'd never doubted she'd give her opinion to him straight. He let out the breath he'd been holding, savouring the unfamiliar praise. Tonight was the first time he'd dared to show her anything he'd painted, despite the fact they'd been seeing each other regularly for several weeks now. Eventually she'd insisted and, being Annie, wouldn't take no for an answer.

He sensed something healing deep within because of her words, reinforcing as they did those of his father. In a few seconds, she'd erased the hurt caused by Ian Bateman's contempt towards his paintings, replacing scorn with approval. A real gift, she'd said. He'd never be able to convey what those few words meant to him.

'I'm spending all my spare time with brushes and paint these days. When I'm not seeing you or my family, that is. That reminds me. I gave Mum one of my pictures yesterday.' The canvas of the woman, girl and child of his memories now graced his parents' home, hung on the wall by his father.

'Best present ever,' Sarah had said, tears shining in her eyes.

Later, Howard took him aside. 'Thanks to you, your mother's got her life back.' He smiled. 'Me, I have a son to be proud of.'

Annie's voice snapped Daniel back to the present. 'I bet she loved it. You thought any more about pursuing your art? Going to college?'

He had. He'd discussed the idea with his parents too. 'Reckon I will. Probably next year.'

'You should.' She picked up the last painting again. 'Your style's changed. I like these later ones better. More life. More colour.'

She was right. No surprise there, he thought. His pictures were a metaphor for his whole being. His abduction and subsequent abuse had coloured his life in dark, sombre hues; now warm reds and yellows had replaced the bleakness. All bound up with the reunion with his family and the solace he'd found in Annie.

More than those two factors accounted for the transformation, though; he couldn't deny the part Laura Bateman had played. A cheap ballpoint pen wielded by his kidnapper had done more to heal his damaged psyche than his secret visits to sex clubs, places as dark and murky as his paintings. He'd not had the urge to screw a man since the attack. No coincidence, that.

Two months had gone by since Daniel had forced Laura Bateman to confront the consequences of kidnapping him. Eight weeks had passed since he'd heard, and understood, what she'd done to put right some of the wrong she'd caused through her actions. Plenty of time to think about what his stepfather's skewered eyeball represented.

Redress was the answer to that question. He'd yelled at Laura Bateman how he'd never get justice for being raped and abused, but he'd been wrong. The woman he'd screamed his hatred at, who he'd believed had ruined his life, had achieved it for him. When he'd heard about the attack, he'd known immediately why she'd done it. Laura Bateman's actions had spoken for her, loud and clear. Her forcing that ballpoint pen into his stepfather's eye had shone light into what had previously been dark, changing his life for the better.

He'd continued to see Annie during that time. The fact they were now having regular sex had altered things, shifted their connection onto a completely new level. Neither of them seemed able to break away from what they had and he didn't think either of them wanted to, not yet. He found such comfort in the sex and even more in the after-sex, when they'd hold each other, the closeness between them healing some of their wounds. They needed each other right now but it wouldn't be a forever thing. They had different priorities. He'd move forward with his life; she'd figure out how to deal with her past and move on as well. Perhaps they'd stay in touch, perhaps not. It didn't really matter. The important thing was what they shared here and now.

He hugged her. 'Thank you. For everything.' His hand slid over her tempting body. God, it had been far too long since they'd hit the sack. Time to put that right.

A couple of hours later, Annie was lying in bed next to him, limp and sated, making pillow talk.

'How're things going with the family?'

'Couldn't be better. Mum spoils me rotten – she says she's making up for twenty-two years of maternal deprivation – and Dad, well, we drink beer together and he's a great guy, Annie. He's the father I always wanted as a child. My grandparents too, they're wonderful. I'm not saying everything's perfect. We've all needed to make adjustments. But it feels right, Annie. I'm exactly where I should be.'

'So the story has a happy ending.'

'Seems that way.'

'You in contact with Katie at all?'

'Yeah. We've swapped a couple of emails, and, you know, I think it's getting easier.'

'Told you it would. You should listen to my words of wisdom more often, young man.' She punched the side of his arm lightly, and Daniel laughed. He liked her straight talking and her strength, wondering how he'd ever endured the airheads he'd been with before Katie and Annie. He no longer noticed Annie's hooked nose; he found the mouth underneath far more interesting. The playboy had grown up at last.

'What about you, Annie?' His expression turned serious as he tilted her head up to look at her. 'Is life becoming easier for you?'

She drew in a breath and let it out slowly. 'Yes. No. Not sure. Yes, mostly. Being with you has helped. I think more about the happy times with Andrew and less about finding him dead in his own blood. I still get days when all I want to do is crawl under the duvet and shut the world out and that's when losing him hurts the most. Been eight months now, and I miss him and our life together every single day and I ask myself why it happened.'

'You ever get any answers?'

'Only clichéd ones about how that's life, and crap like that. You always think tragedies happen to someone else. And then one day you're the one in the news, sobbing into a reporter's microphone. Guess that's how your mother must have felt when you were taken.'

'Yes. She's said as much. My nanny too, when I last spoke to her.'

'You've been in touch with her again?'

'Yeah. We've talked on the phone. I'll go down to Bristol sometime soon, check up on how she's doing. She's promised to come to London too. Mum has her phone number. I'm hoping one day they'll talk.'

'You think that's likely? You said your mother blamed her for what happened.'

'Yes. She does, or rather she did. Now I'm not so sure. I think, in time, Mum might call her. I keep on at her about it and I doubt if she can hold out against my charms for much longer.' He laughed. 'Everything's so good, Annie. With my family, I mean. I don't want there to be hatred and divisions and blame anymore. I think we all need to move on from what happened. We have twenty-two years to make up for, and there doesn't seem much point in agonising over the past.'

Annie smiled. 'Listen to yourself. You're all stoked up because your nanny and your mother might be about to heal the breach between them. You say you don't want hatred and blame anymore. Are you going to apply your new-found philosophy to yourself?'

'You mean Laura Bateman.'

'Yes.'

'Whether I can forgive her.'

'Yes.'

'Not all of us can be saints, Annie. Have you forgiven your husband's killer yet?'

'No. I never said I find all this easy, Daniel. Those days when I want to crawl under the duvet, they're the ones when I want to kill the man who murdered my husband for ten pounds of crack money. On the good days, well, I give it my best shot. That's all I can do. I try to remember he was one very fucked-up young man, human like the rest of us. And yes, I get a bit closer to forgiving him.'

Daniel shook his head. 'You're definitely more of a candidate for sainthood than I am. We're talking here about some murdering crack-head.'

'I'm not perfect, Daniel. Truth is – I find it incredibly difficult most of the time.'

He didn't doubt it. 'Don't write me off as a lost cause, though, Annie. I flipped through one of your books on forgiveness the other day.' He hadn't meant to tell her that. 'Some of what it said made sense.

You asked if I could forgive Laura Bateman. My father asked the same thing. I admit I've thought about it.'

'Have they found out any more about her life before she kidnapped you?'

'No more than the obvious. You were right about some things. Turns out she's had a pretty shitty past in many ways. She spent her teenage years in foster care, after her alcoholic mother died, until she was almost eighteen. Then she went to a new placement and not long afterwards ran away from there. Nobody knows why.'

Annie grimaced. 'Not hard to think of a possible reason. I'll bet you anything some abuse, or worse, went on there.'

'You think?'

'Yep. Told you, that woman has had a tragic life, one way or another. You'll probably never discover the full extent of what happened.'

'Well, she's still not speaking.' Daniel sighed. 'God knows I've tried hard enough to make her talk. Anyway, after she ran away, she lived with her grandmother, and then she had her baby, Daniel Mark Covey, whose birth certificate she gave me. The grandmother died not long afterwards.'

'So she's eighteen, alone, with a tiny baby. I'm telling you, that's rough.'

'Yes. I get that.' He did too. Laura Covey stood in front of him, her judge, in the court of his mind, and time wound backwards, and she wasn't his kidnapper anymore, but a fragile and damaged eighteen-year-old. Protectiveness rose in him then, and empathy.

'What happened afterwards? To the baby? And how did she end up in Bristol?'

'That's the bit nobody's sure about. How she managed to carry out the kidnapping isn't clear either. The police traced her to a waitressing job in Bristol and to where she used to live, but she had no baby with her then. There's no death certificate, so nobody knows what happened.

If her child is dead, they've not found a body. They've done extensive searches, but nothing's turned up.'

'And then four years later she kidnaps you and brings you up as her own.'

'I was a substitute.' Understanding hit Daniel. 'She couldn't live without her child, so she replaced him with me.'

'You had the same name, remember, and were about the same age. You say she's always been a bit flaky mentally – well, I think you did become her son in her mind. And so she took you.'

'Probably, I guess. It's difficult to know.'

'Will she stand trial? For either the kidnapping or for what she did to your stepfather?'

'Hard to say, but it's doubtful. They're still trying to assess her mental state, find out if she's competent to stand trial, and of course these things take time. And everything changed when she stabbed my stepfather.'

'Do you still feel the same hatred towards her?'

'No.' Daniel shook his head. He didn't. Perhaps time had worked its magic, perhaps the joy of being with his family again had too. But it was more than that, as he'd already admitted to himself. He now had the satisfaction, savage and bloody, of knowing his pen had skewered his stepfather's eyeball.

'I told her I'd never loved her,' he said. 'I didn't, not the way she wanted. Some feelings were there, though. Ones similar to love.'

Annie smiled. 'Do you think eventually you might forgive her?'

'Possibly.' He couldn't believe he'd said it, but it was true. The quiet words of the police liaison officer, telling him about the alcoholic mother and the foster homes and all the rest, had sunk in. He might not be able to manage forgiveness yet, but compassion was elbowing out hatred, and it felt good.

'And your stepfather?'

'No.' Daniel's reply was vehement. 'Never. Some things don't warrant forgiveness. I'll never forget the awfulness of that bastard raping me. I can't forgive him and I don't want to.'

'I'm not trying to make you live according to my rules, Daniel. All I'm saying is, forgiveness can be an immense force for good, if you let it.'

'Yes. I can understand that. I think, in time, I'll get there with Laura Bateman. And you know why? Because of what she did to my stepfather. He's lost his eye. They couldn't save it. He's permanently disfigured.'

'Justice, in a way, for what he did.'

'Yes. I had no redress at all before she stabbed him. I'd never, ever, have brought a court case against him. The rapes and the abuse, they were eating away at me, making me hate her, when really I hated my stepfather. I always felt so powerless against him. And then she did that to him, with my pen, and all the anger found an outlet.'

'I can understand that.'

'And I'd rather he was dead, and that's probably what she intended, but as we both know, life's not perfect. I reckon I can settle for what she did to him, though, as a way of tipping the scales back in my favour. He's not talking about what happened – not surprising, really – meaning the police don't know what prompted the stabbing.'

'That's all to the good, don't you think?'

Daniel nodded. 'They tell me he's lost his job as well as his eye. He had to quit; not in good shape mentally, it seems.'

'I can't be the judge of it, but it sounds like justice knocked on his door, without any need to involve the law.'

'The bastard deserved what he got.' Daniel grimaced. 'I hope it hurt like hell.'

'Amen to that. Remember, Daniel, when you think about forgiving Laura Bateman – you did get the answers you always wanted. Just not in the way you expected.'

'You're right. Seems you often are.'

She laughed. 'You'll be glad you made the effort. Remember what you said before; there's no point in agonising over the past. Go and enjoy your art, Daniel, have a blast with your life and when it comes to your stepfather, remember the old saying.'

'Which is?'

'Living well is the best revenge.'

35

BROKEN SILENCE

I stare out of the window. The view isn't as good as the last place but then I'm not here for the scenery but for the added security. Obviously, ever since I attacked Ian, they regard me as a high-risk case and so I ended up being transferred here. The nurses search my room and me regularly in case I've hidden any more pens and intend gouging out someone else's eye. Totally unnecessary, of course. I've never wanted to hurt anyone, not until I found out the ugly truth about the man I married. I have no remorse whatsoever for what I did, though. He deserved the retribution I delivered, and more, and my only regret is not managing to kill the bastard. Still, they couldn't save the eye, so I'm told, and I harbour a certain smug satisfaction at such news.

I wonder how my boy is. By now, the police will have told him the facts of my life and he'll have had time to think. He'll understand what I did for him by stabbing his stepfather.

I yearn for some contact with him. Daniel has always been like oxygen to me. I've thought about writing to him, but that would involve speaking to ask for paper and a pen and I'm not sure they trust me where writing implements are concerned.

I make a deal with myself. If I haven't seen or heard from him by the end of this month, I'll pour my soul out in a letter, even if I have to break my silence and dictate it to someone to get it sent. With a letter, he can read what I've said and let the words sink in, and perhaps his heart will soften a little towards me.

I look at the calendar on the wall. I think today is the fifteenth; I can't be sure when every day is the same. Sixteen days until the end of the month.

On the twenty-fourth, I'm told I have a visitor. Hope floods me; if you don't count the police and the doctors, nobody but Ian and Daniel has ever visited me, and my bastard husband will never come again, that's for sure. I wait as the nurse stands back, and then he's in front of me, my beautiful son, and I stare at him, and I can't get enough of him. I blot out the sight of the man standing in the room with us; he's there to make sure I don't do anything I shouldn't. To me, only Daniel and I are in the room, and I'm so delighted.

I have so much more to make me happy than him visiting me, though.

His eyes are what fill me with exquisite relief. They're not full of hatred anymore. Instead, understanding reaches out from his expression.

He pulls a chair across and sits in front of me. I can't help myself; I lean forward and rest my fingers lightly on the back of his hand. He doesn't pull away.

His voice is gentle when he speaks. 'You've had a lot of shit in your life, and I'm sorry.'

I don't reply. First I need to soak up his words, find out what he's come here for.

'Can you talk about it?' Daniel asks.

I shake my head, a barely imperceptible movement. Not yet, anyway.

'That's OK. You don't have to. I've had shit in my life too, but it's in the past now. Life is good these days.'

I'm glad, even if he means with his new family, away from me. I want him to be happy, whatever that entails for him.

'Been turning everything over in my head for a while now.'

I curl my fingers around his hand and squeeze lightly.

'I'm going to apply for art college. These days I'm painting every spare minute I get.'

I smile and squeeze his hand again. It's not enough, though. My boy is going to do something that means the world to him, something my bastard of a husband cruelly denied him, and I need to tell him how happy I am. To do so requires breaking my silence, but now is the right time.

'I'm glad.' It's all I can manage, but I register his surprise on hearing my voice and I know I've done the right thing.

'You're speaking again,' he says. 'That's good.'

I nod, incapable of further words just now.

'Been seeing a woman.' He smiles fondly. 'She's special. She's been good for me these past few months. We need each other. For how much longer, I'm not sure. What we have probably isn't a permanent thing but she's one hell of a woman. She's suffered too. She told me I should walk in your shoes and find out how they feel.'

I like the sound of this woman. The memory of Emma Carter comes to me. Seems as though my son found his own version of Emma when he needed it most.

'She talked to me about forgiveness. What she said didn't make sense at first. I couldn't understand how I could forgive either you or my stepfather. And whatever she says, I'll never forgive him. Never. But I don't need to. What you did to him. The assault. It made all the difference to me.'

His words deliver comfort. Perhaps I've succeeded to some extent in making amends to my boy. Hope fills me when he next speaks.

'It gave me what I needed to move past all the anger.'

I try to think what his words imply. Does he also mean he's been able to overcome his rage towards me?

He gives me my answer.

'I can't say I'm there yet where you're concerned.' He pauses. 'But I'm not full of my own crap anymore. I don't think about why it had to happen to me. Me, me, me. Annie made me understand that's how life is. Shit happens, and sometimes the crap happens to you, not the other person.'

I guess Annie must be the name of his new woman. I bless her wisdom.

'Been told a lot about your life, how things were for you when you were younger. There's a lot we don't know, though. You had a baby.'

Tears prick the backs of my eyes. I swallow hard and nod.

I speak again, even though the words come out strangled with sobs. The pain is as raw today as it's ever been. Some wounds never heal.

'He was fine when I put him to bed the night before.'

'Cot death. So that's what happened.' The empathy in Daniel's voice brings me exquisite comfort, all the sweeter for me craving it for so long. 'I can only try to imagine how awful your son's death must have been for you.'

The tears recede as I take in what he's saying. My boy is trying to understand, and compassion appears to be taking over from harsh judgement in his mind.

'Something broke inside me when I found him dead.'

He nods. 'You were young and alone.'

'I'd not had it easy up to then.'

'They told me. Your mother. Years in foster homes. The loss of your grandmother.'

'I was raped.' I startle myself. I hadn't meant to tell Daniel that. Nobody but Gran has ever known about what took place that night.

'By the man Social Services placed me with. He should have protected me, but instead he hurt me.'

'Christ. So Annie was right. God knows, I understand, I really do, how awful that must have been.' He turns his hand around so he's holding mine, and grips it tightly. 'Was that how you got pregnant?'

I shake my head. 'No. It was as I told you. Well, mostly. The engineering student. He was the father. But he had no intention of marrying me and he didn't die in a car crash. He didn't care at all about me.'

'He wasn't bothered about you being pregnant?'

'Not in the slightest. I intended to be the best mother ever, to make up for my baby not having a father. My love didn't stop my son dying, though. The pain – it was unbearable.'

'You weren't able to accept he had died.'

'No.' A hot tear slides down my face.

'And you never told anyone.'

Only Emma. And not about my child's burial. 'No.'

'Because it would have made his death real.'

'Yes.' My son really does understand. He gets it at last, how things were for me, and that's all I've ever wanted.

I can see Daniel is weighing up a question and he's not sure how to put it, and so it must be something big.

And it is.

'Your baby,' he says. 'Where is he?'

My mind flies back to the tree that is part of my child, holding his tiny body firmly in its grasp, and I shake my head. I can't bear the thought of him being disturbed, dug out of the ground, the protection of the oak's roots prised away. Burial in some anonymous graveyard, with a proper headstone and a service, won't give him anything he doesn't have already. The wood is where he should remain.

'Leave him be, my love. He's at rest now.' My baby has peace, beneath the oak tree, and that's how it should stay. 'He's safe. I took care of that. There was nothing else I could do for him in the end.'

Daniel doesn't reply, but I know he gets what I mean, and won't ask any more.

Silence for a while.

'He lost his eye, you know,' he says eventually. Relief fills me that we've moved away from the subject of my child's makeshift grave, although my rapist husband isn't exactly safe ground.

'What I did to him. It was like how it was with my baby.' I can see Daniel doesn't understand what I mean.

'It was all I could do for you, come the end,' I explain.

Daniel nods, grasping what I'm trying to convey. 'He deserved what he got and more.'

'You needed redress, you told me.'

'That bastard. That vile bastard.'

'I didn't realise what he was like,' I whisper.

'The anger was eating me up, knowing he'd got away with what he did. Then they told me what you'd done . . . and how he'd lost his eye. In my head, it was as if I had stabbed him, not you, giving me justice at last. What's more, I'd been reunited with my birth family, I'd met Annie, I'd started painting again and somehow I managed to get over myself and all the resentment.'

'I'm happy for you, my love.'

'My mother hated my nanny. Always blamed her for what happened. I never did, though. She was always special to me. I know she did wrong, but somehow that never mattered. I found myself wanting, needing even, my mother to forgive her. So both of them can heal, and move on.'

I don't ask if his mother will ever forgive me. Perhaps absolution from her would be too big, too huge, to hope for and anyway Daniel's forgiveness is the main thing I crave. I realise I should tell him how sorry I am but the words seem inadequate, given what he suffered through my actions.

In time, I might stop hating myself for the devastation I caused in Daniel's life. I thought I was doing the right thing for him, but really I was trying to plug the gaping hole in my heart. I wonder whether he will ever forgive me. The days and nights won't seem so long if I know he's trying.

'Can you . . . ?' I can't go on, but looking at him, I realise I don't need to. He grasps what I'm trying to say. We've never had such understanding between us. I pray it will never end.

'Yes.' The most beautiful thing Daniel's ever said to me. 'I think so. In time.'

I hear the word yes in my head and I turn it over in my heart, savouring the wonder at how one syllable can fill me with such joy.

Silence fills the room again. I sense our time here today is up. We've said so much; all the important things too.

My son presses my hand briefly. 'I should go,' he says.

I look at my boy, so handsome, and love floods through me. 'Thank you. For coming here. For understanding.'

He doesn't reply, but he smiles at me, the most beautiful smile I've ever seen.

'Will you come again?' I have to ask, even though I dread the answer. But even if he doesn't, it's enough for me. He doesn't hate me anymore. In time, he'll reach forgiveness towards me; that's more than I deserve. And sufficient to last me the rest of my life.

'I think so.' He stands up and turns towards the door. 'Probably.'

Dear God. Did my Daniel really say those words?

'We both need it,' he continues, and then I know he will come again.

I can't speak. I smile at him through my tears. Then he is gone.

I grab a tissue, wipe my face and lie down on the bed. The male nurse has left, and I'm alone.

I've got my son back, at least that's how it feels. He may have another family and another life now, but part of him has returned to me and I hug that thought tight, remembering what he said. The joy of *I think so*, married with *probably*. They're the most wonderful words he could have uttered and I can exist on them for all eternity. I have calm in my world now. Daniel brought me that gift today.

I can be at peace, because my boy has moved on from his anger and his future looks bright, what with going to college to do his precious art. If he's happy, so am I. I wonder briefly about this woman of his and I send her silent thanks. Whoever she is, even if she's only temporary in his life, she's good for him. Sometimes the people who touch our lives the most are only passing through. Like Emma Carter.

I've not had a happy life. I've experienced pain, loneliness and tragedy. But I've also known love and what it means for someone whom you adore beyond everything to touch you with their forgiveness, and that's the most beautiful experience, it really is. I'll carry Daniel's compassion with me always, and what it's meant to love him so dearly, both when he was a baby and now he's a grown man. The two are inextricably linked for me and that'll never change.

I lie on my bed for a long time and then I go over to the window and look out.

There's a tree in the grounds, an oak, the same sort I buried my baby under, and it's tall and strong and I draw new comfort as I look at it. I picture another oak, its roots thick, long and winding into the ground, and the beloved child I entrusted to its care, and I smile.

'Sleep well, my darling,' I say.

POSTSCRIPT

I hope that you enjoyed *His Kidnapper's Shoes*!

I'd like to ask a favour. Please would you write a review of *His Kidnapper's Shoes* on Amazon and/or Goodreads for me? It really does make a difference. I'd very much appreciate it – thank you!

Please visit my website at www.maggiejamesfiction.com. My blog is also on my website – I post regularly on all topics of interest to readers, including author interviews and book reviews.

ACKNOWLEDGEMENTS

Thanks to:

Jeanette, Gary, Jeni and Mary for their invaluable help and feedback;

X, for giving me the kick up the backside I so desperately needed;

and finally, to the people of Sucre, Bolivia, where the first draft of this novel was written.

This novel is dedicated in loving memory of Jeni Moss.

OTHER BOOKS BY
MAGGIE JAMES

Fiction

BLACKWATER LAKE (A FREE NOVELLA)

Matthew Stanyer fears the worst when he reports his parents missing. His father, Joseph Stanyer, has been struggling to cope with his wife Evie, whose dementia is rapidly worsening. When their bodies are found close to Blackwater Lake, a local beauty spot, the inquest rules the deaths as a murder-suicide. A conclusion that's supported by the note Joseph leaves for his son.

Grief-stricken, Matthew begins to clear his parents' house of decades of compulsive hoarding, only to discover the dark enigmas hidden within its walls. Ones that lead Matthew to ask: why did his father choose Blackwater Lake to end his life? What other secrets do its waters conceal?

A short (25,000 words) novella, Blackwater Lake examines one man's determination to uncover his family's troubled past.

Blackwater Lake won the award for 'best novella' in the 2016 Bards and Sages eFestival of Words.

THE SECOND CAPTIVE

Stockholm syndrome: the psychological tendency of a hostage to bond with his or her captor.

Beth Sutton is eighteen years old when Dominic Perdue abducts her. Held prisoner in a basement, she's dependent upon him for food, clothes, her very existence. As the months pass, her hatred towards him changes to compassion. Beth never allows herself to forget, however, that her captor has killed another woman. She has evidence to prove it, not to mention Dominic's own admission of murder.

Then Beth escapes . . .

And discovers Dominic Perdue is not a man who lets go easily. Meanwhile, despite being reunited with her family, she spirals into self-destructive behaviour. Release from her prison isn't enough, it seems. Can Beth also break free from the clutches of Stockholm syndrome?

A study of emotional dependency, *The Second Captive* examines how love can assume strange guises.

The Second Captive won the award for 'best novel' in the 2016 Bards and Sages eFestival of Words.

GUILTY INNOCENCE

Two eleven-year-old boys. One two-year-old girl. A murder that shocked the nation.

Ten years after being convicted of the brutal killing of a toddler, Mark Slater, formerly Joshua Barker, is released on parole from prison. Only the other boy jointly sentenced for Abby Morgan's murder, the twisted and violent Adam Campbell, knows the truth. That Mark played no part in Abby's death.

Four years later, Mark's on-off girlfriend discovers a letter revealing his conviction as a child killer. At risk of having his protective cover made public, Mark's need to confront the injustice of his sentence becomes overwhelming. Desperate to find answers, he initiates a friendship with Abby's older sister, something strictly prohibited by the terms of his parole. Rachel Morgan, however, unaware of Mark's former identity, is battling her own emotional demons.

Meanwhile, circumstances have thrust Mark back in contact with Adam Campbell, who, aged twenty-five, is more domineering and chilling than ever. Can Mark rewrite history and confront his nemesis?

A gritty novel examining child murder and dysfunctional families, *Guilty Innocence* tells of one man's struggle to break free from his past.

SISTER, PSYCHOPATH

When they were children, Megan Copeland adored her younger sister Chloe. Now she can't bear to be in the same room as her.

Megan believes Chloe to be a psychopath. After all, her sister's a textbook case: cold, cruel and lacking in empathy. Chloe loves to taunt Megan at every opportunity, as well as manipulating their mentally ill mother, Tilly.

When Tilly, under Chloe's malignant influence, becomes dangerously unstable, the consequences turn ugly for everyone. Megan's world falls apart, allowing long-buried truths to rise to the surface. Her sister's out of control, it seems, and there's little she can do about it. Until Chloe's actions threaten the safety of Megan's former lover. A man from whom she has withheld an important secret . . .

A study of sibling rivalry and dysfunctional relationships, *Sister, Psychopath* tells the story of one woman's struggle to survive the damage inflicted by her sociopathic sister.

Non-Fiction

WRITE YOUR NOVEL! FROM GETTING STARTED TO FIRST DRAFT

Have you always longed to write a novel? In *Write Your Novel! From Getting Started to First Draft*, I aim to inspire you with the confidence to do just that. With this book, I'll be your cheerleader, your hand-holder. We'll work on your mind-set, find sources of support, and deal with procrastination issues. I'll help you carve out the time to write and together we'll smash through the excuses that are holding you back.

What else? Do you need help in finding ideas? Worried where to start? Unsure whether writing software is right for you? Confused how to plan your novel? No problem! We cover all these issues and more. Every section ends with an action plan so you're raring to go!

I've included two chapters on plotting, as well as one containing writing advice. That way, once you've finished *Write Your Novel!*, you'll have an outline in place, one that will inspire you to get going, and you'll know how to start. My aim is to prepare you to write your novel as soon as you've completed the exercises in this book.

So if you've always yearned to be a novelist but you're unsure how to begin . . . why not buy *Write Your Novel!* and get started?

ABOUT THE AUTHOR

Maggie James is a British author who lives in Bristol. She writes psychological suspense novels.

Before turning her hand to writing, Maggie worked mainly as an accountant, with a diversion into practising as a nutritional therapist. Diet and health remain high on her list of interests, along with travel. Accountancy does not, but then it never did. The urge to pack a bag and go off travelling is always lurking in the background. When not writing, going to the gym, practising yoga or travelling, Maggie can be found seeking new four-legged friends to pet; animals are a lifelong love!